Ганите,

алеста нечреш

де урпатонезды

Song of the
Swans

аееае оеер!

баеееты

баеаездер!

Автор: *[signature]*

07.10.17 м.

Song of the Swans

Selection of Plays

Dulat Issabekov

Copyright © 2017 by Dulat Issabekov.
Translated By: Katherine Judelson

Library of Congress Control Number: 2017910232
ISBN: Hardcover   978-1-5434-8623-0
            Softcover   978-1-5434-8622-3
            eBook   978-1-5434-8621-6

All rights reserved. No part of this book may be reproduced or transmitted in any form or by any means, electronic or mechanical, including photocopying, recording, or by any information storage and retrieval system, without permission in writing from the copyright owner.

This is a work of fiction. Names, characters, places and incidents either are the product of the author's imagination or are used fictitiously, and any resemblance to any actual persons, living or dead, events, or locales is entirely coincidental.

Any people depicted in stock imagery provided by Thinkstock are models, and such images are being used for illustrative purposes only.
Certain stock imagery © Thinkstock.

Print information available on the last page.

Rev. date: 07/06/2017

To order additional copies of this book, contact:
Xlibris
800-056-3182
www.Xlibrispublishing.co.uk
Orders@Xlibrispublishing.co.uk
764032

Contents

Song of the Swans 1
    Act One 2
    Act Two 13

The Actress 22

A Man on a Mission 61
    Act One 62
    Act Two 88

The Transit Passenger 130
    Act One 131
    Act Two 163

The Monument 195
    Part One 196
    Part Two 226

Song of the Swans

(ON MOTIFS TAKEN FROM A KAZAKH EPIC POEM)

Dramatis personae

Zhibek – a beautiful maiden
Tolegen – her devoted suitor
Bekezhan – an evil ruler
Chief of the guard
Guards
Zhibek-swan
Tolegen-swan
Bekezhan-vulture
Crow-guards
Old man
Grandson

ACT ONE

(*The shore of a lake. An old man with a white beard and his grandson are talking in a picturesque natural setting*)

GRANDSON: Grandfather, why is our lake called "Swans' Nest"? There aren't any swans here!

OLD MAN: They say that many swans lived here in the old days.

GRANDSON: Where have they gone to?

OLD MAN: They were treated cruelly by people here and flew away to other parts.

GRANDSON: They were treated cruelly by us?

OLD MAN: Compared to our ancestors, it turns out that we have become heartless and cruel. The swans flew off and they decided to stay far away from people like us.

GRANDSON: Won't they be coming back?

OLD MAN: Who knows, my boy? Perhaps they'll come back, when people grow kind again and stop killing them.

GRANDSON: Why did people destroy the swans?

OLD MAN: Oh dear… that's a long story, my boy.

GRANDSON: Tell it to me even so…

OLD MAN: Listen and I shall tell you…

"Long long ago there lived a girl here by the name of Zhibek. She was a true beauty – her lips were like a crescent moon and her eyes were like stars. She loved a young stalwart called Tolegen. Zhibek's parents were planning to celebrate the young couple's wedding, when suddenly Bekezhan stormed into the village with his body-guards. He was a wicked, vengeful man and he took Zhibek prisoner and led her away. Then he locked her beloved Tolegen in a stone dungeon and forced him to make bows. Zhibek meanwhile refused all Bekezhan's advances.

* * *

(*The topsy-turvy stone palace belonging to Bekezhan. He is sitting on a couch of stone and opposite him sits Zhibek, as beautiful as an angel*)

BEKEZHAN: I gave you forty days so that you might think it over and agree to marry me. Thirty-nine of those days have passed and there is one day left. So, what shall your answer be Zhibek?

(*Zhibek does not reply*)

What did you see in that wretched Tolegen? He is only a huntsman who will hardly be able to feed his family with the meat of wild animals and no more… Unless he is a good marksman…?

(*Zhibek's lips are sealed*)

I meanwhile possess fabulous riches (*Bekezhan takes a fistful of gold coins out of a chest, which ring out as he lets them fall back in again*). If that is not enough for you, I shall capture another city and build you a palace of gold and you shall never know cares again. You shall be the most beautiful, the richest and the happiest woman on earth. Is that what you would like?

(*Zhibek sits there in silence*)

What I have to offer is bound to be better than the meat of wild animals and game. (*He laughs loudly and proudly*) Well, do you agree?

(*Silence is her reply*)

Tolegen is dead. He cannot be brought back to life.

ZHIBEK (*in a frightened voice*): No, he's alive!

BEKEZHAN: He died thirty-nine days ago. His parents will be commemorating his death on the fortieth day.

ZHIBEK: It's not true, that is a lie!

BEKEZHAN: You may think what you like, but what difference does it make to you? You will never see him again.

ZHIBEK: If Tolegen has died, I shall die too.

BEKEZHAN (*with a loud laugh*): No, you shall not die. First you shall become my wife and then we shall see… It is best for you not to make me angry. You should be grateful that I was patient enough to wait these long thirty-nine days.

ZHIBEK (*with a note of bitter irony*): Thank you.

BEKEZHAN (*rising from his seat*): Think carefully, Zhibek. I shall come for you tomorrow morning. (*He falls, unexpectedly, to his knees*). You are a clever young girl. Do not take it into your head to refuse me. Here is a gold bracelet (*He fastens it round her wrist*). Dear Zhibek, do not make me use force…

(*Bekezhan rises to his feet and leaves the chamber*)

* * *

(*Zhibek is seated alone. She is singing a long and wistful song. Then she turns to the angels with a prayer*)

ZHIBEK: Oh, holy angels! Help me to break free from this cruel torture! Or send me to my death! I beg you to take pity on me!

VOICE (*that of the old man telling the story or the voice of an angel*): I am listening to you Zhibek. You shall not die.

ZHIBEK: Whose voice do I hear? Who are you?

VOICE: Those who truly love each other are able to turn into white swans. Do you truly love Tolegen?

ZHIBEK: Life is empty for me without him.

VOICE: Think carefully. If you truly love him, you shall turn into a white swan. If your love is not true you shall turn into a vulture.

ZHIBEK: I am ready to accept your terms.

VOICE: Then close your eyes tight. Now stretch out your arms. Your arms have turned into wings. You have turned into a swan. You shall fly freely to the land of swans. If you take off your wings there, you shall once again turn into a girl and when you put them on again, you shall turn into a swan.

(*Zhibek, after turning into a white swan, flies away. She can still hear the voice of the angel behind her*)

VOICE: May you have a safe journey, Zhibek. If you search tirelessly, you shall find your happiness.

* * *

(*Panic reigns in Bekezhan's stone palace*)

GUARDS: Alert! Alert! Zhibek has vanished!

Zhibek has flown away. She has turned into a swan!

BEKEZHAN (*runs in*): What is happening?

CHIEF OF THE GUARD: Zhibek has vanished, Master! She turned into a swan and flew away!

BEKEZHAN: Stop talking nonsense! Where has anyone seen such a thing – someone turning into a swan? Find her for me! You must have helped her escape! Or you will all lose your heads!

(*He starts to hurl objects around as he searches for Zhibek*)

VOICE: People who truly love each other can turn into swans. Your search is in vain, Bekezhan.

BEKEZHAN: Who's that? Where is that voice coming from? Did I hear right?

(*He walks over to the stone door. The door opens of its own accord in front of him. There is no Zhibek. He opens the lid of his stone chest. The chest rolls over of its own accord*)

VOICE: D'you see, Bekezhan? Your efforts are in vain.

(*Bekezhan takes a sabre out of its sheath and hurries off in the direction of the voice. But then the voice is heard from the opposite side of the room*)

VOICE: I told you Bekezhan, do not rampage for nothing. She is not here.

(*Bekezhan is gripped by fear. His guards are terrified and they shout: "A phantom! A phantom! The stone palace is full of monsters and djinns!" Jostling each other in their haste, the guards hurry off*)

BEKEZHAN: Pull yourselves together, you worthless cowards! (*Kicking them with his feet, he brings back in some of the guards who were trying to call out*). No, there are no phantoms! Even if there are, Bekezhan is not afraid of them! Assemble all the good marksmen. Bring them down to the lake – to the "Swans' Nest". Shoot down the swans to the very last one. Zhibek shall not escape me!

CHIEF OF THE GUARD: Master, let us bring Tolegen out of the dungeon. He is an excellent marksman, second to none

BEKEZHAN: So be it. His hour has come. But do not tell him that Zhibek has turned into a swan.

SONG OF THE SWANS

(*On the surface of the radiant lake, known by the people as "Swans' Nest", swans are gracefully swimming. Their trumpeting calls to mind the tune of the song "Gak-ku". They dance joyfully on the water. Tunes ring out. Tolegen appears with a stone block round his ankles and holding a bow*)

BEKEZHAN: Well, show us your marksmanship! If an arrow fails to find its target – I'll rob you of your head. If you bring down the swan with a gold bracelet I shall personally lead you to your beloved Zhibek.

TOLEGEN (*rejoicing*): Is that true Lord Bekezhan?

BEKEZHAN: When has Bekezhan ever lied? (*He pats the young man on his back and laughs excitedly*) I myself will arrange your wedding.

TOLEGEN: Thank you my lord? I shall do my best…

* * *

(*Once again carefree life can be seen on the shore of the lake. The festival of swans continues. Suddenly there is a flash of lightning and a rumble of thunder. The whole scene changes in an instant.*

Bekezhan's guards suddenly appear and merciless slaughter begins as they shoot at the swans

Dead swans cover the smooth surface of the lake. Heart-rending deep-throated calls of the birds. Noisy flapping of white wings)

BEKEZHAN (*with a loud satisfied laugh*): You have triumphed, my guards. There is not a single living swan left on this lake! It is all over, I am pleased. Now you may drink wine and make merry!

(*Bekezhan leads the way and the guards' drunken revels begin*)

CHORUS: We are the guards bold and fleet,
        Bekezhan is our father and master.

No enemy we might meet
can escape from us or run faster.
Our arms shall deal him a deathly blow,
for the sake of our Master and Lord.
If on our way we meet a foe,
he'll be slain by fire and the sword.
We shall crush him underfoot
and capture every town,
as we march through dust and soot
bringing our enemies down.
Sabres, bows and spears at the ready,
The world rolls along, but our hands are steady.

CHIEF OF THE GUARD: Hail to our hero Bekezhan!

GUARDS: Hail to our hero Bekezhan!
　　　　Hail!
　　　Hail!
　　Hail!

CHIEF OF THE GUARD: Bekezhan. It is not right for Tolegen to make merry with us.

BEKEZHAN: Why?

CHIEF OF THE GUARD: He has not fired a single arrow. Look, his quiver is still full of arrows.

(*Bekezhan inspects Tolegen's quiver*)

BEKEZHAN: You have not fired a single shot. Whom did you take pity on?

TOLEGEN: It is not the custom to shoot at swans, Lord Bekezhan.

BEKEZHAN: Foolish boy! There is nothing more precious than man in this world. If necessary we shall shoot every swan on earth. You did not keep your promise.

TOLEGEN: Why? I was looking for the swan with the gold bracelet.

BEKEZHAN: How could you ever have found her in all the confusion of the shooting? You simple didn't shoot at a single swan. What punishment can we devise for you?

CHIEF OF THE GUARD: A crime like that you always used to punish by death.

BEKEZHAN: You are right. So be it.

CHIEF OF THE GUARD: How do you command that we kill him? Should we strangle him or cut off his head?

BEKEZHAN: First strangle him… and then cut off his head…

(*The guards drag Tolegen away, when the cry of a swan rings out overhead. The merry-making immediately stops and all raise their heads to look at the sky. Above the sky is hovering a white swan adorned with a gold bracelet*).

CHIEF OF THE GUARD: Bekezhan! A swan! One has survived!

BEKEZHAN: It's the swan with a gold bracelet! Bring it down!

(*Everyone starts shooting arrows but they fail to hit the bird*)

CHIEF OF THE GUARD: Bekezhan! The swan is flying high, the arrows can't reach it!

BEKEZHAN: You must reach it, sleepy good-for-nothings!

(*Again they shoot and again they fail to strike the bird*)

BEKEZHAN: Your turn has come, Tolegen! Shoot! If you bring down the swan, your life is spared.

TOLEGEN: Take the stone block off my foot. Otherwise I cannot shoot.

(The guards set Tologen free)

BEKEZHAN: Hurry up and shoot!

(Tologen slowly raises his bow)

BEKEZHAN: Shoot, I tell you!

(Tologen takes aim slowly, but he cannot bring himself to shoot. The swan flies off)

BEKEZHAN: You wretch! The swan's moving off! Everyone run after it!

(They all hurry after the swan. Tolegen, seizing the moment, runs off)

* * *

(Zhibek-swan is flying quietly above the green steppe)

ZHIBEK-SWAN: How beautiful it is here! From high up above. How wonderful life is! The emerald grass, the green forest and flowers fluttering in the breeze. A feast for the eyes! A miracle! But where is the "Swans' Nest" down there? I can see the lake but no swans.

(The lone swan circles above the green world below her)

* * *

(On the shore of the lake Tolegen keeps track of the lone swan. Unexpectedly the swan alights on the ground next to him. Tolegen picks up his bow)

TOLEGEN: The swan with the gold bracelet! Why has this bird come to rest in front of me?

(*Tolegen takes aim at the swan*)

ZHIBEK-SWAN: Shoot me quickly, Tolegen!

TOLEGEN: You can speak the language of men?

ZHIBEK-SWAN: Can't you hear me?

TOLEGEN: But how do you know my name?

ZHIBEK-SWAN: I know it and have known it for a long time.

TOLEGEN: That's miraculous! But why are you asking me to shoot you?

ZHIBEK-SWAN: Because then you will regain your happiness.

TOLEGEN: And where does my happiness lie?

ZHIBEK-SWAN: To be forever with your beloved.

TOLEGEN: Perhaps you'll tell me her name?

ZHIBEK-SWAN: She is called Zhibek. But now she is Bekezhan's prisoner.

TOLEGEN: That's right, swan. And if I shoot you down, Swan with the gold bracelet, Bekezhan will hold a wedding-feast for me and Zhibek.

ZHIBEK-SWAN: What are you waiting for? Shoot.

(*Tolegen does not know what to do. He lifts up his bow and then puts it down again*)

ZHIBEK-SWAN: For the sake of your beloved, you will probably not take pity on a swan.

TOLEGEN: What a beautiful bird you are! How should I choose? Zhibek or a swan? A swan or Zhibek? (*He raises his bow*). No, I cannot shoot. My hands are shaking and my eyes are clouding over.

ZHIBEK-SWAN: Then I shall fly away. And you will not meet your beloved.

TOLEGEN: I have no other way out, my beautiful swan. She is the finest creation in the world of men, you are the finest creation in the world of birds. I shall remain a hapless creature. Zhibek has been told long since that I am no longer among the living. Perhaps she will still be able to find happiness. And if I were to kill you, Zhibek would never forgive me anyway. Farewell. Be happy, talking bird!

(*Tolegen sits down and presses his forehead against a stone*)

ZHIBEK-SWAN: Tolegen! Lift up your head and open your eyes!

(*Tolegen raises his head and sees Zhibek before him and falls down unconscious. Zhibek splashes his face with water to bring him round*)

TOLEGEN: Am I awake or is this a dream? What is this miracle? Zhibek? You are my dream, Zhibek!

ZHIBEK: This is real.

TOLEGEN: Zhibek! My little swan, Zhibek! (*He embraces her*)

ZHIBEK: Tolegen!..

ACT TWO

A detachment of Bekezhan's guards. They are all looking for Tolegen.

BEKEZHAN: The earth can't have swallowed them whole? There is no sign of the prisoner, or that swan!..

CHIEF OF THE GUARD: Perhaps our prisoner has turned into a swan? I have heard that people who are truly in love can turn into swans.

BEKEZHAN: Enough of that, you numbskull! If the son of some pauper can turn into a swan, why then do I not turn into a phoenix? Look for them. Find them and bring them to me!

CHIEF OF THE GUARD: They are not here, Master. There is some mystery afoot. I feel uneasy, my Lord!

BEKEZHAN: Are you shaking, you coward? I remember now, how last time you were the first to try and slip out of the palace. I shall have you beheaded, so that you do not spread panic. (*He pulls his sabre out of its sheath*)

CHIEF OF THE GUARD (*hiding his head in his hands*): You cannot kill me, Master!

BEKEZHAN: But why not?

CHIEF OF THE GUARD: Because it was I who wrote the words and composed the music for the song: "Bekezhan is our father and master".

BEKEZHAN: So that's it! Imagine that such a coward should write heroes' songs! All right you cunning fellow, find me the fugitives! If they are not found, everyone shall be hung! Look for them!

(*Zhibek and Tolegen are on the shore of the lake, walking through the beautiful landscape. Together they are singing the well-known song by the composer Ibrai - "Gak-ku"*)

ZHIBEK: Tolegen! Tolegen! Look, there lie the dead swans! Look – one, two… three. There are ten, twenty of them. You can see the arrows that pierced them. Who killed the birds?

(*Tolegen says* nothing)

Why do you not reply, Tolegen? Here swans have been slain! Poor luckless birds… My beautiful swans! My dear swans!

(*Zhibek kneels down and weeps. Tolegen embraces Zhibek and tries to comfort her*).

ZHIBEK: Was it you who were killing the swans?

TOLEGEN: Yes… We were…

ZHIBEK: Do not come near me! You are a true villain!

TOLEGEN: Zhibek! Dear Zhibek, listen to me! After you ceased to be Bekezhan's prisoner, turned into a white swan and escaped from him, in his fury he gave orders for all the swans on the lake to be destroyed. He dragged me out of the stone dungeon. He was looking for you.

ZHIBEK: So that means I was the reason for the death of the swans? Then I am ready to die. I cannot be the only one from the "Swans' Nest" to enjoy happiness.

TOLEGEN: And me? What will become of me? Are you ready to take your leave of me so fast, so easily? You and I have endured such torture and injustice on our path to happiness… Must we be torn apart?

ZHIBEK: How can we be happy when the swans have been slain and the "Swans' Nest" is empty? I would rather throw myself from the rocks into the lake.

(*She clambers up the rocks. Tolegen rushes after her*)

TOLEGEN: Stop Zhibek! We shall die together…

ZHIBEK: No, Tolegen. You were shooting at swans. There is no place for you among pure souls.

ZHIBEK: I wasn't shooting, Zhibek! Because of that, Bekezhan sentenced me to death.

ZHIBEK: There's no need to justify yourself, Tolegen! After that slaughter of the birds we cannot be happy. Farewell, Tolegen!

(*Zhibek is about to throw herself into the lake when the Voice is heard*).

VOICE: Stop and think, Zhibek! Do not leave Tolegen on his own. For your sake he has suffered so much pain.

ZHIBEK: A voice, that very same voice? My protector, answer me. I am to blame for the blood of those slain birds. How can I count on any happiness?

VOICE: Calm yourself. At least a little. You yourself will come to understand…

(*Bekezhan's guards approach*)

CHIEF OF THE GUARD: Bekezhan, they are here. They are trying to escape us! There they are, climbing up the rocks.

BEKEZHAN: The cursed fugitives! So you're caught at last? Kill them both!

(*At the very first shots Zhibek turns into a swan and flies away*)

BEKEZHAN: Catch Tolegen!

(*The guards rush after Tolegen and surround him. A fight begins but the guards prove unable to take Tolegen prisoner*).

BEKEZHAN: Pathetic weaklings! Give him to me! I shall test the strength of the young stalwart insistent on winning Zhibek's hand.

CHIEF OF THE GUARD: That will be for the best, Master! We shall step back.

(*The guards move away and form a circle round Tolegen. The rivals engage in single combat. Tolegen gains the upper hand*)

BEKEZHAN: Do not kill me, Tolegen! You have won and I am defeated. It is a dishonourable for a warrior to cut off a bowed head. Let me go and we shall be friends.

(*Tolegen lets Bekezhan go*)

TOLEGEN: I am always ready for friendship.

(*They embrace. Bekezhan does not keep his word. As soon as Tolegen turns away, Bekezhan shoots an arrow at him. The arrow pierces Tolegen's shoulder. Tolegen, now fatally wounded, falls to the ground. He sings a song as he bids life farewell. At that moment Zhibek-Swan flies over the heads of the people on the lake shore*)

CHIEF OF THE GUARD: Bekezhan! Bekezhan! The swan!

(*Zhibek-Swan casts down the gold bracelet, which Bekezhan had given her. It falls right in front of him and Bekazhan picks it up*).

BEKEZHAN: This is the swan who was wearing the gold bracelet! Shoot!

ZHIBEK-SWAN: Do not shoot, Bekezhan! You have drowned the "Swans' Nest" in blood. You betrayed Tolegen and killed him. That is enough!

BEKEZHAN: And how, do you think, I should act now? I abandoned my sense of honour. I knelt before you and begged you to be my wife – but you would not listen. My love was no less than the feelings of Tolegen – you preferred not to understand it.

ZHIBEK-SWAN: You have shed the blood of innocent creatures.

BEKEZHAN: Forgive me, Zhibek.

ZHIBEK-SWAN: I intend to insist on my own conditions.

BEKAZHAN: I am ready to accept any conditions from you, dear Zhibek.

ZHIBEK-SWAN: Then shut your eyes and wave your arms like wings. If your feelings are pure, like mine, you will turn into a swan as I have. If you are deceiving me, then you will turn into a vulture. Do you accept?

(*Bekezhan is at a loss and does not know how to reply*)

ZHIBEK-SWAN: I do not hear your reply, Bekezhan. Are you not sure of yourself?

BEKEZHAN: Why not? I am sure...

ZHIBEK-SWAN: Then answer, do not hesitate.

BEKEZHAN: Just a moment... Just a moment...

CHIEF OF THE GUARD: Answer her, Master!

BEKEZHAN (*throwing him a rapid glance, enough to kill him...*): You dastardly hypocrite...

ZHIBEK-SWAN: Close your eyes.

BEKEZHAN: I have closed them.

ZHIBEK-SWAN: Stretch out your arms.

BEKEZHAN: They are stretched out.

CHIEF OF THE GUARD: Stretch them out properly! (*He helps Bekezhan*). Like that...

ZHIBEK-SWAN: Now wave them up and down.

(*Bekezhan waves his arms and immediately turns into a vulture and flies off*)

CHIEF OF THE GUARD: He has turned into a vulture! Bekezhan is now a vulture! Farewell, Master Bekezhan! (*He looks round at all the others*). Come now guards, come over here! Now instead of the song "Bekezhan is our father and master" we shall sing our other song, which I wrote long ago.

CHORUS OF GUARDS: When suddenly his wings appeared,
he vanished over the hill.
The villain hitherto so feared,
he would be fighting still,
but now with beasts and not with men.
Our lives had been in his cruel hands
and his power beyond our ken.
Today we have shaken off those bands
and you can be sure my brother guards,
it is I who shall the orders give.
Let us feast and drink and all play cards,
and tomorrow decide how we shall live.
We shall not grieve in vain today
Just follow my lead, come what may!

VOICE: Feast, make merry! Sing loudly and caw!

CHIEF OF THE GUARDS: We shall feast, make merry, sing loudly and caw!

VOICE: You shall turn into black crows!

CHIEF OF THE GUARDS: Into crows? Cr…Crows…Caw!

(*The guards turn into crows and cawing as they go, fly off and away*).

* * *

(*The lifeless body of Tolegen lies on the shore of the lake. Zhibek sits down next to him. She passes her hand three times across Tolegen's face*)

ZHIBEK: Open your eyes Tolegen! Rise to your feet!

(*Tolegen opens his eyes. He stands up and looks around him in astonishment*)

TOLEGEN: How long did I sleep? Night is falling.

ZHIBEK: You must wake up, Tolegen. Can you hear the calls of the swans?

TOLREGEN: Yes I hear them. Their calls sound sad.

ZHIBEK: The swans have come back to life and now they are bidding farewell to their home. They will not be coming back here.

TOLEGEN: And what shall we do?

ZHIBEK: We shall leave together with them.

TOLEGEN: You shall fly away, but I shall remain.

ZHIBEK: No we shall leave together. There is no place for us here.

TOLEGEN: But how can I follow you? Surely I shall not turn into a swan?

ZHIBEK: Bekezhan turned into a vulture, the guards turned into black crows.

TOLEGEN: How did it happen?

ZHIBEK: I shall tell you later. And now, close your eyes. First raise your arms and wave them up and down like wings. Just watch what you are turning into.

(*Zhibek looks at him with a smile. Tolegen waves his arms three times and turns into a magnificent white swan. Zhibek turns into a swan as well and they soar skywards together*)

VOICE OF ZHIBEK: Farewell, mirror-lake!

VOICE OF TOLEGEN: Farewell "Swans' Nest".

VOICE OF ZHIBEK: We shall not return till people grow kind again and begin to love all that lives on this earth. Farewell!..

(*The old man and his grandson are sitting on the shore of the lake. The old man has finished telling him the legend about the "Swans' Nest"*)

OLD MAN: Because of men's cruelty the white swans left their home forever. Beautiful Zhibek and Tolegen and other young men and girls who loved each other truly, they too are said to have turned into white swans so as to escape from mankind's cruelty. Bekezhan and heartless people like him have turned into vultures and crows.

In those far-away times the swans deserted our lake and just the black crows now remain.

GRANDSON: Grandfather, are there people living among us who could turn into white swans?

OLD MAN: I do not know, my boy, perhaps there will be some. People who could not be together because of the intrigues of evil men. They say that lovers turn into swans. That is why nobody ever shoots at swans.

(*All of a sudden the boy jumps to his feet and claps his hands*)

GRANDSON: Grandfather! Grandfather! Look, white swans! Look there are two of them circling above the lake and singing. What are they singing about, Grandfather?

OLD MAN: They are singing about their sad past and how joyful they are to be together at last.

GRANDSON: Fly over here, dear swans! Fly over here! Come back to the nests where you belong! We have been pining without you, beautiful swans!

(*The boy runs down towards the lake*)

THE END

Dulat Issabekov, Holder of a State Prize of the Republic of Kazakhstan

The Actress

Dramatis Personae:

The Actress – Aigul Asanova
The Director
Erlen-1
Erlen-2
Company director
Actors taking part in the Rehearsal

In general, this is just a story – the biography of an actress. Her creative path. To put it briefly, a portrait of her life on stage.

The other characters in the play – as the theatre sees fit – could be presented in the form of just one person. That is up to the theatre company. The main aim is to create the image of the Actress.

So there she is – the Actress – on stage. She is dressed in an attractive housecoat, shown in an everyday setting at home. Her housecoat is not buttoned up – there is no-one in the house apart from her. As she walks round her home setting, sometimes the housecoat flaps open. The Actress often attempts to close her gaping housecoat which keeps flapping open. At other times she does not even notice it. She is talking or rather addressing the audience, sharing her innermost thoughts with them.

THE ACTRESS

When the curtain goes up the Actress is sitting in an armchair with one leg crossed over the other and talking on the telephone.

ACTRESS: Hallo. Yes, speaking. Who d'you need to speak to? Yes, it's me. You're saying you're a journalist? What d'you want to ask about? I'm sorry, but I haven't any free time at the moment. Get in touch later, tomorrow…

She replaces the receiver and then turns to the audience again. He says he's a journalist. He's probably planning to ask questions about my love-life again. Some correspondent turned up last year: I thought we'd had a meaningful conversation, but when I read what he'd written after it came out… It was shameful! He mixed everything up and exaggerated it all: the gossip, the emotional suffering, the men I'd found attractive and the ones who had been kindred spirits. He came out with all sorts of idle chatter, undermining everyone's honour and self-respect. There was hardly a word about parts in the theatre, it was all so superficial. He must have thought that if someone's a beautiful actress, then all they think about round the clock is Love… Let's leave all that to one side for the moment. Let me introduce myself: my name is Aigul Asanova. [!!!At this point the actress can give her actual first name and surname!!!]

I have not been working in this theatre for very long. The theatre is my second home. Or perhaps Home pure and simple…? The only thing I don't do here is sleep. The rest of my life goes on here. That's how it's been for thirty years. Theatre, rehearsals and home. Touring. I've starred in fourteen films. I had the starring role in nine of them and supporting roles in the other five. In most of the plays in our theatre's repertoire I've had leading parts. Talking about all of that is easy…but as for the ups and downs in everyday life! Quarrels, in-fighting, rivalry, jealousy, hatred… What can you say…? Sometimes all you want to do is turn your back on it all and live the life of a simple, ordinary woman. Sometimes I long to complete an ordinary nine-to-five day, drink some tea and relax in peace and quiet with my family. I even tried it out, seven years ago.

When our new chief director appeared, after listening to some evil gossip or other, he began to ease me out. He would always make a point of criticizing me at meetings of the artistic committee. He started taking away my leading parts and giving them to other people. The arguments and wrangling between us were becoming more and more heated. The atmosphere in the theatre was impossible by this time. The other actors started taking sides and forming cliques. All our talents and energies were focused not on the plays but the 'dramas' going on backstage. The chief director would not budge and neither was I prepared to give in. In the end, realizing that all the bitterness between the actors was approaching boiling-point, I handed in my resignation and left that theatre. Rumours about "Aigul Asanova having been driven out" spread almost that very same day to all the theatres of Kazakhstan and my 'friends', yes – my 'friends' in inverted commas – celebrated their victory with great relish. Especially the 'friends' in our theatre! I've almost lost my wits over these last eighteen months spent without (or outside) the theatre. Sometimes I felt I didn't even have enough space to move in when I was at home. But there was enough work in the theatre and on television. It turns out there is good money to be earned from a single advertisement. To put it another way, I even began earning more money than I had back in my days as an actress in the theatre. Yet…I found out that I cannot live without the theatre. As soon as I shut my eyes I start dreaming about it. I kept on dreaming about the theatre, longing to be back there, even if only as a doorman. Various newspapers kept writing about "Aigul Asanova turning her back on the theatre". Not long afterwards the chief director was dismissed and in his place a young director appeared, who invited me back again. I've been here ever since. The company's on holiday at the moment, but I'm not having any time off. My husband and I are busy preparing a new play, *Princess Turandot*.

Incidentally, my husband is working in our theatre now as well: he's working as one of the directors. He's my second husband.

THE ACTRESS

The first was a top-class pilot working for Aeroflot. He was too jealous. Unfortunately for him, all the parts I played involved love stores: Karagoz Bayan, Aktokty, Juliet, Cleopatra, Katharina the Shrew, Medea, Desdemona, Lysistrata, Beatrice and Mrs. Patrick Campbell. Each performance made his hair turn greyer. After one of my performances he turned up without warning at our theatre. I and the director were on our own, preparing the staging for Petruchio and Katharine in *The Taming of the Shrew*. The director was a young man, a striking young man. As soon as a man and a woman found themselves on stage alone, he was convinced they would embrace and start kissing each other. According to the stage directions, Katharina should only kiss Petruchio on the cheek. The director, on the other hand – to make matters worse he was playing Petruchio as well – made that scene last incredibly long. He began to embrace me, to paw me all over, kissing my face, my eyes and on the lips. He paid no attention to my objections, to my insisting "there's no scene with kissing on the lips, it would be against the author's idea". After declaring "to start with Shakespeare's long dead and won't be coming to the première, so he won't be able to argue about it: secondly in Shakespeare's day things were different. Today things are no longer the same. We have to stage the play in the light of modern requirements. That's why we turn to the classics nowadays". To make it clearer I can repeat the scene for you if you like (*looking towards the very back of the stage, the actress calls out in a loud voice*).

ACTRESS. Samat! Where are you Samat!

SAMAT. I'm here. What's happening?

ACTRESS. We're going to repeat the scene – that very same passage.

(*In comes Samat. He now has to play director, actor and the actress' husband*)

SAMAT. You've only just been telling me you were tired. I haven't even had time to shave.

ACTRESS. Never mind, you'll be able to shave your other cheek after the rehearsal I've just come over all inspired!

SAMAT. Wonderful! In that case we'll get down to work! Lights! Where are the damn lights?!

ACTRESS. Remember, we're going to play this scene according to the old version.

SAMAT. What d'you mean? You've already divorced your husband as a result of that staging. D'you want to divorce me too now?

ACTRESS. You can read into it what you want. I want to repeat the original staging. I'm coming round to like it more and more.

SAMAT. An actor shouldn't indulge in ad-libbing, but follow the director's instructions to the letter.

ACTRESS. But Monsieur Samat! An actor is not the director's mute slave, who just does what he's told…

SAMAT. Are you going to start giving me orders now…Don't forget I'm your husband, after all…

ACTRESS. Yes, you're my husband, but after the play's over. During the play we're both quite different people. Come on now, let's get started! Otherwise we'll quarrel and a whole day will have been wasted.

SAMAT. A man's virtue lies in his ability to put up with women's whims! (*He kisses her hand*). Well, my dearest, let's get started. Light! Lights! Bring on the lights! Light up the stage!

(*The stage is lit up by a beam of light.*) [The actors' costumes are a question of their personal taste. If they think they should be dressed as in Shakespeare's day, so be it].

EPISODE

KATHARINA. Just think, my friend, how might this game play out?

PETRUCHIO. An apt remark. But first kiss me on the cheek, Kate.

KATHARINA. How? Out in the street?

PETRUCHIO. No-o! God forbid! I would be ashamed to kiss you!

KATHARINA. Then let me begin the kissing…Just a moment… Wait

PETRUCHIO. There is nothing wrong with this, is there? Is it so unpleasant? Come now, come now, dearest Kate! It is better if what is good can be enjoyed all the sooner. There's a good side to everything!

AIGUL. Now that's the Shakespeare version. D'you remember how we used to play that very episode?

SAMAT. I remember… of course I do!

AIGUL. In that case let's repeat the close of this scene. When you are embarrassed, blushing red with shame and begin to kiss my face. You come up to me…like that…

SAMAT. There's no need to tell me how. I can manage just fine…

(*By this time the two of them are immersed in their roles again.*)

KATHARINA. Now I kiss you…Wait, just a moment. (*This time Petruchio after suddenly kissing Katharina, begins to kiss her neck, her lips, her breasts.*)

PETRUCHIO. Well, how was it, surely you weren't disappointed? So then, dearest Kate. It would be best if all that is good reached completion right away. There's a good side to everything… (*He hurls Katharina down on the bed and begins kissing her for all he is worth*)

(*There is a knock at the door. They both leap up from the bed. Petruchio-Samat leaves by the other door. Aigul walks over towards the audience. On her way she buttons up her housecoat so as to cover her exposed breasts. She attempts to tidy her tousled hair*).

AIGUL. Would you believe it, at that very moment my husband comes in?

(*Samat comes back, but this time in the role of Erlen – Aigul's husband. He looks at Aigul, who is looking rather helplessly at her crumpled bed.*)

ERLEN. Who's here?

AIGUL. Who are you talking about?

ERLEN. I'm asking you about that devil, who's dared to touch you up in my bed.

AIGUL. He's not a devil, he's an actor.

ERLEN. So he's an actor you say? But of course. Given he's an actor, he couldn't possibly be a devil. That's why, Mademoiselle Actress, I want to make my deepest apologies for disturbing your ardent passion by tactlessly appearing without warning (*He makes a deliberately low bow*). Just to think – how difficult it must be to cope with unexpected bursts of feeling! You couldn't even find an opportunity to shut the door properly, could you?

AIGUL. It wasn't passion. It was a scene with Katharina and Petruchio. Written by Shakespeare, no less!

ERLEN. No. my sunshine, you yourselves were the authors of that parody of a play. In the play *The Taming of the Shrew*, which I've had the opportunity to see, there is no scene where Petruchio touches up Katharina in bed.

AIGUL. What can I do if the director putting on the play is a screwball? If he's such a wild partner and out of control?

ERLEN. So that's why you decided to lie down and romp in the bed. How aw-ful for you!

AIGUL. You were meant to be in Uralsk though… Had you run out of kerosene again…? Was your plane out of action? Or was it like last time, when you declared a strike, demanding a salary increase?

ERLEN. Listen to yourself, just listen to what this crafty wench is saying! As if nothing had been happening. It turns out that a woman, who has known plenty of strangers' embraces, has also learnt how to brush things under the carpet. Don't you dare put the bed to rights!¬ You're trying to hide the traces of your misdemeanours, as if nothing had happened. No-o! You're not getting away with it! I'll make sure everyone knows. That'll be the proof of your crime!

AIGUL. (*who has only just realized that her husband is really very worked up*) Erlen, you don't really mean it, do you?

ERLEN. Until today I hadn't paid attention to the gossip, to the idle talk. I didn't even take seriously what friends and family were thinking, when they said: "While you're flying around in a dream world, down here on earth your wife's leading you a dance: get away from that wretched woman." Now I've seen it all for myself. I can't live with you any more.

AIGUL. What? Erlen... Out of the blue... You've decided to divorce me?

ERLEN. Yes... you've got it in one, Aigul. I can't stand it any more. It's tough for me too, living with suspicion all the time.

AIGUL. Erlen. You're barking up the wrong tree. You're beside yourself... I've never been unfaithful to you, even in my thoughts – let alone in reality!

ERLEN. Ha, ha, ha (*pointing at the bed*) No, never. You insist you haven't been unfaithful. How much more proof do I need?

AIGUL. But I keep telling you. That's part of the play. That's Shakespeare. Being in his plays is what every actor dreams about!

ERLEN. Shakespeare, Auezov, Mursepov, Gol... Gol...

AIGUL. Goldoni.

ERLEN. That's the one... There's no end to them. It's crazy passion every time. In all their plays you're lying there in bed after it all or kissing someone as if your life depended on it.

AIGUL. What can I do about it if all the parts are like that?

ERLEN. It's hard to believe that back in the past and today the writers could find nothing else to put in their pays but Love?

AIGUL. How were the poor fellows to know that the Kazakh actress, Aigul Asanova, was going to be acting in their plays and that she would have a very jealous husband?

ERLEN. That's it. I've had enough of all this wrangling. (*He makes for the door*).

AIGUL. Erlen. Where are you off too? Are you really going? And me... What about me?

ERLEN. You've got your beloved theatre… For you it's sweeter than honey…you've got your parts. Your interest in them will never fade. Every year they'll be several new plays. New parts, new characters…!

AIGUL. Erlen, you're a pilot. You should be able to look at all this from way up high…

ERLEN. My eyes are worn out, looking down on all your plays from up in the sky. My heart's worn out.

AIGUL. But wait, Erlen! Don't go! I can't live without you. You know that perfectly well. If things have gone this far, I can call in the actor and the director. For God's sake, nothing was going on between us…

ERLEN. Oh, yes! It's not the first time I've heard those words! Let go of me!

AIGUL. I can't let you go! You know I'll love you till my dying day. I could never be unfaithful! How on earth? If you want to hear me say it, I've got nobody besides you!

ERLEN. There's no other way out for me…

AIGUL. The children are about to come home from school. What do I say to them?

ERLEN. You should have thought about that before…

AIGUL. Erlen! You're accusing me of something I've never done. If you want me to, I can turn down this part and just play witches. You know I make a first-class witch.

ERLEN. I can imagine.

AIGUL. You praised me too, when I played the Witch in *Golden Cudgel*. That was in my first graduation play. You used to joke saying "You make a splendid witch!"

ERLEN. So you see at last – that's how it's turned out.

AIGUL. Let go of the door handle. Take your clothes off (*Aigul starts taking off his jacket*).

ERLEN. It's not worth the effort, Aigul! However guilty you may have been, don't start begging, falling down on your knees…

AIGUL. From the way you're playing hard to get… you have clearly got someone else. Isn't that right Erlen? If that's the case, there's no need to hide it.

ERLEN. So you're now going to tar me with the same brush?

AIGUL. No, Erlen. Look at me, straight in the eye. I beg of you! Look straight at me.

(*Erlen, with a rather sheepish expression, looks Aigul straight in the eye*)

All right… that's clear. No more explanations needed. You've found a kindred spirit this time… All you needed was an excuse. Now you've got one. .. All of a sudden, out of the blue… And now you can go. There are plenty of women who manage to exist without a husband, you know. I'll just be one of them. There's no need for you to have second thoughts. Somehow I'll cope with bringing up two children. I've been up against it before, when I and my small sister were stranded as orphans after the death of our parents. There were tears sometimes, but despite it all we pulled through. We'll get used to the hard times, there's very little that we poor wretched women can't learn to cope with. So, good riddance!

ERLEN. Aigul….Why are you accusing me?

THE ACTRESS

AIGUL. It's probably for the best if I move off now, before I come across you wrapped round another woman…

ERLEN. Aigul!

AIGUL. You're a pilot, I'm an actress. You're up in the skies and I'm down here on earth. Soon we'll be as far apart as Heaven and Earth… only, it appears, I poor wretch was not aware of it. Farewell (*Aigul pays no more attention to him and starts reciting Azhar's monologue from the play "Abai"*).

ERLEN. Aigul! What's up with you? What are you on about? We're divorced. Don't you understand? (*Aigul continues reading. Erlen shrugs his shoulders and walks off.*)

AIGUL. That was how we went our separate ways. Life at the theatre went on as usual. Soon after that there was the première of *The Tamong of the Shrew*. It was a great success. At that time Moscow was the capital of our enormous country. The play was taken on tour to Moscow and shown to the capital's public. The papers, radio and television praised our production to the skies. In the years that followed we put on productions of Goldoni's *Servant of Two Masters*, Chekhov's *Seagull*, Ostrovky's *Storm*, Auezov's *Black Eyes*, Musrepov's *Tragedy of the Poet* and a play based on Nurpeisov's novel *Blood and Sweat*. The name of our theatre was becoming internationally famous. We often toured abroad. Delhi, Prague, Cairo, Tehran, Riga, Kiev, Budapest, Minsk and then Moscow once more. To put it briefly, we covered half the world over four or five years. I was given the title "People's Artist". In those days every new play we put on was a great occasion. Countless congratulations, warm embraces and armfuls of flowers! The standing ovations showed how much respect the audiences had for our art: our boundless devotion to the theatre and love for what we did helped people forget about the problems in their everyday lives. We were bringing them joy and we felt like the happiest mortals on earth. I have two sons. The youngest has a degree in law and is working in a Kazakh embassy abroad. When he can get away, he comes home for visits. Three days ago he sent me 85 roses as a present for my birthday. The same evening he telephoned and when I asked: "My son, why did you send me 85 roses, what should I do with them all?" he replied, "I've already been working here for 85 days, Mama, and it turns out that over all that time I hadn't bought you a single flower. So this makes up for what I owed you over all that time!" At that he started laughing as well. How difficult was life with them, worries and endless struggles, especially when I had to be away on tour. I often had to separate them, persuade neighbours to look after them or take them off to stay with distant relatives. You should have seen how they wept and shouted "Mama, Mamochka!" when I came back after a long tour!... Best not to think back to it all… When I start reminiscing, tears start pouring from my eyes. Only a woman who's been on her own with small children can understand what that's like…

[HUMAN WEAKNESS]

Feeling split in two is something all living creatures experience. Nobody can live relying just on ideas. Goals and noble aspirations are one thing: ordinary everyday life is quite different. So it was for this actress.

Her ideal was to be able to devote her whole life to the stage, to bring alive characters and while on that path to turn her back completely on trivial details of everyday life, on its colourful temptations. The life of ideas and emotions is one shaped by our brain, by our consciousness.

Flesh makes very different demands. To survive everyday life, certain conditions are essential. Often the individual becomes a slave to the situations in which he has to survive. Those situations often leave little room for his essential spirit, for his ideas to flourish.

THE ACTRESS

(*The Actress appears to be dreaming or perhaps she really is asleep*) [that choice would be up to the director]]

VOICE. Aigul Asanova! You truly deserve the titles and honours accorded to the masters of the stage! Your deep devotion to your craft and your talent are on a par with those of great actors from other countries. Yet you are in a different world. You are an actress in a poor country. You are not a creator – you are a performer. Like any performer who does not mind what he is asked to perform, you are used to all manner of parts, one after the other. Deeply rooted in your consciousness is the thought that "someone from the world of art has to live in poverty and hardship". That is not a thought you will be able to shake off. You were educated in a patriotic spirit. A patriot, as we all know, is someone who is used to hardship and takes a poor view of prosperity. Despite poverty and privations in the past you steadfastly put your art before everything else. All praise and credit to you, may your creative labours be crowned with success...

(*The actress has woken and asks where the VOICE had come from? Was someone actually speaking or were those thoughts all her own...?*)

AIGUL. (*clutching her head*) What was all that? Where did that voice come from? Who was speaking or were those my own thoughts? You shut your eyes and there's one person there, you open them and there are two. Why is a person split in two, like two parts of a single whole! What a delusion!

VOICE. There's nothing out of the ordinary about that! Who's ever known someone who never changed and always remained true to himself? Ever since Man was created he's led a double life, surely? What he says is one thing and how he acts is another. So Aigul, it was not for nothing that your ancestors used to say: "Every whole has two halves".

AIGUL. (*Seeing people around her, she suddenly takes fright.*) Who are you? How did you turn up next to me?

AIGUL-2. I'm with you all the time. I am you.

AIGUL. Are you a woman or a man?

AIGUL-2. I shall be whatever you think I am.

AIGUL. (*Scared*) I really think I'm losing my mind…

AIGUL-2. Don't be frightened Agul! I am just your inner voice, but in human form. It's only now that you are beginning to notice me and take note of what I say. Until today you only existed so as to carry out someone else's instructions, but now you've begun to reflect. You now have plenty of doubts and questions. You're becoming more aware.

[**REHEARSAL.** Which scene and which play to choose for the rehearsal – that depends on the director's own choice. It could be *The Taming of the Shrew*, *Tragedy of the Poet* or even *Carmen*.]

CARMEN

DIRECTOR. I repeat. Once more!

ACTRESS. Oh…I'm dead tired. If only we could have a tiny break?

DIRECTOR. No! You haven't really found your way into the part. Come on now, we'll start the scene again from the very beginning. One sentence is repeated several times. Again and again.

ACTRESS. Sir! You're starting to turn me into a tool for your own idea.

DIRECTOR. An actor is the fruit of the director's imagination!

ACTRESS. No-o! I'm the fruit of my own thoughts. What would become of me, if I were to turn into the fruit of a hundred different directors!

DIRECTOR. There'll be nothing left, just a skeleton. D'you know what a Kazakh says when he entrusts his young child to the mullah for his schooling? He uses the words: "Your body (literally flesh) is yours but your bones are mine". If you set off to the next world with nothing but bones, then you won't burn in hell! Ha-ha-ha! Let's get down to work now...

[*The rehearsal continues, but how long it lasts is up to the Director*]

(*The "Carmen" dance*)

(*The moment of Carmen's death*)

(*The Actress is beside herself with anger by this time. She is completely exhausted, at the end of her tether.*)

DIRECTOR. (*He is also tired by this time*) Well, that's enough for today. Tomorrow it's the première. We probably need to save up all our energy and willpower for tomorrow.

ACTRESS. I've already used up all my energy and willpower on this rehearsal. I haven't got the strength to come out for the première.

DIRECTOR. What's that meant to mean?

ACTRESS. Just what it says! I can't appear in front of the audience tomorrow.

DIRECTOR. But the première was announced a month in advance. It's been a complete sell-out. That would mean we'd have to come out in front of the audience and announce "Dear Friends, you can all go off home now. There's not going to be a première today. The reason is that our People's Artist, Aigul Asanova, tired herself out at the rehearsal. If it's not too much trouble, do come back tomorrow".

ACTRESS. Your sarcasm's completely out of place! An actor isn't some kind of mechanical clock, which you only have to wind up for it to start ticking again and counting out the time. An actor's a living being!

DIRECTOR. What are you trying to say?

ACTRESS. You should have started the rehearsal earlier and you kept on putting thing's off. You were having a fine time…

DIRECTOR. We were not having a fine time…

ACTRESS. All right, all right. You were raising money… Travelling round the country… and now you're letting off steam at me for all the problems you've encountered.

DIRECTOR. (*cheering up all of a sudden*) My precious, Aigul Asanova. When the première's over tomorrow I'll present you with a gold necklace! I'll fasten it round your neck with my very own hands in honour of your peerless work and rare talent!

ACTRESS. Don't keep telling me fairy-stories, Sir! It's not the first time you've told me that. I think you and I have long since left behind us the time when we might deceive each other with jests like that.

DIRECTOR. So what's going to happen?

ACTRESS. Let it be (*she laughs*)… See you tomorrow! At the première!

(*The Actress is now alone*)

ACTRESS. The première was a tremendous success. The grateful audience wouldn't let us actors leave the stage … They went on clapping for fifteen minutes, clapping for all they were worth. Some prominent politicians were among them. They all congratulated us and shook my hand. Incidentally…

AIGUL-2. Yes and on that day someone gave you a complimentary ticket…

ACTRESS. Oh yes, it had completely slipped my mind. Go on then, read it our!

AIGUL-2. *(Reading out loud)* "Dear Aigul Asanova. The limited construction company "Gimarat" has the great honour of inviting you to attend a function to mark the tenth anniversary of its founding. You would be doing us a great honour if you would agree on this occasion to perform some of your songs or an extract from one of your favourite plays. These celebrations will be taking place in the Blue Hall of the Ankara Hotel. A group of our staff members will be there to welcome you at the entrance to the hotel, as will our gift to you of a new car.

Yours faithfully – the Gimarat Company"

So, Aigul Asanova, off you go! Fly away! As fast as you can! In two hours you'll be the owner of a foreign car, which you could never afford sweating away for your whole working life "for the sake of Art, for the sake of the People".

(*In the Blue Hall of the Ankara Hotel. High-ranking guests. Young men are dashing nimbly about. Young women trying to show how sophisticated they are. Music.*)

TOASTS. "Here's to the company's 10th Anniversary!"
"May ten years lead on to a hundred!"
"May Kazakhstan's economy blossom!"
"Long live the company's President"

YOUNG MAN. Long live our special guest, our star artist, the pride and joy of our nation, Aigul Asanova! We now invite Aigul Asanova to proceed to the centre of the hall!

(*The guests welcome Aigul with applause. She moves into the centre of the hall and bows to the public.*)

ACTRESS. Ladies and gentlemen! The President of your limited company… "Gimarat" has invited me to your celebrations. This is not just an honour for me personally but for Kazakh art in general, so I should like to express my deep gratitude to you all…

YOUNG MAN. Ladies and gentlemen! Hip hip hurrah! Let Aigul Asanova now sing us one of her songs. Let us all greet her with our applause!

ACTRESS. I'm not a singer, I'm an actress. A serious actress.

YOUNG MAN. And we're a limited company. Do sing a song for us.

ACTRESS. Why "limited"?

YOUNG MAN. That means that we don't answer unnecessary questions. We only ask questions. We consider that as you are an artist, you will sing a song without fail. So please will you carry out our request.

ACTRESS (*looking at him in astonishment*) And who might you be?

YOUNG MAN. I'm just me…

ACTRESS. How strange… Your voice is familiar, but you look different…

YOUNG MAN. Ladies and gentlemen, let's applaud once more!

THE ACTRESS

(Aigul taks up position centre stage. [She performs a song or an extract from a play, as the Director sees fit. He can choose either option, taking into account circumstances or time.]

YOUNG MAN. Bravo, bravo! Long live Kazakh art! Ladies and gentlemen, please raise your glasses to Kazakh culture! Now, allow me, in the name of the whole company to thank our star of the Kazakh stage, pride of our people, Aigul Asanova, for the honour she has shown us by attending our celebrations, and to present her with the keys to a foreign car. (*He claps and hands her the keys – a short silence for the solemn moment with the keys*).

ACTRESS. My heartfelt thanks to you for this honour and for the deep respect you have shown me!

YOUNG MAN. May I congratulate you on the prize and may I kiss your hand.

(Aigul is still looking at the young man in surprise as she holds out her hand. At that very moment the young man takes a wig off his head)

ACTRESS. It's you…Is it really you? The voice was familiar, but you looked like a stranger. Why did you have to go and put a wig on? To make a laughing-stock of me? Or was it some kind of revenge?

YOUNG MAN. This is where we are now, Madam Aigul the Beautiful! In the Soviet era you were so obstinate and hard to please. You would never allow anyone to get close to you, you were always the star up so high that you were out of reach. The government spoilt you, it kept singling you out for praise, conferring titles on you, singling you out for praise rather than anyone else. There was a time when you would not even deign to look at me, someone who was desperately in love with you and ready to fall at your feet.

But now the times are different. Now you depend on me. If I give you my support, you'll still enjoy the big time. If I feel inclined,

I can send you off on a foreign tour. If your glory is fading, I can make sure that you still sparkle like the brightest star in the sky. These sublime beauties here tonight are clustering round me too (*he points at the beautiful women surrounding him*).

Yet I am an obliging fellow, with a big heart. Tonight I have, as it were, rekindled the sincere feelings I once had for you by inviting you here for this grand occasion and showering you with every consideration. If you want to, I could take you with me next week to Antalya. We could spend a few days there on holiday.

ACTRESS. You have that much power…?

YOUNG MAN. Yes!

ACTRESS. Despite the "limited responsibility"?

YOUNG MAN. The responsibility is limited, but the possibilities are limitless… (*He laughs*).

ACTRESS. What sly laughter…!

(*The young man drops a key down the cleavage of one of the girls and leaves the hall.*)

ACTRESS. Pathetic non-entities! (*She leaves the hall*)

ACTRESS AND THE DIRECTOR

DIRECTOR. Well, how was the party?

ACTRESS. Wonderful! Their show was more successful than the one our theatre put on.

DIRECTOR. I heard rumours that the business-man had at one time been in love with you.

ACTRESS. Yes!…

DIRECTOR. Did he really invite you to Antalya?

THE ACTRESS

ACTRESS. Yes, he did. Yes he invited me! To Antalya, to Madagascar, to Karlovy Vary and the Ivory Coast.

DIRECTOR. And you agreed to go?

ACTRESS. Yes, I agreed! On our return he intends to give me by way of compensation for everything a hundred thousand dollars. How do you view all that, my intended. Will you let your wife set off? When I return you'll have a hundred thousand dollars. In hard currency!

(*The Director thinks it over*)

Why don't you say anything? Has real money made your head spin?

DIRECTOR. I...I... Your thoughts...

ACTRESS. So that's it. (*She slaps him on the cheek*) Gasbag! You're all hot air!

DIRECTOR. Thank you, Aigul! You're the very proudest of women! You're a veritable Medea! You're a modern version of Tomyris. I wanted to put you to the test (*He puts his arm round the shoulders of a now weeping Aigul.*)

ACTRESS. He doesn't need me. He only has one idea in his head, he wants to take his revenge, causing me as much pain as he can. O Lord, how sad is the prospect that in the future we'll be living among those self-satisfied money-bags, who only see everything in terms of cash!

DIRECTOR. Don't get upset, Aigul! Their wealth is in the hands of the fraud police while your wealth is in the hands of God himself (*He wipes away her tears*). I'm going to be putting on *Medea* soon and I'll dedicate it to you, my dear. Be prepared!

ACTRESS. D'you really mean it?

DIRECTOR. (*with a smile*) This time it's for real (*he puts his arms round her shoulders*).

* * *

ACTRESS. After *Medea* our theatre put on the play *Princess Turandot* by the Italian dramatist Gozzi. With that play we went on tour the following year to Cairo, where we took part in a drama festival for Asian countries. The play was a tremendous success. I was given the main prize of the festival for my performance as Turandot.

[If the director sees it as appropriate he can show Aigul being presented with the festival's Grand Prix]

Two days later we came back home and received a warm welcome from members of the government, who met us at the airport.

We were given armfuls of flowers. There were cheers, laughter and countless congratulations.

From the airport I took a taxi and drove straight to the hospital. My son who had been involved in a motor accident in the past was still suffering from the consequences of his injuries and had found himself back in hospital. A week before my trip to Cairo, his right leg had started going numb and he had had to go back to hospital a third time. When he saw me I could see he had tears in his eyes as he murmured: "Mama, are you really back home? I was already thinking I wouldn't see you again". According to the doctors it was essential that he be sent to Germany for treatment. The operation in a foreign clinic would cost forty thousand dollars. I turned with a request for help to one of the members of the government who had come out to meet us at the airport, but he just said by way of reply: "We'll have to see, we'll discuss it and let you know what decision is taken". Since then over two months of horribly stressful waiting have gone by.

THE ACTRESS

(*The director comes in beaming with joy*)

DIRECTOR. Aigul! Congratulate me, Aigul!

ACTRESS. Congratulations! What's the good news? Tell me, quickly...

DIRECTOR. I've just been received at the Ministry.

ACTRESS. And what was the good news he gave you?

DIRECTOR. I've been invited to take the production of *Princess Turandot* to the Italian city of Turin. Here's the actual invitation! In two days' time I'm to fly to Italy to sign the contract!

ACTRESS. Congratulations! (*Although it is clear from her face that she is not thrilled by what she has just heard.*)

DIRECTOR. I'm travelling there with two ballet dancers, one opera singer and two cellists. They're going to sign long-term contracts as well. Aigul, what don't you like about it? Why are you forcing yourself so hard to smile.

ACTRESS. Two dancers, two cellists and a director. So they need talent and we don't... Who'll still be left here in two years' time?

DIRECTOR. The Kazakhs are a talented people. They'll be plenty of talent springing up in these parts...

ACTRESS. They'll also be setting off for America, or England, Belgium, Denmark, Spain, Germany, France...

DIRECTOR. Once I get there and have settled in, I'll send you the papers so you can join me.

ACTRESS. Thanks for the noble intentions... I... I am an actress in the Kazakh theatre, speaking Kazakh. A language is not like a cello, simple to export. I was born on the Kazakh stage and I shall take my last breath on it.

DIRECTOR. After the contract's signed I shall… send you the forty thousand dollars required for the operation.

ACTRESS. You only received the invitation for Italy today. And when did that conversation begin…

DIRECTOR. (*Hesitating as he tries to decide how to reply…*) As regards that…

ACTRESS. What sorry creatures we're all becoming! I can't even trust my own husband. How did you keep from exploding with all the effort of keeping silent about the plan…?

DIRECTOR. I didn't want to shout about it from the rooftops before everything was finalized.

ACTRESS. But, of course.. One shouldn't mention incomplete plans even to a wife… That all had to be kept to yourself, to be kept secret (*there is a shake in her voice by this time*)

DIRECTOR. Aigul, surely you're not hurt by this!? Don't be silly! Off we go to Italy. What's still of interest here nowadays? "In the name of the country, our nation, our people!" – all those are meaningless words, empty slogans. There's nobody here who would be ready to give his all for our people. Even if you were to work abroad as a cleaner you'd be ten times better off than here.

ACTRESS. "A hero for his native land…"

DIRECTOR. "Dogs run after the biggest bone…". The days for proverbs like that are long since past. Just think for a moment!

ACTRESS. No, thank you for your good intentions. **I…I** am an actress in the Kazakh theatre, playing parts in the Kazakh language. A language is not like caviar, the poor thing can't be exported. I was born on the Kazakh stage and I shall close my eyes for the last time on that same stage…

DIRECTOR. How wonderful Soviet propaganda was here, able to fill everyone's consciousness with noble patriotic sentiments!

ACTRESS. Kazakhs knew how to love their country before the days of Soviet propaganda...

DIRECTOR. And what will you do if tomorrow your theatre stops being needed by anyone anymore...?

ACTRESS. If that's the case, I shall be the last actress, playing the last part in the Kazakh language in front of the last Kazakh theatre-goer!

DIRECTOR. It's a golden cage and you're the parrot, who despite all possible hardships and privations will not be able to desert your golden cage!

* * *

AIGUL. After divorcing my husband with whom I had spent twelve years, for a long time I remained single. I did not want my young son and daughter to be dependent in any way on a stranger. My former husband did not return from abroad. I did notice though that he was sitting among the audience during the première of *The Taming of the Shrew*. I haven't seen him again since then. Perhaps he's sitting in the audience now as well...

ERLEN-2. (Sitting in the stalls). Yes, I'm here!

AIGUL. Who's that? Who's calling out?

ERLEN-2. It's me. Erlen the Second (*He gets up from his seat and walks up on to the stage*)

AIGUL. What d'you mean – Erlen the Second? Whoever you might be, you can't come up here. Go back to your seat and sit down. You can see perfectly well that a play's in progress.

ERLEN-2. Our whole life is nothing but drama. Each one of us has his own part to play…

AIGUL. You can spout your philosophy somewhere else! Leave the stage! Call the manager! Where is he?

ERLEN-2. I beg of you, don't call anyone to come and help you. I'll leave in just a moment. After all, surely ordinary mortals ought one day to be able to spend a moment on stage (*He looks out at the audience*). Be generous with your forgiveness, just for a moment. Well, didn't you recognize me?

AIGUL. I don't know you and I don't want to know you. If you want to introduce yourself, come and see me after the play. Now leave!

ERLEN-2. It won't be of any interest after the play. Don't push me - that's very impolite. I'll leave, but just let me say one thing before I go. If I say it to you while there are just the two of us, nobody will hear apart from you and me. I had the urge several times to speak to the playwright as well. But all those folks would try and do would be to make us kiss. I've had the urge to say that to the director several times, but couldn't bring myself to…

AIGUL. If you were a playwright, you would be bound to be the most talkative one of all. Tell me what you want to say, but then leave straightaway!

ERLEN-2. In that case…please listen. I love you. I've loved you ever since I was a child. Since then I have never missed a single play, in which you took part. I know all the details of your life, complete with all the nuances. In a word, I'm your shadow. I have loved you from the moment I saw you. I'm still in love with you now and shall be for always.

AIGUL. (*laughing*) One can expect everything from you Kazakhs. The one thing that was missing in my life was a Don Quixote, like you. Thank goodness, you've turned up now!

ERLEN-2. Don't make fun of me. You have a separate life of your own. You have your work, your husband, your children, your interests. You have no other thoughts in your head. But there's someone out there who worships you madly, who dreams of coming up to you and taking hold of your hand. He bows his head in reverence before your art and is ready to idolize you for the rest of his life. That person in the distance wishes you might flourish and prosper on every front, that disaster should pass you by. D'you really think there's anything bad about that?

AIGUL. And are you that person?

ERLEN-2. Yes! It's me!

AIGUL. In that case, you're not just a human being but an angel, protecting me at a distance.

ERLEN-2. Call me what you wish, the choice is yours.

AIGUL. And those eccentric feelings you managed to suppress and keep to yourself all through your life? Surely there must have been some convenient opportunity when you could have told me about them?

ERLEN-2. I was reluctant to do that.

AIGUL. For whose sake?

ERLEN-2. For the sake of my feelings. I was afraid that one fine day I might muddy the waters accidentally.

AIGUL. How can you?! Honeyed words like that make my blood run cold. Please leave... I beg of you, leave now.

ERLEN-2. That's because people like us aren't around anymore. They're not used to sweet words any more. They regard them as something alien today. Here, have a look at this photograph.

AIGUL. (*She takes hold of the photograph*) There's a young girl here and a boy aged seven or eight. But I don't know them.

ERLEN-2. It's a photograph of you and me.

AIGUL. But when did you and I have the photograph taken?

ERLEN-2. When I had just been discharged from hospital. Perhaps you remember. You meet so many different people, wherever you go. But as for me, to this day I can't forget that encounter.

AIGUL. But please hurry up. My husband's meant to be coming any moment.

ERLEN-2. When did you marry him?

AIGUL. You say you follow me around day and night… How could you have missed my marriage?

ERLEN-2. What's his name?

AIGUL. Erlen-2, Erlen-3… What difference does it make? Go on with what you have to say, but make it quick.

ERLEN-2. When I fell in love with you after seeing you for the first time, I was only six and perched on my mother's back.

AIGUL. Where did you say were lying?

ERLEN-2. Across my mother's back. Our state farm was on the far side of the Syr Darya at the edge of dense vegetation. In those days we kept pheasants along with the chickens and at the edge of our village whole herds of wild boar used to graze, like so many sheep.

THE ACTRESS

(*Aigul starts listening attentively to his story*)

Theatre people only appeared in our village once in a blue moon. They virtually never came. Suddenly some unexpected happy news found its way to us: "Actors are coming to the village". Everyone was so excited. We could hardly cope with the suspense as we waited for the great day when you would arrive. At that time there was no bridge across the Syr Darya. People had to use a ferry to get from one bank to the other. At last, the small long-awaited bus with the actors appeared! The village children – all and every one – rushed down to the bank. They were brown from the constant sun. They thought there'd never be such a blissful day as that one again! Everything about you – the way you climbed down from the bus and stepped carefully along the dusty road, the way you laughed and talked – it seemed to us like something from a different world.

Then the play we'd been waiting for began. In those days there was no electricity in the village. As darkness fell four or five of the young men lit big dung-cakes, after first dipping them in kerosene, and that was the light we had for watching the play.

The performance began. There's not going to be anything orderly about people out in the steppes. As soon as you squat down on the ground, someone's going to loom up in front of you, pulling themselves up to their full height. Since I couldn't see anything, my mother lifted me up on to her back so that I could look over her shoulders. She stood like that until the whole play was over. From time to time she asked, if I'd fallen asleep. I couldn't possibly have done that, but I just answered "No". I don't know what the play was that you had put on for us, but to judge from the way my mother kept bursting into tears or laughing, it must have been quite a good show...

I took to you straightaway. You were wearing a white dress. The others were of no interest to me. I was waiting impatiently for you to come on.

AIGUL. Are you sure you didn't invent all this?

ERLEN-2. No. You can tell at once if a story's been made up.

AIGUL. And after that?

ERLEN-2. As I lay there, perched on my mother's back, I fell for you (*laughing*). I was so shameless that instead of taking pity on my poor mother, who was tired after work, I didn't get down from her back. But fell in love with someone!

AIGUL. So you were obviously already a lost cause from a very young age. Falling in love at the age of six is ridiculous. Nobody would believe you.

ERLEN-2. I have a friend called Beksultan. It turns out that he fell in love aged only four. And, just imagine, it was a woman who already had two children.

AIGUL. Come now, spin me another………!

ERLEN-2. I swear to God, by all that's holy! (*Both of them laugh*) Would you like to know what I was thinking about as I lay perched on my mother's back?

AIGUL. It would be interesting.

ERLEN-2. No, I don't think I should. I'd feel ashamed of myself.

AIGUL. You weren't ashamed when you told me about the love you felt at the age of six, so why should you be ashamed as soon as you start telling me what you imagined…? Go on, you've already spoilt the flow of the story…

ERLEN-2. All right then, you're not one to give up easily. So I'll tell you. I imagined how the young actress would lose her way while she was walking through the dense thickets by the river, tire herself out and start crying. Then she would encounter me and hug me in a wild rush of joy. After that I lifted her up on to my back and carried her out onto open ground..."

AIGUL. There were you, perched on your mother's back, planning to lift someone else up on top of you! But wait a moment! Wait a moment! You were day-dreaming about me getting lost.

ERLEN-2. Yes (*with a laugh*). Love makes people imagine all sorts of things....

AIGUL. (*laughing again*) Love! Poor old love reduced to a child's game! So, you carried me out of the thicket. And what then?

ERLEN-2. After that there was another thicket.

AIGUL. And then?

ERLEN-2. After that there was another thicket.

AIGUL. And when do your thickets come to an end?

ERLEN-2. They don't, they go on and on. In the end I started imagining how I found myself in an unfamiliar one and by that time the two of us were lost there forever.

AIGUL. All right, let's imagine that your dream came true and that the two of us were lost in the thickets. But in the end you grew up and became an adult, looking like you do now. So, what do you plan next?

ERLEN-2. To live arm in arm with you for the rest of time. I would look after you, on our own, far away from prying eyes. Even if I had found a way out of the vegetation, I would make sure that we remained 'lost'. We would become each other's prisoners for ever more.

AIGUL. Heaven forbid! I'm starting to feel afraid of you. Your feelings are more like those of a beast of prey than tender human love.

ERLEN-2. Unfortunately you're right.

AIGUL. Do you… have a wife?

ERLEN-2. No! I only love you! I don't need anyone but you.

AIGUL. But I'm already spoken for.

ERLEN-2. You said…

AIGUL. Have you never attempted to marry?

ERLEN-2. No, perhaps after this I shall…

AIGUL. That's interesting. Tell me, if it's not a secret, who the lucky woman is?

ERLEN-2. So that's how it is…? You think that the woman I'm planning to marry really is a fortunate person?

AIGUL. But of course!

ERLEN-2. But it's you. Aigul Asanova, I've been your 'slave' since I was a child!

AIGUL. (*By this time she is really agitated and almost at a loss for words*) You… My God… D'you realize what you're saying? I'm way older than you.

ERLEN-2. (*As if he's not listening to what she is saying*) But then, for the record, when you were putting on a concert after the play, I climbed down from my mother's back and sat down near the children who were at the front. We were very near the burning dung that had been soaked in kerosene and was spitting sparks. All of a sudden the people at the back started pushing forward and the burning oily dung was about to fall on you. I leapt up straightaway to knock the pole with the burning dung on it out of the way and some of it fell onto me.

AIGUL. Yes – yes, it's coming back to me now. That would have been impossible to forget. Then I stopped singing and hugged you. You were yelling loudly and your mother came running up to us. We saved you by plunging you into the water of the canal which ran past the farm office.

ERLEN-2. Then you carried me into the office building and you took some cream out of your bag and started rubbing it on to my burns.

AIGUL. Yes, and after that they took you off to the hospital.

ERLEN-2. I was discharged from the hospital two weeks later. By then you'd finished your touring and on your way back to Almaty you found me and came to say good-bye. It was then that the doctor took the photo of the two of us. That's the very same photo I showed you.

AIGUL. Surely that very same little boy can't have been you? It's not for nothing that people say "It's a small world", when they meet by chance after long years have passed… Who'd have thought it.

ERLEN-2. D'you remember how, when you said good-bye in the hospital you added: "When you grow up, come and see me in Almaty. It's easy to find me in the theatre". I was sniffing as I said to you in tears: "I love you". D'you remember?

AIGUL. (*Troubled by all of this but not able to remember any more*). Perhaps…

ERLEN-2. You remember it all but you seem to feel awkward about saying you do… You laughed and said: "Ooh, it's the first time a small boy has ever said he loves me". Then you added: "I love you too". D'you remember that?

AIGUL. How silly it all seems – remembering words that were said so long ago... Yes, yes, I really did say them. And the small boy, can that possibly be you?

ERLEN-2. If you don't believe me, I can show you my scars (*He lifts up his trouser legs to show her the scars*).

AIGUL. You dear little fellow, ready to throw yourself into the flames to save someone (*She strokes his hair, as if she is caressing him*).

ERLEN-2. (*He freezes motionless, pressing her fingers to his hair*) (*Aigul pulls her hand away*) Why shouldn't I?

AIGUL. I said no and it means no. An actress never speaks from her own script. Throughout her life she is caught up in a struggle against herself, placing limits on her behaviour whatever she is doing. After one part, there follows another. If you start to let go, you lose everything. The stage is my whole life. I remember once when the theatre was getting ready to put on Kilty's play *Dear Liar*. There are only two characters in the play – the Irish playwright Bernard Shaw and the actress Mrs. Patrick Campbell. The story of their magnificent love affair. An hour before the première I was informed that my son had been in a road accident and was in hospital in a serious condition. What should I do? No dramatist on earth would have been able to describe the state I was in... Even if I were to rush straight to the hospital, I wouldn't have been able to see him at that stage. Disrupting a première would kill off an acting career. I thought about it for a long time and I stayed on in the theatre. I had to hide my feelings and give nothing away till the performance was over. That's what our lives are like, my boy who was prepared to brave the flames for me...

ERLEN-2. Neglecting a child who could be on his death-bed, that's sacrilege.

AIGUL. That's what art is, my darling. We have to turn our back on many of the fine things life might offer us for the sake of occasionally being able to bring joy into people's lives.

ERLEN-2. Turning your back on me as well?

AIGUL. (*with a laugh*) Of course on you as well! Roll your trouser leg down again: my husband, the director, mustn't see that and then ask me for my next divorce. Tell me, before you go though, what's your name?

ERLEN-2. It's Erlen. God in his wisdom made sure I had the same name as your husband. I wasn't joking when I called myself Erlen the Second. Tell me, may I call you up on the telephone sometimes?

AIGUL. No! There's no need for that. I don't want you to disrupt my life, which has only just sorted itself out.

ERLEN-2. A serene, calm life doesn't suit an actress like you.

AIGUL. That happy stage of my life is long over, my boy.

ERLEN. Haven't you been telling people till you're blue in the face, on radio and television that "all ages are to love submissive".

AIGUL. Perhaps those words are to some people's liking, but NOT MINE. D'you understand, Erlen the Second?

ERLEN-2. (*taking hold of Aigul's hand*) Your first Erlen dreamt of a different kind of happiness, when he simply looked into your beautiful, tender eyes, as beautiful as the new moon, holding these very palms in his hands!

AIGUL. That's enough young man! Yes, he did have a dream!

ERLEN-2. What kind of dream?

AIGUL. His dream is what you might call jealousy. He was jealous of everything. Even of my roles in the theatre.

ERLEN-2. Of course he was, I would have been jealous too.

AIGUL. That's because your name's Erlen. That name must mean that you resemble each other. You too are a prisoner of your emotions – jealous, self-centred, ambitious. Isn't that the case?

ERLEN-2. How d'you know that?

AIGUL. People in my family can often see into the future…

ERLEN-2. May I…may I make a suggestion?

AIGUL-2. To go off with you to the thickets by the river?

ERLEN-2. Yes… No… Ye-es. For me to kidnap you and carry you off?

AIGUL. (*laughing at the top of her voice*) That's all I need. And where do you plan to carry me off to?

ERLEN-2. To my estates.

AIGUL. To your estates? You own estates?

ERLEN-2. Yes and what's surprising about that? My older brother is a well-known land-owner. On the banks of the Syr-Darya he has two thousand hectares of land, three and a half thousand cows, twelve thousand sheep and around a hundred racehorses. More ducks, geese and chickens than you can count. There are several swimming pools there, a sauna and tame pheasants. In a word, it's a real paradise on earth. There's even room to set up a private theatre.

AIGUL. Theatre?

ERLEN. Yes, a theatre. It can all be agreed if we escape there now. Perhaps there's no need to carry you off, you might just go of your own accord? If you agree, I'm ready to go straightaway.

AIGUL. And then my boy, once you've accomplished your dream, then you'll hide me away in a stone castle?

ERLEN. The wedding could be held on boats on the smooth waters of a man-made lake.

AIGUL. Stop it now, that's enough day-dreaming…

ERLEN-2. You are my truly Beloved on earth… my truly Beloved…

AIGUL. I'm old enough to be your aunt!

ERLEN-2. You're truly cruel, you've forgotten how to nurture and respect another's feelings…

AIGUL. So it would seem. I have no more time for this now. Please leave…

ERLEN-2. In that case…in that case I'll return on another occasion. Whatever happens you're incapable of leaving your golden cage. Time will pass and then your attitude will change. That would seem to be when I should come back again.

AIGUL. That would probably be better. Now, good-bye.

ERLEN-2. In that case can you grant one last request?

AIGUL. I shall if I can. What is it?

ERLEN-2. You'll be able to… Sing me the song, which made me first fall in love with you.

AIGUL. What song was it?

ERLEN-2. "Waltz of Love" by Beken Kamakhaev [The choice of song is up to the director].

AIGUL. My voice is not what it used to be. But nevertheless I shall try to grant your request.

(*Aigil sings the song, "Waltz of Love". Her solo voice gradually gives way to the orchestral accompaniment. Aigul and Erlen begin to waltz... Their dance vanishes amidst a crowd of dancers. When the music draws to a close, Aigul and Erlen part with regret, letting go of each other's hands. Erlen-2 moves away to a dark corner of the stage*)

FINALE

AIGUL. Farewell, my young saviour, who kept his heart and soul radiant and pure! People like you would nowadays be called eccentric or mad. If there were no people like you, our world would split apart at the seams and people would have long since all turned into cruel predators. Wherever you are, may you be safe and sound, my blessed madman. Farewell, farewell.

(*Erlen comes in unexpectedly, wearing his old pilot's uniform. Aigul is astonished. Erlen holds out a bouquet to her*)

ERLEN. Who was that young man? Not another new director?

AIGUL. O-oh, it's a long story...

ERLEN. Well then...Shall we go home?

AIGUL. Where to? Where did you say?

ERLEN. I said home.

(*Aigul does not really know what to say. She rises to her feet and stands as if rooted to the ground. She is crying silent tears.*)

THE END

Dulat Issabekov, Holder of the State Prize of the Republic of Kazakhstan

A Man on a Mission

(A PLAY IN TWO ACTS)

Dramatis Personae

Baluan SHOLAK – poet and minstrel of the steppes
Tatyana – college student in Omsk
Terentii Dyakovich DOLGONOSOV – Head of the Kokshetau District
Elizaveta – his wife
Semyon Trofimovich TROITSKII – Head of the Akmola District
Ekaterina – his wife
Akylbai – friend of Baluan SHOLAK
Mikhail – representative of MAMONTOV, Governor-General of Omsk
Balkash – wife of Baluan SHOLAK
Galiya – Baluan SHOLAK's beloved
Sutemgen – TROITSKII's servant
Pan Nurmagambet – former chief sultan, aristocrat of the steppes

In the crowd scenes the following individuals also take part: guard, Baluan SHOLAK's parents, a maid etc..

ACT ONE

The famous Fair – held annually in the town of Kyzylzhar (mod. Petropavlovsk) – is in full swing. Those taking part have assembled from seven districts: Kokshetau, Atbasar, Akmola, Karkaraly, Kereku, Kyzylzhar and Omsk. After selling their wares, obtaining all that they need for their household and work activities and also watching performances of various actors and singers, they are clustering together in a large crowd and waiting impatiently for the ceremonial 'crowning' of the victors among them.

The herald strides forward into the centre of the crowd and addresses them in a voice loud and grand.

HERALD. Good people! Our Kyzylzhar Fair, which has lasted several days, is almost over. Thousands of people from various places in the Kokshetau, Atbasar, Akmola, Karkaraly, Kereku, Kyzylzhar and Omsk regions have taken part. This has indeed made it a celebration for the whole of our people. In these last few days we have watched horse races and been witness to the art of singers and wrestlers. Now we shall announce the winners of all these contests.

VOICES FROM THE CROWD. Nurmagambet! Nurmagambet!

HERALD. The winner of the wrestling competition we declare to be Nurmagambet, son of Baimyrzy, who twice defeated the supreme champion of Kordabai and who recently defeated Koren, twice declared world-champion, breaking two of his ribs. I call for calm good people! Would Nurmagambet, son of Baimyrzy, please come forward!

VOICES FROM THE CROWD. Make room for him so he can stand here in the middle of us all, so we can have a closer look!

VOICE. Who says God is not generous?! Such a great gift for the poor home of Baimyrzy, who is always eking out such a wretched existence!

HERALD. Where is he? Let Baimyrzauly come forward!

A well-built, thick-set and muscly young stalwart moves into the centre of the crowd, which greets him with ecstatic cheers. When the crowd catches sight of the young man's pleasant features, the excited cheering grows ever louder.

VOICES FROM THE CROWD. There's a really strapping fellow!

So handsome! And look how he's built!

They say that he writes songs as well and performs them too!

What's more, he has a splendid horse and goes hunting with birds. He's the young horseman who at fourteen had a fierce tussle with a full-grown wolf and almost lost four of his fingers to frost-bite when he tried to skin his victim!

In the very middle of the crowd sits the resplendent and proud figure of Pan Nurmagambet, surveying all around him with arrogant disdain: in the past he had been the sultan-in-chief of seven districts – an austere aristocrat held in high esteem by the people.

He calls someone over to him.

PAN NURMAGAMBET. It would seem that women from the clans of Argyn, Kipchak, Kerei and Waq cannot bring forth worthy sons. You're just sitting there calmly giving the main prize to some upstart Uisun. How can you bear the shame and disgrace!

At that moment a young man by the name of Nurmagambet comes into view. He is wearing a waisted caftan made of white camel hair camel, edged with a border of black and coloured silk, and a beaver collar four fingers wide. His white 'tymak' head-dress, made of lambskin and with green silk at the top, is pulled down over his right ear at a dashing angle. On his feet he is wearing Kosai boots of Kazakh design. Pan Nurmagambet is somewhat taken aback at the sight of this brave young stalwart.

NURMAGAMBET. Your Honour, who in the past was the sultan of eight districts, I know that I need your permission to greet you. Do you allow me to shake your hand, Pan Ata?

The elder gives a brief nod, as if to grant permission. Nurmagambet shakes his hand in greeting.

PAN. Whose son might you be?

NURMAGAMBET. Baimyrzy's, your Honour.

PAN. And what is your name?

NURMAGAMBET. Nurmagambet.

PAN. Hm-m! So the mongrel's now called a wolfhound! Which clan are you from?

NURMAGAMBET. Not from a local one. I'm from the Ai clan. Descended from the Uisun tribe. In the hard years one of my ancestors fought alongside Ablai Khan and, when he was out in those parts, he married a girl from the Kerei clan and then settled here. Families from that line now run into dozens.

PAN. Your attire does you proud.

NURMAGAMBET. Thanks to the care taken by my mother Kalampyr. She sold her only cow, fitted me out as required, reminding me all the time "you will be competing in front of other people and perhaps you will need to greet the highly esteemed Pan Ata".

A MAN ON A MISSION

PAN. "A poor man makes do with a copper pot!..."

NURMAGAMBET. Pan Ata! What is amiss if a poor man is ambitious? You called me an upstart just now. Perhaps I am, but my ancestors on my mother's side are from the Kerei clan. As a wrestler I have upheld the honour not of the Uisun clan, not of the Kerei clan but that of Kazakhs. When I was up against a famous French wrestler, I competed not in the name of my clan but as a Kazakh.

PAN. You speak well and you are right to do so. You are not only endowed with heroic strength but you have a way with words. I still want to give you one piece of advice though.

NURMAGAMBET. I am listening, Pan Ata.

PAN. It turns out that you and I bear the same name. But from now on you shall be called "Baluan" - the Strong. If that is not enough for you, then you can add the word "Sholak" – the fingerless. Without more ado, people will know you as Baluan Sholak from now on!

NURMAGAMBET. Let that be as you wish, Pan Ata! Let the whole of my prize be a gift for you.

PAN. What foolishness! How will you acquire wealth if you throw it all away?

NURMAGAMBET. My aim in life is not to acquire any kind of wealth. I devote my life and skills to the people. I shall not take even a crumb of the prize!

PAN. You are a real hero youth, of whom your mother can be justly proud. Well done! I wish you every success! Let the herald share out Baluan's prize among all the poor and needy here. It is not without good cause that they say: "The brave man's spoils fall to his people!"

Thrusting his way through the crowd, Baluan Sholak heads over to his parents. They call out with tears in their eyes: "Dear boy! Thanks be to Allah for giving you to us!"

At the very moment when Baluan is making his way through the crowd, a beautiful young woman, appearing out of nowhere like an angel, walks up to Baluan. She is of medium height and is wearing a silk dress, fine boots with high heels and gold crescent-shaped earrings. She places a richly embroidered silk caftan round Baluan's shoulders and hands him a white silk scarf.

GALIYA. This gift may not be very grand, but it is from the bottom of my heart. Accept it as a sign of my respect for your noble gesture, for your courage!

Dumbfounded by the young woman's irresistible beauty and her gesture so bold and unexpected, of a kind rare among Kazakh women, Baluan hesitates for a moment, not knowing what to say. While he seeks to regain his calm, the young woman vanishes without trace. All he can see before him now is the cheering crowd.

VOICES FROM THE CROWD.

Where on earth did that young woman spring from?

What is her name? Does she have a husband? If she does, he must be half-blind. What kind of husband would let his wife place a caftan round a stranger's shoulders. Then she just climbed into a coach and drove off home… The midget sitting next to her – that must be the husband…

By the way her name's Galiya and her husband's Elzhan. They live in Akmola. They're on their way home from the Tashkent bazaar!

AKYLBAI. Whatever you may say, it looks as if she's taken a shine to our Baluan.

BALUAN. How do you know?

A MAN ON A MISSION

AKYLBAI. You can tell from her eyes! Eyes never lie! They were on fire with passion for Baluan.

What has just been happening resembles a dream and Baluan, feeling bewildered, is now deep in thought. It would seem that the passing glance from Galiya's ardent eyes has left an undying flame in his heart.

BALUAN. Galiya! Galiya! Was that a dream or was it real? Who could believe that that angel was a human being! Akylbai!

AKYLBAI. Here I am, Baluan!

BALUAN. You are my most loyal friend. Go out and search for Galiya, who appeared so suddenly like a vision. Where does she live? Does she or does she not have a husband? How did she know who I am? In a word you must help me meet her.

AKYLBAI. If I do bring you together, what then?

BALUAN. Don't worry about the rest. I'll see to it. What you must do is bring me and Galiya together.

AKYLBAI. It was only last year that you married Balkash. You carried off a poor girl, whose parents had a dowry ready to marry her off. D'you intend to marry again? So you've decided to turn your attention to every girl in the district!

BALUAN. Akylbai, she has lit an undying flame in my heart.

AKYLBAI. D'you remember the desperate fight your marriage led to last year? By way of a warning you had to spend time in Atbasar prison. This time, your venture could well lead to outright war.

BALUAN. If that is my fate, we shall indeed experience war. Akylbai, make ready to set off!

* * *

Baluan Sholak's house. There is a low table with four legs in the place for honoured guests. Round it there are small chairs. Balkash enters carrying a brass samovar. Baluan is rummaging through the contents of chests, looking for something and appears agitated. Balkash is making ready to pour out tea.

BALKASH. Baluan, what's the matter with you? Ever since yesterday you've been restless, extremely worried and running round in circles. What's happened?

BALUAN. Balkashzhan, you yourself know how tense everything is all around us. The local elder, Syzdyk, is planning to turn over our village to settlers who have moved here from Russia.

BALKASH. And where shall we be sent?

BALUAN. We don't know. We'll probably be made to leave the places we grew up in. We'll just have to follow our noses…

BALKASH. Surely they could have found somewhere else for the settlers in the Kyzylzhar district?

BALUAN. Our village, Kairakty, was the only one which voted against him being put in charge of the area. Syzdyk has since gained power and now he's out to take his revenge.

BALKASH. Let things take their course, we'll have to wait and see, along with everyone else. Sit down or the samovar will get cold.

BALUAN. (*Listening to noises outside the house*) Listen, can that be the thunder of horses' hooves?

BALKASH. Perhaps you've invited the mullah here to celebrate a marriage rite?…

Baluan bangs the lid of the open chest shut and looks at Balkash in astonishment.

A MAN ON A MISSION

BALUAN. So that's it! I was wondering why you had seemed out of sorts recently. It turns out there was a reason. Balkashzhan what could have put that idea into your head? So let us drink water blessed by the mullah. (*He opens the chest again*). Is that what you're longing for? **BALKASH.** (*in a tearful voice*). I had been a spoilt girl, cherished by my parents and ready to be married off at a moment's notice, when I met you. I trusted you. I shut my eyes to everything else. It all turned out badly for me… I just followed you. Now just look at the life I'm leading!… It couldn't be more humiliating!

BALUAN. Balkash, what are you saying?! What's humiliating about it?

BALKASH. I know what you're looking for in the chest. A silk caftan Galiya gave you at last year's fair. You're wasting your time. I cut it up into pieces and threw it into the Ishim river.

BALUAN. Balkash, what are you talking about? After all, you're a sensible woman.

BALKASH. No, I'm not. I've been out of my mind ever since. You were planning to put on that silk caftan and set off to Akmola to look for Galiya, weren't you? In that case it'll be my turn next.

BALUAN. What d'you mean – "my turn"?

BALKASH. The river that swallowed up your caftan could swallow me up too.

BALUAN. Balkash… Come now! You're talking nonsense… It's horrible!

BALKASH. A woman just obeys, while a man gives the orders. A woman without any freedom is hardly likely to be capable of anything!

BALUAN. Don't cry, dear Balkash! Soon we're going to have a child. Perhaps we'll have time to celebrate our wedding properly before that...

At that moment Akylbai comes rushing in out of breath. Baluan leaps to his feet, worried that Akylbai, who had ridden to Akmola to find news of Galiya, might blurt something out in front of Balkash.

BALUAN. Oh, Akylbai! Where have you sprung from, as if you're being chased? Has something happened? Is everything all right?

AKYLBAI. Everything's fine! I was off on your errand... (*after looking over towards Balkash*) that took me to Akmola...and now I've come back... **BALUAN.** For old Pan?

AKYLBAI. Yes. He was sending a letter to the district chief in Akmola, to Troitskii...

BALUAN. I hope you gave it to him safe and sound?

AKYLBAI. Yes, I did!

BALUAN. And what was his reply?

AKYLBAI. He said he'll dispatch it with a courier.

BALUAN. (*with a sheepish expression*) Well done, Akylbai! And what next?

AKYLBAI. We'll see about all that later. That's it for now... Horrors at every turn! Baluan, it seems the end of the world is upon us!

BALUAN. What are you on about?

AKYLBAI. The settlers are coming this way. There are so many of them, you'd think it was a swarm of ants. Just looking at them is enough to scare you. They're being led by a Cossack detachment of 30-40 men. I only just managed to get away.

A MAN ON A MISSION

BALUAN. So that's what's happening! It turns out that for the sake of his position, our local elder Sydyk is ready to give up our lands to newcomers from far away.

AKYLBAI. Our men are all fired up... they're mounting their horses and collecting in the birch grove at the foot of a local hill. Pan Nurmagabent is among them. They asked me to come and they're waiting for you. They're armed with cudgels.

Baluan Sholak quickly takes off his ceremonial garments and replaces them with clothes comfortable for riding.

BALUAN. Akylbai. Ride over to them now and tell them that they shouldn't attack the armed detachment until they hear from me. Otherwise there could be pointless sacrifices...

AKYLBAI. And where are you going?

BALUAN. To the district chief! A messenger came over from him the day before yesterday – Sutemgen. He said: "The district chief is inviting you over". As the proverb says: "Before the wild ass has time to scratch, the trigger's been pulled". I'll go and see him, as if it's an emergency, and if he's not in his office, I'll go straight to his home.

AKYLBAI. What if he locks you up in his dungeon?

BALUAN. If that happens, I'll tell my men to get hold of the dozens of old rifles hidden in blacksmith Sharip's barn and arm themselves. There aren't enough of the weapons of course, but those guns are still better than sticks and cudgels. Forgive me Balkash, but I've got no time now for drinking tea. Don't stick your nose out of doors, stay inside the house.

BALKASH. How can I sit here calmly when there's all this commotion outside!? I'm the wife of Baluan Sholak!

Baluan Sholak casts a long glance at his wife, as if he had only just come to understand her. Then he strokes her head and walks with rapid steps out of the house. Akylbai runs after him.

* * *

The imposing house of Terentii Dyakovich DOLGONOSOV, Head of the Kokshetau District. It is built of red brick and set in a shady pine wood on the edge of the town. Recently, in the wake of growing discontent among the local population over the introduction of Russian settlers which has led to clashes between Russians and Kazakhs, Dolgonosov has started to feel worried and he has taken steps to make sure his residence is better protected.

On this day high-ranking guests are visiting Dolgonosov's home. At the dinner table are sitting Troitskii, Head of the Akmola District, with his wife and also the director of the local circus and a curly-haired young man of 25-26 wearing a pince-nez. Dolgonosov, head of the local district, and his wife Elizaveta are playing host to them, but seated in less prominent places at the table.

Walking to and fro so as to replenish tea-glasses is Marfa, the maid. There is a sentry each side of the main entrance at the back of the stage armed with a rifle and standing to attention.

ELIZAVETA. Marfa, take a look out of the window and see if you can see Tatyana…

MARFA (*looking out of window*) No Elizaveta Petrovna, no sign of her.

ELIZAVETA. I'm worried something might have happened to her…

DOGONOSOV. Did she leave on her own?

ELIZAVETA. No she went with Selivan, the coachman. I asked her to stay at home, saying she could go out after the guests had left, but no, she insisted on doing things her way. What can you do… Papa's one and only beloved daughter (*she leans her head coquettishly up against Dolgonosov's shoulder*)? Tatyana left at dawn to drive round the fair-ground. It's nearly midday now and she's still not back.

TROITSKII. Don't worry, Elizaveta Petrovna, she'll be back soon. She's probably missing her home by this stage.

ELIZAVETA. (*with a smile*) She was born in Orsk. The local Kazakhs call it Zhaman-kala.

TROITSKII. Zhaman-kala? What does that mean?

EKATERINA. My dear husband, it's already fourteen years that you've been living amongst Kazakhs. Surely you know what the word "*zhaman*" means in the local language?

TROITSKII. That's not the point…! I know what the word means, but why do the Kazakhs call the town "Zhaman-kala". Circus director, perhaps you can explain it?

CIRCUS DIRECTOR. As I understand it, the first military fortifications built by the Russians in the West Siberian region were precisely in that place. It led the local Kazakhs to start calling the town "Zhaman-kala", namely the "evil city". Who would enjoy a place where uninvited people are setting foot in lands that don't belong to them!

DOLGONOSOV. It's not like that at all. The Kazakhs have no grounds for grumbling at us. We brought them literacy and education. We introduced them to a settled way of life and taught them to build towns.

TROITSKII. But, Terentii Dyakovich, don't you think that those virtuous efforts of ours were in vain? Having mastered the Russian language, aren't they perhaps – in the fullness of time – going to start trying to teach us things? Some of them have already started contradicting their teachers…

EKATERINA. For heaven's sake leave politics out of it today. We haven't met up like this for a long time. Given that we've come to visit friends of the family, let's get away from it all and enjoy ourselves – listen to music or dance. Yes, and we haven't seen Tatyana for a long time either! How many years ago is it now that she left to study in Omsk?

MIKHAIL. Five years. She will finish training as a teacher next year. To be exact – she has been in Omsk five years and four months.

ELIZABETA. A-ha! It turns out that we don't need to worry about Tatyana, if the Omsk Governor-General's representative responsible for Siberian peoples' affairs knows exactly how many years and months… (*giving her husband a meaningful look*) our daughter has been gone!

MIKHAIL. Those are most apt words of yours, dear Elizaveta Petrovna! How could we…I…not turn our attention to Tatyana, who is about to graduate with honours from the Omsk college, when the wife of the Head of the Akmola District – Ekaterina Naryshkina – my first cousin once removed – is on very close terms with the Dolgonosovs? In addition, His Excellency the Governor-General always speaks in the most flattering of terms about Terentii Dyakovich.

After hearing about such fulsome praise from the Governor-General of Western Siberia, all those seated at the table, including Dolgonosov at its head, rise instantly to their feet.

DOLGONOSOV. I should like to drink a toast to the plenipotentiary representative of our illustrious sovereign here in Western Siberia, Governor-General Timofei Matveyevich

A MAN ON A MISSION

Mamontov, so energetic and diligent in his efforts to transform our beloved motherland Russia into a great nation!

All present clap, clink glasses and then drink their champagne.

MIKHAIL. I felt truly moved by the good wishes expressed by Terentii Dyakovich. On my return to Omsk I shall make a point of conveying your sincere and heart-felt sentiments to the Governor-General!

They all sit down.

CIRCUS DIRECTOR. (*addressing Mikhail*) You were just saying that Ekaterina Naryshkina was your first cousin once removed. Tell me is that surname linked in any way with the renowned Naryshkina, who followed her Decembrist husband to the town of Chita – or is it just a coincidence?

Silence descends over the table.

EKATERINA. Yes, she is my distant relative. She did indeed follow her husband, who had been banished to Siberia. It was there that she buried her daughter Ekaterina and later, after the death of her husband, she came back to St. Petersburg. In 1830 she married for a second time and gave birth to another daughter. In order to keep alive the memory of her first-born, she gave her second daughter the name Ekaterina as well. She was my mother and that makes me the third Ekaterina. Are you satisfied with my answer, Mr. Director.

CIRCUS DIRECTOR (*He stands up again and continues in an emotional voice*) Yes, a beautiful and such a sad story. I made a point of going to visit the house where the Decembrists lived, when our circus was on tour in Chita. It was there that Pushkin's famous poem *A Letter to Siberia* was first recited. And it was your great-grandmother who took it to Chita! I stood for a long time by the grave of Ekaterina, who had died when she was only two. I can still remember the sad figure of your grandmother weeping tears born of suffering and grief, as she stood by the grave of her infant daughter. Whichever way you look at it, that was part of our history – the history of our great country. Let us raise our glasses now to that history, to Russian mothers undaunted in spirit, for our third Ekaterina, sitting here with us, for her and her husband!

MIKHAIL (*in a jovial tone*) Gentlemen officers! Let us rise to drink this toast as well! (*Turning to the circus director*) Thank you, we are deeply grateful to you for such warm and flattering words referring to our dynasty!

TROITSKII. The reason for my having been banished to the Kazakh steppes (*noting the disapproving expression on his spouse's face*), or rather for my transfer to these parts is the same "cruel history", which you mentioned. On learning that my dear wife was from the Decembrist dynasty, my superiors in the Department denied me my comfortable post in St. Petersburg… and banished me to Siberia as well.

Troitskii was about to attempt a laugh, so as to turn his words into a jest, but after noticing the dismayed expression on Mikhail's face and that of his wife, he immediately fell silent.

EKATERINA. Marfa! Is your duck ever going to be ready? How long are you going to be walking about just filling up our guests' glasses with *kumiss*?

MARFA. (*calling out from the kitchen*) I'm coming now, right away!

DOLGONOSOV. Is that "now" Russian-style or Kazakh-style?

MARFA. Terentii Dyakovich – this time it's Russian-style.

DOLGONOSOV. If that's the case we'll wait! (*looking round at the others*). When it's Kazakh style, then we're in for a long wait before we see our meal.

At that moment the door swings wide open and in comes Tatyana, pushing past the sentries and all out of breath. She appears flushed and beautiful. Her eyes are radiant as she returns from her drive out in the fresh air. After running in, Tatyana suddenly stops in her tracks, gasping for air like a frightened fawn as she looks round at the guests seated at the table: her gaze is one of astonishment with a touch of nervousness. The small group of people, whose minds are eaten up by politics while their feelings have long since been blunted by endless problems and worries, falls silent for a moment, staring at the new arrival confronting them with this epitome of beauty and innocent purity.

The first person to break the silence is Ekaterina.

EKATERINA. Oh-oh! What a marvel you are Tanya! A real beauty! Come over here and let me kiss your cheek! (*She embraces Tatyana and kisses her on the cheek*).

ELIZAVETA. Tanya, d'you recognize your aunt Ekaterina?

TATYANA. Yes. I have a photograph of her in my album.

EKATERINA. Really, where was the photograph in your album taken?

TATYANA. Don't you remember, we had a group photograph taken before I left for Omsk. At that time, you all seemed young...

TROITSKII. Yes, it's not for nothing that people say: "A man ages when he looks at the younger generation". We've aged, Terentii Dyakovich, we've aged...

DOLGONOSOV. Yes, Semyon Trofimovich. We can't call forty-one a small number anymore! Before we've even had time to blink, our youth has flown by. Well my daughter, how was your drive?

TATYANA. Wonderful, Papa! A real treat! The horses seemed to be flying. As soon as we came out into the square, Selivan the coachman gave them full rein. He must have wanted to show off his skill as an experienced horseman. The dust was rising up in clouds – we must have galloped round the fairground twenty times.

ELIZAVETA. And meanwhile we were all worried about you, fearing that something might have happened to you. Thank goodness you're safe and sound. Why are you just standing there… come and greet our guests.

Tatyana still breathing fast as she walks, goes round the table greeting each guest in turn. Then she suddenly freezes over, when she comes to Mikhail.

TATYANA. When…when did you come over from Omsk? You hadn't said you were going to come here.

MIKHAIL. (*Slightly taken aback*) It was an urgent assignment from His Excellency the Governor-General… and I was also missing my second cousin and my in-laws…

TATYANA. Missing your in-laws? (*Laughing as she continues*) Semyon Trofimovich is a worthy man, deserving of your devotion. But tell me, Uncle Semyon, have you ever experienced heartache from missing your brother-in-law?

TROITSKII. You mean drunken Epiphanii in Kereku? God help us!

While the guests are all laughing, Marfa finally brings in a splendidly presented roast duck and goose, which she places on the table. At that very moment Dolgonosov's messenger, Sutemgen, comes in. His face has an air of agitation about it.

DOLGONOSOV. Sutemgen. What's the matter? Has something happened?

SUTEMGEN. I'm in a bit of a fix, your Excellency! Baluan Sholak, who had been invited to come yesterday, has turned up. He's asking to be allowed in.

DOLGONOSOV. (*In an aside to Troitskii*) Semyon Trofimovich, it appears that the minstrel of the steppes has turned up, who is a famous wrestler in these parts. If you don't object, I should like to exchange a few words with him. Nothing confidential, a perfectly ordinary conversation.

TROITSKII. A-ah, Baluan Sholak! Yes I've been hearing about him... let him come in. We'll see what kind of a customer he is!

ELIZAVETA. They say he is an insolent rebel. It's not a good idea to admit him when we have visitors.

Before Elizaveta has even had time to close her mouth, Baluan Sholak marches in, without bothering to wait for any special permission. The sentries attempt to block his path, but Dolgonosov makes a gesture, signifying that he should be let in. Scared by Baluan's weather-beaten, swarthy appearance, Tatyana almost collapses in fright onto her mother. The others present also look at him with a good deal of apprehension and suspicion.

DOLGONOSOV. We had invited you to come yesterday... Why didn't you come then?

BALUAN. It was impossible for me to come, Your Honour. I couldn't possibly set off yesterday, because my father was laid low, he's seriously ill.

DOLGONOSOV. D'you know this man?

BALUAN. Yes, I do. He's the circus director.

DOLGONOSOV. The message is short. We're planning to send you to Omsk for you to train there for six months at the wrestling school. After that you'll be able to perform in the circus and your name will be famous throughout the world.

CIRCUS DIRECTOR. Your monthly wages will be 15 roubles. We'll set something aside for your parents from the circus takings.

BALUAN. Thank you for your trouble, but at the moment I can't think about any training.

CIRCUS DIRECTOR. You don't seem to have heard me properly? Fifteen roubles a month! In this part of the world nobody has been receiving large sums like that. We are always very pleased to note your major success on the wrestling mat. That is why we have decided to grant you such substantial wages. In my opinion there's nothing here to hesitate about.

BALUAN. In another situation I might have devoted some thought to that. But at this moment I can't accept your offer.

DOLGONOSOV. And your reason?

BALUAN. The reason is that settlers intend to take over the lands of our clan. Hordes of them have turned up there. People do not want to leave the lands of their forefathers of their own free will and this is going to lead to fierce clashes. Out in the steppes there's terrible turmoil at the moment. People are in despair: you can hear crying children and weeping women wherever you go. Meanwhile you're just sitting here, calmly sipping your cold beer and enjoying your strong *kumiss*.

TROITSKII. Ye-e-es, so now our wild man of the steppes is coming out with seditious turns of phrase. It looks as if we're going to have to take steps to make sure he comes to a sorry end!

DOLGONOSOV. So what is the request you have come to us with?

BALUAN. That you should send the settlers somewhere else. There are other places they could go in the Kyzylzhar District. Don't drive the people here to panic. Turn back the armed detachment accompanying them, otherwise you'll be responsible for fierce clashes and bloodshed between Kazakhs and Russians.

DOLGONOSOV. Interesting and in whose name have you come here?

BALUAN. I've come here in the name of the mothers weeping in distress and the children crying in fear.

DOLGONOSOV. Ah, so that's it! You must be the leader of the insurgents, the trouble-makers. It was I who decided on these places, the man in charge of the area. Go and talk about your worries and grief to your own village leader, Syzdyk.

BALUAN. I have no wish to talk to a man who has betrayed his people and his lands for the sake of his career. You must issue a decree calling back the settlers and the detachment of soldiers!

ELIZAVETA. Just listen to the way these savages dare to lay down terms!

BALUAN. In the first place, when a wife interrupts what her husband is saying, it shows a lack of proper manners. Secondly, we are not savages.

ELIZAVETA. At the time when people in Europe were eating raw meat and running round naked, the Turanian Empire was already flourishing out here in the steppes!

TROITSKII. So here we have it! Terentii Dyakovich, I was warning you about all of this only the other day! Here are the fruits of all your good works! Just you go on teaching them, training them and spreading enlightenment!

BALUAN. If you do not satisfy my demands...

TROITSKII. It's interesting to hear what you have to say... you've started so you'd better finish. So, what have you in mind, if your demands are not satisfied?

BALUAN. Who is this bald fellow, who keeps interrupting me?

TROITSKII. (*leaping to his feet and spluttering with rage*) T...T... Terentii Dyak... Dyakovich! Silence the wretch. Otherwise I shall leave immediately!

BALUAN. The way is open... if you wish to leave... (*Addressing Dolgonosov*) I need to speak to you on your own at once.

Dolgonosov is beside himself by now.

DOLGONOSOV. This is no stranger from outside, but the head of the Akmola District. Speak out and don't get carried away, or I'll be sending you straight to prison.

BALUAN. So here we have it... head of the Akmola District? In that case, my apologies! God willing, I shall perhaps soon be a visitor to your *aul*. Make sure you stop calling us savages... How can a people capable of creating wonderful art be termed savage.

Without warning Baluan begins to sing a song. He renders the song "Buryltai" in his fine tenor voice [at this point a recording of a professional singer's performance is required]. *When the first verse is complete, Ekaterina and Tatyana have in part regained their calm: by now the expression on their faces is no longer one of fear but undisguised interest, while they listen, positively enchanted.*

TROITSKII. (*To his wife*) So here's some music for you. Listen away, to your heart's content! That's what you wanted, after all!

His wife is not paying attention to what her husband is saying. She is quite carried away by Baluan Shokal's singing. When the song comes to an end, she and Tatyana do not even notice how they are applauding enthusiastically, calling out "Wonderful!" rapturously as they do so.

BALUAN. (*Addressing Troitskii*) You call us "savages", but we "savages" do not talk while we are listening to music.

EKATERINA. Very well said!

BALUAN. (*Turning now to Ekaterina*) There are hundreds, thousands of songs and tunes like that to be heard out in our steppes. Surely referring to a people, which has created such rich musical art, as "savage" is savagery in itself?

The answer to that question comes unexpectedly from the circus director.

CIRCUS DIRECTOR. Indeed, that's how it is!...

He has had his say, but sensing that his words have not really been to the liking of the local dignitaries, he looks round the room apprehensively. Ekaterina sits there fanning herself energetically, her eyes full of admiration as she gazes at Baluan, who has been taking real liberties.

EKATERINA. Nevertheless… To behave so uninhibitedly in front of two high-ranking dignitaries requires a rare degree of boldness! This Kazakh is a real daredevil!...

TROITSKII. There's nothing bold about him… He's a brigand and a trouble-maker!

BALUAN. In my place you would have done very much the same. We live in our own lands, we have not invaded other people's territory and broken our word by doing so. Then outsiders appear, intending to seize our houses and drive us out from the land of our ancestors. Your Honour, Chief of the District, you are right: my action is not heroic, simply the result of desperation!

TATYANA. (*to Baluan*) Do sing us another song, please!

DOLGONOSOV. Tatyana! We did not gather here to 'appreciate' songs. Go to your room and we'll call you back when we see fit.

TATYANA. Papa, I'll be bored on my own!

DOLGONOSOV. As for you – you special Kazakh, you – get out of here! Your demands cannot be met! That's all there is to it. Messenger, see our uninvited guest off the premises!

Sutemgen tries to steer Baluan in the direction of the door, but Baluan pushes him roughly aside. Unable to contain themselves after being confronted with this outrageous insolence, the sentries rush to the aid of the messenger. Meanwhile Baluan, as if keen to demonstrate his singular strength, lifts them up off the floor by the scruff of their necks, holding them aloft for a moment or two like helpless puppets, before dropping them down again and then marching in a calm and dignified fashion out of the building.

TROITSKII. (*Regaining his composure after the shock*) A very dangerous customer! Its people like that who sow the seeds of trouble encouraging people to defy the authorities.

DOLGONOSOV. Sutemgen! Take two men and follow that bandit! D'you understand?

SUTEMGEN. At once, Your Excellency!

* * *

In a pine wood not far from Kokshetau, Baluan and Akylbai are seated by some folded rocks. Baluan broods in silence while Akylbai is looks around nervously.

AKYLBAI. Yes… The village has been burnt to the ground. Everyone has been driven out, they went off in all directions. Our lands have been seized – by outsiders. Resistance was cruelly put down and a fair number of innocent people perished. Our respected elder, Pan, could not bear the wicked treachery and he died, unable to bear the pain and sorrow. We ourselves had to flee. So here we are out in the woods, trembling at every rustle of the wind, like frightened hares.

Baluan still says nothing.

There is no brave, upright man able to rally people together and lead them… Surely – after the era of Ablai – success can't have turned its back on the Kazakhs. All the prisons are overflowing with our fellow tribesmen. Yes, we managed to get away, but what use was it? Here we are sitting it out as if driven into a trap. Where are our people, where is everyone – the old people and the children, our families, our friends?

From behind the pines appears Sutemgen, Dolgonosov's messenger.

AKYLBAI. Halt or I'll kill you straightaway! Who are you?

SUTEMGEN. I'm Sutemgen, the messenger of the District Chief.

AKYLBAI. Wretched traitor, where have you sprung from? Drop your weapon!

SUTEMGEN. This is not the moment to sort things out, to decide whether I'm a traitor or my master's guard dog. Where's Baluan?

On catching sight of Baluan sitting on a boulder, Sutemgen walks over to him timidly. When he sees the gloomy figure of Baluan, deep in sad thoughts, Sutemgen can hold back no longer. He unexpectedly bursts into tears.

SUTEMGEN. I never thought I'd see you in this state!...

AKYLBAI. Stop wailing, you groveller!

SUTEMGEN. Akylbai, please don't talk like that. How would you have behaved in my position?

AKYLBAI. I would have finished myself off, drunk some poison!...

SUTEMGEN. If I had died, what use would that have been? D'you think I have an easier time of it?

AKYLBAI. And what d'you want out here? Have you come to betray us?

SUTEMGEN. You must leave here and as quickly as possible. Men sent out to follow you are on their way.

AKYLBAI. And how did you find us?

SUTEMGEN. I found out from the local shepherds.

BALUAN. What's the district chief planning to do?

SUTEMGEN. He's waiting for the armed detachment from Akmola, sent out to support him.

BALUAN. And where's Tatyana?

SUTEMGEN (*Not really understanding the point*) She…Where else would she be… she's at home of course…

BALUAN. Does she continue to go out for drives in a carriage?

SUTEMGEN. Yes, every God-given day. She's not alone either, but with their guest from Omsk. They were planning to go out for a drive today as well.

BALUAN. So that's what's going on!…

AKYLBAI. Listen, what do you need that girl from Omsk for? You don't even manage to make the journey to visit your beloved Galiya! No way is that girl your equal!

BALUAN. (*in a bolder tone*) You should leave us your horse, your rifle and the file.

SUTEMGEN. (*With a frightened look on his face*) And what's to become of me?

BALUAN. Yes, and take off your clothes as well.

SUTEMGEN. God help me! - the mosquitoes will eat me.

BALUAN. You'll survive. Ride off at a gallop over to the village, raising clouds of dust… That'll keep the mosquitoes away.

A MAN ON A MISSION

Akylbai laughs loudly but, realizing how out of place such a reaction was, he stops laughing almost immediately.

SUTEMGEN. And what shall I say to His Excellency, if he asks where my horse and rifle are?

BALUAN. Tell it like it is. Baluan Sholak took them. Now undress and be quick about it!

Sutemgen hastens to obey and soon he only has his underwear on. He begins to slap at the flesh on his stomach and shoulders, so as to drive the mosquitoes away.

SUTEMGEN. Remember, hero-leader, they're not going to leave you in peace. Don't expect any mercy from them. As they understand it, you alone are to blame for all their disasters and misfortunes.

BALUAN. I know! And now, be off with you and quick about it! Run out there and shout at the top of your voice: "I've been robbed!". I'm sorry! (*He slaps him across the face*).

Sutemgen with his eyes rolling and still slapping himself all over his body, sets off straightaway at a gallop, screaming out in blood-curdling fashion "O horrors, bandits! They've robbed me!"

AKYLBAI. It's beyond me! What's this all about? We now have a horse each but what are you going to do with that toady's animal?

BALUAN. It'll be for Tatyana.

AKYLBAI. Tatyana?! But why? What for? Why on earth is she coming to join us?

BALUAN. You'll find out later. But only under one condition: don't ask too many questions and carry out all my instructions to the letter. Off we go!

ACT TWO

The summit of Mount Okzhetpes, where no man has set foot. Although it does not seem particularly high from a distance it takes a man on horseback almost a day to reach its foothills. What mere mortal would make so bold after grappling with sharp stones, deep gorges and sheer cliffs to conquer that summit, let alone any frail individual who has decided to renounce this transitory world of ours.

In a small forest consisting of sparse pines interspersed in places with red juniper trees, three travellers pause for a while. One of them is Baluan Sholak, the second is Akylbai and the third Tatyana.

Tatyana's hands are tied and her mouth gagged.

While out enjoying a drive one day, Tatyana had suddenly been ambushed: two horsemen had galloped up to her, hurled the coachman to the ground with a single blow and seconds later the official representative of the Governor-General of Omsk had been sent head over heels to the ground. Despite the heart-rending scream from the girl, she had been tied up and had a scarf thrust into her mouth before being led away up into the mountains. After reaching the summit of Okzhetpes and making sure that they were out of danger, the weary fugitives had dropped exhausted to the ground and fallen asleep straightaway.

They are lying separately, each one of them at some distance from the others. Tatyana no longer has the strength to move: she is lying there as if lifeless. The wordless quiet does not last for long. The first to lift his head is Akylbai.

AKYLBAI. Any further and we would have killed the horses and hurtled down into the gorge, Baluan. We've had some rest now though and we need to talk to this wilful daughter of the district chief.

A MAN ON A MISSION

Baluan Sholak walks over to the girl. She fails even to notice him. He tries to rouse her by nudging her several times, but she is not even prepared to open her eyes. Baluan unties her arms and removes the gag from her mouth.

BALUAN SHOLAK. Tanyusha! Tanyazhan… That's enough now, up you get.

AKYLBAI. She doesn't respond at all. It's as if in her terror she gave up the ghost…

BALUAN. No. It seems she's just fallen into a deep sleep, intoxicated by the fresh clean air of the mountain. Tanya, come on… up you get.

With her hands now free of the rope, Tatyana opens her eyes and stretches in delight. Then, remembering, that she is no longer free to do as she pleases, she jumps to her feet and tries to hide behind a stone boulder.

AKYLBAI. It looks as if she's worn out by all the jolting of the long ride. Her lips have even turned blue. I'll give her some water right away.

He lifts a leather jug to her lips, but Tatyana cries out and refuses to let him anywhere near her.

TATYANA. Don't you dare! Keep away from me!

AKYLBAI. You're desperate for a drink. Have some water… at least a sip.

TATYANA. I'll die before I start drinking out of your filthy jug. Keep away from me!

BALUAN. No need to be frightened. We're not going to do you any harm.

TATYANA. What could be worse than what you've already done to me! You'd have done better to kill me than humiliate me like this. Go ahead, finish me off!

BALUAN. No, we're not going to kill you. Why should we deal your parents such a bitter blow?

TATYANA. My parents are already weeping and distraught about their daughter disappearing without trace while out for a drive! After beating up the coachman, two savages kidnapped their daughter. They still don't know whether their daughter is alive or dead.

AKYLBAI. Yes, the young man from Omsk had a raw deal, but we had no choice…

TATYANA. He's not my suitor, he's a mentor. What a disgrace! How shall I be able to look people in the eye, if this terrible news reaches Omsk!

BALUAN. Tanyazhan, from the moment I saw you, I realized you were an intelligent girl.

TATYANA. What did you say?

BALUAN. Tanyazhan.

TATYANA. What kind of a word is that?

BALUAN. It's an affectionate term of address in the Kazakh language.

TATYANA. I don't need a horrible name like that. I already have a name of my own!

BALUAN. All right. Have it your own way. First of all you need to calm down a little. Come over here and sit down (*Baluan spreads out a saddle blanket on the boulder. Tatyana sits down*).

TATYANA. What did you bring me here for? To shame me to your heart's content? Just you try! You'll both rot in prison with all your friends and family. Didn't you have enough brain to realize that?

BALUAN. Akylbai's going back to the city now. I shall give him a letter to hand to your father. You and I shall remain here, until I receive a reply from your father. Whether we have to stay out here for a long time or not depends on how fast your Papa takes to write his reply.

TATYANA. What kind of letter?

BALUAN. It doesn't concern you. The content is of quite a different kind. Our village has been seized by your fellow countrymen. When people tried to resist, the whole village was burnt to the ground. After losing their homes and everything of value, the inhabitants had to wander off and roam through the steppe. Anyone who dared to stand up for themselves was brought down with a gun. All my close relatives have been thrown into jail. I was declared a trouble-maker and a rebel and locked up in jail as well. Yet I managed to escape and began to look for you. You were out enjoying yourself, while my people were roaming through the steppe in sorrow and grief. I have already had to spend time in jail on four occasions. Each time it has resulted from your father's harassment. So I decided to make off with his beloved daughter. There was nothing else for it. D'you understand?

TATYANA. I don't know, I'm not in a fit state to take things in at the moment. I need to come to…

BALUAN. You see, it looks as if we're beginning to understand each other. Akylbai!

AKYLBAI. I'm here. I'm collecting dry branches so as to cook something to eat for this evening.

BALUAN. You're living up to your name – Akylbai – "clever and resourceful". You understand everything without having to be told. Light the fire, bury the potatoes in the hot ashes and in the meantime I'll write the letter. The evening banquet will be a little on the late side Tanyazhan... Oh drat, I meant to say Tanyusha! Make the supper, Akylbai!

AKYLBAI. Your orders will be carried out... Sir and...Madam!

* * *

The house belonging to the head of the district. An angry and agitated Dolgonosov is striding impatiently up and down the room. His wife is in tears, cursing her husband and blaming him for all their misfortunes.

ELIZAVETA. It's getting light already! And there's still no news of our vanished daughter. My little dove, my sweetheart – how you must be suffering in the hands of those brigands! My precious, you must have been crying your heart out, calling "Papa, Mama!" What news is there from the search party? What are they saying?

DOLGONOSOV. There's no news!

ELIZAVETA. What does her mentor say, the visitor from Omsk? Where is he?

DOLGONOSOV. He set off at short notice to Akmola. To his aunt's. It appears he's planning to report the incident to Troitskii.

ELIZAVETA. His aunt kept on boasting haughtily that they were of Decembrist stock, but why did Mikhail fail to behave like a hero? What kind of man must he be, if he couldn't even protect a young girl sitting by his side?!

DOLGONOSOV. There'll be hell to pay, if the Governor-General in Omsk hears about all this...

ELIZAVETA. The Governor-General shouldn't be your concern! You should be thinking about your poor little daughter! Oh, God in Heaven, what are we going to do?!

DOLGONOSOV. Lisa, calm down. News is bound to come.

ELIZAVETA. That's all there is for us to do, sit around and wait for news, watching the grass grow under our feet!

DOLGONOSOV. Who's just sitting around? A whole detachment of soldiers is out searching for her, scouring the hills and valleys. Troitskii's sent out another armed detachment from Akmola as well! What else d'you insist I do?!

ELIZAVETA. All this turmoil is the result of your softness! You let off all those wild savages! It's got to the point where nobody fears you, nobody is in awe of you. If that brigand had any respect for you, he would not have burst in here in the presence of two high-ranking dignitaries. To make matters worse, he behaved in an insolent, cocky way: he started singing, doing just as he pleased. It was horrible! He made a laughing-stock of us all.

DOLGONOSOV. Don't forget how Ekaterina and Tatyana were applauding the savage, calling his singing "splendid"?!

ELIZAVETA. Of course, it was all the same to Ekaterina! If that unseemly scene had taken place within her walls, her husband would immediately have arrested the upstart. You even stayed silent when he was insolent enough to make a mockery of your servants, pushing them aside like so many puppets. And now they've carried off your daughter in broad daylight. What insolence! How dare they! My poor little dove, beloved daughter!

At that moment Sutemgen, rushes in, panting. Desperately gasping for breath, he cannot get his words out in his haste and agitation. He has a bruise under one eye.

ELIZAVETA. You should have sent that Kazakh packing too. You failed to do anything, you were like a little child believing what he said - "Baluan Sholak stripped me bare". But perhaps they were working together?

DOLGONOSOV. Lisa, what's come over you!? Calm down, at least a fraction. Whatever state you're in... if there is any news, come out with it and fast!

SUTEMGEN. Sir, there's a messenger... a messenger's come from Baluan Sholak!

Dolgonosov and his wife cannot help shouting out in their alarm.

ELIZAVETA. What? From Baluan Sholak!?

DOLGONOSOV. Should he come in?

Enter Akylbai with a rifle over his shoulder and a document folder in his hand.

DOLGONOSOV. (*Recognizing the folder Akylbai is holding*) That's a folder from my office. How has it ended up with you?

SUTEMGEN. (*Trembling from head to toe*) Your Excellency... Sir. They grabbed it last time... when they looted my home.

ELIZAVETA. What are things coming to! Why are you just standing there? Tell us. What's the news? Is our poor daughter alive?

AKYLBAI. She's alive. You could say she feels fine.

ELIZAVETA. Thank the Lord!

DOLGONOSOV. Out with it!

AKYLBAI. Baluan Sholak has sent you a letter. It's here, in this folder.

A MAN ON A MISSION

(*After opening the folder, Dolgonosov takes out the letter written on headed paper from his own office and looks through it*)

DOLGONOSOV. It's written in the Arabic alphabet...how can I read it?

AKYLBAI. I can't help you there Sir!

DOLGONOSOV. Sutemgen, perhaps you'll read it to us? After all you were trained in Muslim studies at Orenburg.

(*Sutemgen takes the letter and looks it over at length*)

DOLGONOSOV. Why are you just standing there? Read it and quickly!

SUTEMGEN. Your Excellency, I can't...!

DOLGONOSOV. Why?

SUTEMGEN. If I read it out, you'll lock me up.

DOLGONOSOV. There won't be any punishments. Read everything out that's written there.

SUTEMGEN (*reads*) You, the district chief, are a son of a bitch. You've been hounding us for years. Our land was seized and our village burnt down on your instructions. (*His voice starts shaking*) Your tax-collectors drove away our livestock. You, personally, have had me locked up on several occasions. Why are you hounding me, as if I'd killed your father....

DOLGONOSOV. (*In a threatening tone*) Read on!

SUTEMGEN. To hell with you... Am I just a blood-thirsty murderer? I, incidentally, am living in my homeland, while you are outsiders. Yes, I did carry off your daughter. I accuse you of real crimes though, because you locked up innocent people in jail. Remember this, district chief – if you don't release innocent people from prison, I shall slit your daughter's throat, like a piglet's. Now everything is going to depend on your choice. Either you release innocent people from prison or you'll lose your daughter. In addition you must sign an officially stamped letter stating that you won't lay a finger on me or my relatives in future. If you don't comply with these demands, the price will not just be losing your daughter. If you refuse to make concessions, I shall carry you off as well and your spoilt wife. Don't waste any time before responding to my demands. However many soldiers you send out after me you won't find me. Soon you'll be begging for my help. That's all there is to it".

The bold tone of the letter frightens not merely Dolgonosov himself, but his wife as well. Elizaveta is quaking in the grip of terrible fear.

ELIZAVETA. Set them free! D'you hear me – set them all free! That savage is capable of anything.

AKYLBAI. Baluan is not a savage! He's a singer, a musician, a wrestler, a hero and a minstrel. As you would see it – a gallant knight! You probably wouldn't be able to find another like him in the whole of Russia!

ELIZAVETA. I don't object… call him a knight. But please just tell me, where is my little dove, my beloved daughter?

AKYLBAI. I can't tell you that.

ELIZAVETA. They're already starting to talk down to us. For those vile words alone, you ought not just to lose your tongue, but your head as well.

AKYLBAI. If you kill me, you won't be seeing your daughter again. **ELIZAVETA.** Tell me, is she safe and well? Will I see her alive again? I beg you (*she throws herself down at his feet*). O God, how low have we sunk, having to beg vermin like this for mercy!

AKYLBAI. Everything is clearly stated in the letter. There's nothing for me to add. (*Turning to Dolgonosov*) So, Your Excellency, district chief... I think I shall wait for you later outside. It would be bad manners for me to stare at the back of a man's neck, while he writes a letter. (*Moving towards the door*). The faster you write your reply, the sooner you shall see your beloved daughter. I warn you – if you send out your people to follow me, you will not see your daughter alive again.

(*Akylbai leaves the room*)

ELIZAVETA. It's humiliation pure and simple, downright humiliation! Merciful Creator, protect us from these monsters! Oh, Jesus – only you can help us!

(*She walks over to the icon above which hangs Christ crucified. Meanwhile Dolgonosov totters over to his desk with his head in his hands and then sits down*)

* * *

In the house of Troitskii, Head of the Akmola District. His Excellency is sitting at the table with his wife and drinking tea. After taking several sips from his tea-bowl, Troitskii stands up and moves away from the table.

TROITSKII. Why do you make a song and dance everywhere about the fact that your distant relatives were connected to the Decembrists?

EKATERINA. I didn't mention it just anywhere, but within the walls of a close friend's house. And you still can't forget about that? What was so special about it?

TROITSKII. What was special about it? Don't you remember how your 'harmless' phrase almost put an end to my career?

EKATERINA. Then you made a mistake right at the start when you married me. Yet even now it's not too late. The Governor-General in Omsk is living with a second wife.

TROITSKII. Stop all this back-biting. There are forty people on one side and just one stubborn mule on the other. Just remember how while at the Dolgonosovs you applauded some brigand or other so wildly. Had you never heard anyone sing like that before?

EKATERINA. Of course I hadn't! You won't hear a baritone like that either in Petersburg or anywhere else in Russia. If he were to have specialist musical training, not just Russia but the whole of Europe would be applauding him.

TROITSKII. Poor Europe doffing her cap to all manner of upstarts! And then... what's making your second cousin such a frequent visitor to the Dolgonosov's house? He had come out here to visit you, his relative, not the Dolgonosovs. I had the impression they had invited us to visit them last time so as to play host to Mikhail.

EKATERINA. But why not?... He's a visitor, from far away... What also needs to be taken into account is that he is a trusted member of staff working for your immediate superior, Mamontov...

TROITSKII. Ye-es. The Dolgonosovs don't invite people over just like that. Everything's carefully calculated well in advance. If your young nephew were to marry Tatyana, they would have closer links to the Governor-General than we do. Recently it was rumoured that Mamontov was to be promoted and would soon be going back to St. Petersburg. It looks as if Dolgnosov aspires to the office of Governor-General. **EKATERINA.** I don't think that Tatyana is showing much interest in Mikhail.

TROITSKII. It's not really up to her. Mikhail is twenty-seven years old, mature and with good prospects. The Dolgonosovs are not likely to let a son-in-law like that slip through their fingers.

A MAN ON A MISSION

EKATERINA. The poor wretches must be weeping desperate tears over their kidnapped daughter. But you in the here and now... Have you sent out a search-party?

TROITSKII. Oh yes! ...But it's hard to predict how the Governor-General will view any intervention on my part in this situation...

EKATERINA. You're mind's on very different matters! Perhaps you're even happy that Baluan Sholak has carried off Tatyana, assuming now that Mikhail won't be paying any more attention to her? In your eyes it's fortuitous that this tragedy has befallen the Dolgonosovs...isn't that so?

TROITSKII. Ekaterina...Naryshkina! You're talking all kinds of rubbish, just so as to wound someone else.

EKATERINA. I am deeply grateful to observe that sometimes you recall my surname, at least in conflict situations like this one. Coming straight out with the truth is second nature to us.

TROITSKII. It would seem that it is by no means necessary to have Decembrists among your distant relatives in order to confront people with the truth. D'you know what Elizaveta said – a woman who was born here in the land of the Kirghiz-Kaisaks?

EKATERINA. What did she say then?

TROITSKII. She criticizes your nephew, boasting: "We are descendants of the Decembrists", but their current descendant can't even try and defend a young girl sitting next to him... Can you even call him a man?

EKATERINA. Did she really say that? They're just parasites with no talent for anything except being blood-suckers, like so many leeches, and raking together riches for themselves! They have no interest in art or education, they don't understand anything about music, they might as well be tone deaf. In future I'm going to punish Mikhail and stop him setting foot there again. Elizaveta's husband asked for military support. Don't you dare to send them any! Let them sort their problems out themselves!

Troitskii rings a small bell as loud as he can and a sergeant of the guard comes running in.

TROITSKII. Call back immediately the military detachment that was sent out to help in the Kokshetau District!

SERGEANT. Yes, they'll be summoned right away, Your Excellency! (*He makes a rapid exit*)

* * *

The summit of Mount Okzhetpes at night. Tatyana is alone.

Tatyana is looking fearfully around her but there is nothing to be seen. The sounds of wild animals start to be heard in the distance making her more frightened than ever – the distant hooting of an owl, the howling of wolves, also the sound of falling stones. She stands up and begins looking for Baluan Shokal, but there is no sign of him.

TATYANA. Hey… hey!

Not a sound by way of reply.

TATYANA. Is there anybody there?

Nobody responds.

TATYANA. Where on earth have you got to?

The howl of a wolf is heard in the distance.

TATYANA. How will things turn out, if they abandon me here at the top of the mountain? Am I really going to perish as prey to wild animals and horrible creatures? Perhaps there are even lions and bears out here…

A MAN ON A MISSION

The howl of a wolf is heard once more, but this time somewhere nearby.

TATYANA. Come out and rescue me, you wretch! I'm scared...

Another howl is heard, this time very near, from behind the rock on which Tatyana is sitting. After leaping to her feet in terror, Tatyana stands leaning against a pine tree as far as she can from the rock.

TATYANA. What a monster! He may be a savage, but there must be something human in him. Why did he leave me on my own, where's the wretch got to? What a rogue he is! Come out here... I'm scared the wolves are going to start gnawing at me...!

At that very moment Baluan Sholak leaps out from behind the rocks in front of Tatyana. Terrified out of her wits by this time, she swoons and falls to the ground. Baluan Sholak places her head on his knee and looks into Tatyana's face as she begins to regain consciousness.

BALUAN. How beautiful she is! This dear creature has been blessed with such rare beauty! She's like an angel, who's come down from Heaven.

At that moment a voice is heard echoing through the mountains. It could be a ghost.

GALIYA'S VOICE. You womaniser, you said things like that to me, when we met! It's not fitting for a real man to scatter round words like that. It turns out that you can't resist anything beautiful...

BALUAN. (*looking all around him*) Who's that? Where's the voice coming from?

GALIYA'S VOICE. It's me – Galiya. I hope to meet you soon. I waited impatiently, but you didn't come that day. What did that mean?

BALUAN. Galiyazhan! You've probably heard about what's happening here. As soon as I get out of this trouble, I'll find you. Galiya, I haven't forgotten you! For me you're the most beautiful girl in the world!

GALIYA'S VOICE. How can I believe a seducer's words like that? Who is that woman sitting there in front of you?

BALUAN. A girl, our prisoner!

GALIYA'S VOICE. Is she more beautiful than I am?

BALUAN. No, Galiya! She is not more beautiful than you. While she might be compared to the Moon, you are the Sun!

Tatyana raises her head. At that moment Galiya's ghost disappears. Realizing that she is lying on the outlaw's lap, Tatyana leaps to her feet in fear and hides behind the rock.

TATYANA. Where did you disappear to, leaving me here on my own?

BALUAN. I went to fetch water from the spring. It's clean and as cold as ice. We haven't eaten anything for two days. At least have a drink of water.

TATYANA. I'd rather die of thirst than drink your water.

BALUAN. Then I'll leave you on your own again (*He rises to his feet*).

TATYANA. No, please, don't leave me alone. I'm horribly scared of being on my own, even when I'm at home.

BALUAN. Then drink the water and have something to eat.

TATYANA. What kind of food? Raw meat?

BALUAN. You've never eaten such tasty food in your life. Meat cooked on an open fire, potatoes baked in hot coals.

TATYANA. Potatoes baked in hot coals?

BALUAN. Yes. A pheasant cooked over hot coals as well.

TATYANA. No. I'm not going to eat that...

BALUAN. It's up to you. I for my part am really hungry.

Baluan takes the pheasant and some potatoes from the hot coals and devours large pieces of them hungrily. He enjoys his food, deliberately licking his lips.

BALUAN. It's a waste of time being so stubborn. Surely you must have realized over these last two days that I have no evil intentions. You're an innocent girl, as pretty as an angel. It would be wrong for me even to touch you – a tender young girl as beautiful and timid as a forest doe. D'you want to eat some warm potatoes? I can serve you some.

TATYANA. Don't come near me! Throw me one or two over here.

BALUAN. Aha! Now I'm hearing something sensible!

He throws two or three potatoes over to Tatyana and a leg of the roast pheasant. Tatyana, who had not had even a crumb to eat for two whole days, starts to eat the soot-stained potatoes and meat greedily.

Struck by Tatyana's child-like delight in the food, Baluan looks closely at Tatyana's sweet face in his surprise.

BALUAN. I can throw you meat and potatoes, but what shall we do when it comes to the jug full of water? It could break on the stones. But now, have a drink, otherwise you might choke by mistake... Don't be afraid of me: I'm not a wolf, I shan't eat you.

Baluan hands Tatyana the jug. She does not seem to be as frightened as before and takes the jug from Baluan's hand. She presses her lips to it and then drinks with desperate thirst, splashing and spilling the water as she does so.

TATYANA. A little while ago, when you weren't here, there were wolves howling horribly. One of them started howling right behind that rock. How terrified I was! Why aren't they howling now?

BALUAN. Because there aren't any wolves here.

TATYANA. But where are they? They were howling just a little while ago. Did they run away because they were frightened of you?

BALUAN. It was me howling like a wolf.

TATYANA. You? You know how to howl like a wolf?

BALUAN. Yes! I began trying to howl like a wolf, when I started hunting at the age of fourteen and was setting traps for wolves. Once, out of the blue, a full-grown wolf attacked me.

TATYANA. How awful! What happened then?

BALUAN. We fought.

TATYANA. And then?

BALUAN. I strangled the wolf and skinned it.

TATYANA. (*with a rippling laugh*). Surely not! Munchausen of the steppes!

BALUAN. Who was that?

TATYANA. The Germans had a famous liar, just like you!

BALUAN. I'm not lying. That happened on a frosty winter's day. In the heat of the struggle I didn't even notice that my fingers were frost-bitten.

A MAN ON A MISSION

TATYANA. You're not lying again?

BALUAN. That was when I lost four fingers to frost-bite.

TATYANA. At fourteen!... that's not possible!

BALUAN. Ever since people seem to have forgotten my name is Nurmagambet and they began calling me Baluan Sholak, Baluan "the Fingerless".

TATYANA. You're a really brave man! Will a wolf appear if you start howling like a wolf?

BALUAN. I've already told you, there aren't any wolves in these parts.

TATYANA. Really? Try and start howling!

Baluan Sholak imitates a howling wolf. Frightened by the sinister howls suddenly ringing out in the night, Tatyana throws herself into Baluan's arms...

PAUSE

Baluan Sholak is thunderstruck, rendered almost senseless by the girl's unexpected behaviour. A moment later he recovers his calm, puts his arm round Tatyana's shoulders and strokes her hair. Then he steps back a little from Tatyana and looks her straight in the face.

BALUAN. You seem to have enjoyed my wolf howls. If you like I can roar like a lion.

TATYANA. You... You are an honourable man. Someone else in your place might have...

BALUAN. Tanyazhan, there's no need to talk of that...

TATYANA. Tanyazhan? For some reason that affectionate name is starting to grow on me... Say it again...

BALUAN. Tanyazhan, you are like a tulip opening up in the rays of the morning dawn! Tulips do not like rough treatment. They quickly fade…

TATYANA. By the way you were talking to somebody else, when I fainted…and was lying here…with my head on your lap. Who was it?

BALUAN. Oh, that's a long story. Not something you'd understand.

TATYANA. Why? I can understand everything. I have read all Turgenev's novels.

BALUAN. Novels are one thing, real life is something else. They're two very different things.

TATYANA. But all the same, tell me who you were talking to.

BALUAN. To Galiya.

TATYANA. And who's she?

BALUAN. I only saw her once.

TATYANA. Is she beautiful?

BALUAN. There's no other beauty like her in the whole wide world!

TATYANA. More beautiful than I am?

BALUAN. Yes…

Tatyana slaps Baluan's cheek.

TATYANA. So that's it! I shan't touch your potatoes and meat any more. So there! (*She scatters the food*) And I shan't drink your water either! (*She tries to hurl away the water jug as well, but at that very moment Baluan embraces her*)

BALUAN. Tanyazhan you can scatter everything you like, but not the jug. Otherwise we'll have nothing to drink!

TATYANA. Don't try and win me round by calling me Tanyazhan! Don't you dare call me that again! It's not right... you must understand you shouldn't do that!

BALUAN. All right, if it's not fitting, I won't use that name any more. Did you really need to get so angry about it? Calm down a little! If you want me to, I can grunt like a camel or crow like a cock.

TATYANA. You can bray like a donkey for all I care!

BALUAN. You're such a small creature but so proud! I told you that you were a tender flower like a tulip that was just opening its petals – an innocent angel. She on the other hand already has a husband!

TATYANA. (*calming down straightaway*) She's married? You're in love with a woman who already has a husband?

BALUAN. Yes...

TATYANA. How could you fall in love with a married woman?

BALUAN. The fair at Kyzylzhar was in full swing. When I had defeated the reigning champion, I then brought down the famous wrestler Koren, breaking two of his ribs. A beautiful, really impressive woman came up to me, wrapped a silk caftan round my shoulders, and said "I am a true admirer of yours". Then she climbed into a cart and disappeared, without telling me who she was.

TATYANA. Yes, but where was her husband?

BALUAN. Where you'd expect – at her side.

TATYANA. Hasn't he challenged you to a duel?

BALUAN. Not yet (*laughing*). Perhaps he'll get round to it later…

TATYANA. And where's the caftan?

BALUAN. The caftan… My wife cut it up and threw it into the river.

TATYANA. That's terrible. Are you married?

BALUAN. Yes.

TATYANA. Where is she?

BALUAN. In jail. My close relatives – my father and mother – they're all languishing in jail. I have already managed to land in prison four times myself. And now, so as to have innocent people released from prison and brought back together again in their ancestral lands, I was obliged to kidnap you. I think that I shall soon receive an answer from your father…

TATYANA. (*in an excited state*) You are a real hero. A truly honourable knight, like those in Alexandre Dumas' novels!

BALUAN. And who is Dooma.

TATYANA. Not Dooma, but Dumas. He's a famous French novelist. His novels are full of all sorts of adventures like yours.

BALUAN. They imagine those adventures. In the Kazakh steppes they're happening for real every day.

TATYANA. To be honest…

BALUAN. What about?

TATYANA. I'm starting to get used to you… I'd like to eat some of your hot potatoes, if you'd give me some.

BALUAN. So that's it! That must mean you're not angry any more. Just a minute!

He runs off and comes back with two or three potatoes straight from the fire.

TATYANA. I don't want to get my hands covered in soot. Could you peel them.

Baluan peels the potatoes with care.

TATYANA. Put half a one into my mouth.

Baluan cuts one of the hot potatoes in two and puts one of the halves in Tatyana's mouth.

TATYANA. How tasty they are! How romantic eating out here on the mountain…

BALUAN. You're scared of dirtying your hands, while your lips are covered in soot… Tell me, why are you so angry sometimes and then friendly the next moment?

TATYANA. I don't know. Sometimes I just don't feel capable of sorting out my own emotions. Are you going to marry Galiya now?

BALUAN. I don't know! Perhaps it would be interesting just to be in love like this for the rest of my life…

TATYANA. Like Don Quixote!

BALUAN. And who's he?

TATYANA. He was a Spanish knight, who spent his whole life dreaming about a girl whom he had never seen, not even once… You too, like him…

BALUAN. Wait a moment, Tanyazhan! There is everything you could wish for out here in the steppe. You just need to know how to see it, how to listen to it, how to love it. Only then will all life's secrets be revealed.

TATYANA. I'm going to make a point of telling my father and my mother about all of this. What a good thing it is that you carried me off. Otherwise I would never have learnt about all these things.

BALUAN. Over these past two days you have grown wiser…

TATYANA. That's true. You've gradually become someone close to me. I think that there would be nothing to fear if I were beside you, nothing to worry or to feel sad about. Perhaps Galiya too, with her feminine intuition, sensed those noble qualities in you. Tell me, is it possible to fall madly in love the moment you set eyes on someone?

BALUAN. There is no such expression as falling in love at the third or fourth encounter. If someone falls in love, it's probably that very first time…

TATYANA. Do you think you're really in love with her?

BALUAN. Perhaps I am…

TATYANA. If you meet her again, are you going to marry Galiya? To have a second wife?

BALUAN. Ever since that meeting she has been my dream. My feelings for her ring out like a song in my heart.

TATYANA. Like a song? Do you make up tunes as well?

BALUAN. They surge up like a wave… dreams and longings cannot help but burst from my heart in song.

TATYANA. How interesting! Do sing me the song… I beg you!

BALUAN. No, Tanyazhan. Now's not the time for singing songs.

TATYANA. Why? It's the perfect time. Here we are at the top of a mountain on a moonlit night. All around us there is wordless silence. There is probably nobody else but God watching over us. If you don't agree to my request, I shall cast myself down from these rocks. Like this...

BALUAN. All right now, Tanyazhan. You'd be capable of doing that... The song is called "Galiya".

Baluan climbs up on to the rock and sings. His powerful voice resonates all around them. His voice sounds particularly enchanting on this occasion. Tatyana listens to him intently and with great interest, as if bewitched. All the time she is peering straight at Baluan's face. The song comes to an end. When it is over Tatyana remains sitting there without saying a word.

TATYANA. Sing another song. Just one more...!

BALUAN. Now I think I'll sing you a song called "Starling" the work of a bard from the steppes called Akin.

Baluan sings Akin's song "Starling" and its gentle melody echoes through the mountains and gorges. Baluan sings with inspiration in his powerful voice from deep in his chest, perhaps because of the beautiful scenery all around him and the moon shining down on him and Tatyana together in a world of their own. This song makes an even deeper impression on Tatyana.

TATYANA. *(truly moved by what she is hearing)* Wonderful! The tune is so full of mystery! What a sense of freedom! You...you (*she starts crying*).

BALUAN. Tanyazhan! What's the matter? Why are you crying?

Tatyana throws her arms round Baluan's neck, unable to control her strong emotions. She is weeping, choking back her tears. Baluan is stunned by the fervour of the beautiful young girl: he stands there unmoving and silent, wrapping Tatyana in a firm embrace.

* * *

In the house of Dolgonosov, who has written an official stamped document agreeing to all the demands made by Baluan Sholak. The general atmosphere is one of total chaos. The district chief, well aware that his daughter's life depends on the results of his actions, is striding up and down the room in a state of painful despondency. He feels unable to tolerate the cruel humiliation and disgrace, which have befallen him.

ELIZAVETA. My poor desolate little dove! Who could have imagined that we should have to go through this disgrace!

DOLGONOSOV. Stop the wailing! D'you think I'm having an easy time of it?

ELIZAVETA. You're the one who's to blame for everything! That scoundrel could appear here any night and do away with us all. That's all we need. Isn't that the case?

DOLGONOSOV. It'll serve us right, let him do away with us. It would put an end to all our problems and humiliation.

ELIZAVETA. Don't be in such a hurry, my dear. That day may well be something we have to reckon with in the end! I know that my poor daughter is in the clutches of that savage, weeping bitter tears and pining for us, for her "Papa and Mama"! Your father who should be rescuing you is spineless. He's not capable of anything. All he knows how to do is shout at me!

DOLGONOSOV. What's got into you? Stop it at once, you make it impossible to think. Your daughter will be back, safe and sound.

ELIZAVETA. How do you know? Have you dreamt it, or seen it in the stars? Even if that savage releases her still alive, it will no longer be our innocent, chaste daughter. My head's like a sieve... why on earth did I let Tatyana go out for a drive that day?!

DOLGONOSOV. You're a fine one to talk about all of this. Why do you have to make that man of the people an enemy, referring to him as a "savage". How many times do I have to ask you to put that word out of your mind? As I see it, he's a man of his word. You'll see that he'll bring Tatyana back to us safe and sound.

ELIZAVETA. You just wait and see how the wolf will have mercy on the lamb!

Sutemgen runs in all out of breath.

SUTEMGEN. Your Excellency. It's ba-ad news.

DOLGONOSOV. What else has happened? Out with it, quickly!...

SUTEMGEN. Your Excellency, Mr. Troitskii...

DOLGONOSOV. What's up with him?

SUTEMGEN. When the men were only halfway there, he called back the detachment, which had been sent out to support us...

DOLGONOSOV. What nonsense is he talking? What does he mean?

SUTEMGEN. Your Excellency, I can't understand what's going on!..

ELIZAVETA. So now he's decided to turn his back on us, has he? He must be planning something. They're a really cunning pair...

DOLGONOSOV. In these parts I know every pine tree. I'll manage with my own people. But I can't help wondering why he turned back his detachment when they were halfway there? What's behind it all? But just a moment! It's at this very point that

Governor-General Mamontov is being transferred to St. Petersburg. Last time he was put out by Mikhail informing him that the Governor-General had a very high opinion of me. This rebellion taking place in my district plays into Troitskii's hands. He'll be keen to fan the flames and hoping that we don't find our missing daughter. In this situation he's counting on my having to abandon any hope of a Governor's post and that I shall even have my work cut out to stay on in my current one... He's obviously determined to overtake me with regard to the Governor's favour. His calculations are cunning ones, aimed at securing his long-term future!...

ELIZAVETA. Now they definitely won't let Mikhail visit this household any more. He did not even bid us farewell when he set off for Akmola.

DOLGONOSOV. He was clearly too ashamed to show his face here again, when he failed to protect Tatyana.

ELIZAVETA. It's clear that after this he'll do his best to keep as far away from us as possible.

DOLGONOSOV. Yet I still have not understood what he's up to. He doesn't openly say what he thinks. He's not prepared to have an open conversation. He behaves like someone who has a great deal of experience despite his youth. He is either a very clever young man or really stupid. I've heard that he did not even go and pay his respects to his aunt.

ELIZAVETA. Yes, to Hell with them all... don't talk to me about them. O Lord, all we can do is sit here quite helpless and lament our fate. Meanwhile time flies past mercilessly. My poor little dove... how she must be suffering in the hands of that heartless savage, that cruel monster. Every minute we wait seems like an hour! Why don't they dispatch look-outs after the brigands? We have to do something... are you head of a district or not?

DOLGONOSOV. I'm wracking my brains to find a solution too. We need to tread very carefully. Otherwise we might lose our daughter. What we must avoid is making them angry. If we do that, there'll be no stopping them.

After thinking long and hard, Dolgonosov rings his small bell.

SUTEMGEN. I haven't gone off anywhere, Sir. I'm here. What do you want me to do?

DOLGONOSOV. Leave half a dozen soldiers here to protect the house and let the rest make ready to set off. Prepare my field uniform and saddle the horses!

SUTEMGEN. Yes Sir!

Sutemgen leaves the room. After hesitating briefly, as if anxious to say something to his wife, Dolgonosov eventually leaves the room without a word, after noticing that Elizaveta is crossing herself in front of an icon.

* * *

At the summit of Okzhetpes, which has become a temporary shelter for Baluan Sholak and Tatyana. Today is the third day they have been there. During those three days they have become used to each other to some degree.

After climbing up onto the highest boulder, Baluan looks down. Tatyana is stirring the ashes in the hearth, which had been hastily built out of the available stones.

BALUAN. Today is the third day. Perhaps Akylbai will be returning soon. What kind of answer will he bring back from your father?

TATYANA. What will you do to me if my father rejects your demands? Will you kill me?

BALUAN. And what do you think?

TATYANA. If you are going to kill me, don't drag it out. Can we agree on that? Just say: "Tanyazhan, jump down from that rock over there". Then I shall shut my eyes tight and jump, without thinking twice about it!

BALUAN. Don't go rushing into jumps for the moment. First of all, let's read the answer.

TATYANA. Hey!... For some reason I keep on saying "Hey" to you. It's time to tell me what your name is by now, isn't it?

BALUAN. It's Nurmagambet. But everyone calls me Baluan Sholak.

TATYANA. Nur-ma-gambet! Balvan...

BALUAN. Not Bal-v-an, but Baluan and don't forget the Sholak!

TATYANA. Those are names that are really hard to say. But at the same time I don't want to call you Sholak. I want to...want to call you Mergen – the marksman! Yesterday it seemed like a trifle to you when you brought down that pheasant flying over our heads.

BALUAN. All right, call me whatever you like. We shan't be meeting again in the future.

TATYANA. (*with a shiver of fright*) That means... we shan't see each other again? Ever again? It'll all be over?

BALUAN (*walking up to her*) Yes, Tanyazhan! I shall make my way back to my burnt out village, rally together the people who had scattered in terror... then I shall set free my relatives and friends from the prison, while you go back to your parents, who have been sitting and weeping for the last three days and three nights mourning their lost daughter, and bring joy back into their lives...

A MAN ON A MISSION

TATYANA. They're unlikely to need me anymore.

BALUAN. What d'you mean?

TATYANA. What honour can a girl still have who has been held captive for three days and three nights? The terrible news of the "district chief's only daughter captured by brigands" will be exciting not just Akmola and Kokshetau, but will be doing the rounds of Kereku and Semipalatinsk as well. Bad news always spreads quickly: if not today, then tomorrow it will have got as far as the Governor-General in Omsk. He, in his turn, will have to report it back to St. Petersburg. After all that, who will have anything to do with a girl acquiring that kind of "bad name"? Balvan you've ruined my whole future!

BALUAN. You were calling me Mergen just now...

TATYANA. With your marksmanship, incredible strength, gift for singing, heedless courage... on top of all that you're mad, Balvan. My Balvan... you've ruined everything...forever. Mad, Balvan...!

Unable to speak any more through her sobbing, Tatyana puts her arms round Baluan's neck. He wipes away her tears with the scarf he had used earlier to gag her.

BALUAN. Tanyazhan, stop, don't cry anymore! Everything will be all right. Your parents are sure to realize that their daughter has returned to them chaste and pure as before. Soon you'll set off to Omsk and take up your studies again. Time is the best doctor, it will heal everything. Soon all will be forgotten. You'll marry your Mikhail...

TATYANA. I have to acknowledge that he came here on this occasion so as to introduce himself to my father and mother. You made sure he did that all right...

BALUAN. If he isn't sitting at your side anymore, he only has himself to blame!

TATYANA. He is very reserved by nature. He's too clever to be anything else. When I'm in his company I feel as if I'm under official escort. But now he'll have no need for me anymore either...

Taking her arms down from Baluan's neck, Tatyana suddenly starts giggling.

TATYANA. Whichever way I look, I see that your talent is for rescuing maidens about to be married off. To judge from what you've told me, you carried off a certain Balkash, who was about to be given away in marriage. And then later on there was an opportunity for you to carry off Galiya. Now here am I sitting as a captive on a mountain, where not a soul has set foot before.

BALUAN. Perhaps to people who don't know me I do look like a brigand. But judge for yourself, the girl was not even sixteen and her parents, after noting the groom's fortune, were planning to give her away to an old man of eighty. I walked up to a young girl on a swing set up for the young people in her village, when she suddenly burst into sobs. Despite the spies keeping an eye on her, she managed to tell me about her sad fate. Weeping as she spoke, Balkash began to beg: "Agatai – my honoured brother - take me away from here tonight. Even if you won't take me as your wife, I'm ready to be your servant. No-one can rescue me but you. Even if people find out that I've run away with you, none of them will dare to give chase". At that time I was a bachelor and the girl really appealed to me. So at dawn I made off with her.

TATYANA. Did they come after you?

BALUAN. Of course they did. They too have their honour to safeguard. They were hot on my heels – nine young men armed with cudgels caught up with me.

A MAN ON A MISSION

TATYANA. Really! How did they get the girl back?

BALUAN. Why should I have given her back? The fighting started. I brought all nine of them down with their own cudgels and by mid-day I had restored the girl to her parents, much to their amazement.

TATYANA. And then?

BALUAN. After that the injured parties submitted a complaint and your father locked me up in Kokshetau prison.

TATYANA. Weren't those nine young men ashamed to complain that they had all been brought low by just one opponent?

BALUAN. D'you think that nowadays people have a sense of honour and a conscience?

TATYANA. How could the court have believed what they said?

BALUAN. The complainants weren't concerned with honour and the judges were not God-fearing ones. Nowadays people are slaves to their desires; they'll do anything for the sake of profit. On top of everything, all nine of the injured men were sitting there in court without a twinge of conscience. Some had teeth missing, others had suffered blows to the head, broken arms or legs… As if to prove my guilt!

TATYANA. You reckless minstrel from the steppe! (*Tatyana kisses him on the cheek*). If Gogol were to hear about that, he would have written a splendid comedy.

BALUAN. Yet another of your writers is he?

TATYANA. A great Russian writer. You don't know anything about anything. Every time I mention someone, you ask: "Who's that?". When we get down the mountain I'll have to start work on your education!

BALUAN. You have your studies and I have mine. I write using the Arabic alphabet and you write in Russian. Because we don't write in the Russian alphabet, your parents call us illiterate savages. Each one of us needs to grow up with the traditions of his own people. You see that magpie up there sitting at the top of the pine tree?

TATYANA. Yes, I can see it.

BALUAN. Go and call out: "Hey, Magpie, I'm human, I'm me!" What was the name of that last writer…?

TATYANA. Gogol…

BALUAN. Yes, try and say to the Magpie: "I'm Gogol. I'm a genius. Shall we change places?" Go on now for real, try and say that to the bird…

TATYANA. Here we go! (*She runs over to the tree and lifting up her head calls out to the magpie perched at the top of* it) Hey there Magpie! I'm human, I…, I… (*looking over towards Baluan*) What should I call myself?

BALUAN. Just say: "I'm human".

TATYANA. I'm human!

BALUAN. Tell the Magpie: "I'm the prettiest, happiest girl in the world"!

TATYANA. I'm the prettiest, happiest girl in the world!

BALUAN. Tell the Magpie: "I'm being kept prisoner by a Kazakh rogue and I hate him".

TATYANA. I'm being kept prisoner by a reckless Kazakh minstrel of the steppes … and I like him.

BALUAN (*looking at her intently*) Tell the Magpie: "But soon I'll be set free. Would you change places with me?"

TATYANA. Sadly I'm going away soon. Would you change places with me? Tell me, would you…? (*With a rippling laugh*) At that very moment the bird flew away! Not even willing to listen to all I had to say!

BALUAN. So you see, everyone's only interested in their own life. Why did you change round the words I'd told you to use?

TATYANA. I just wanted to… Tell me, Mergen.. Would you have married me, if you'd been single?

On hearing those unexpected words, Baluan feels bewildered for a moment.

BALUAN. Of course. Even if it meant going back to prison. But you and I have different paths to follow in life. Your path leads to a church and mine to a mosque.

TATYANA. And if I were to go with you to the mosque?

BALUAN. Tanyazhan, you're saying this swept along by your feelings, because you're so young. I'm used to hardship… I'm a stubborn wild mustang from the steppes used to lunging without growing tired, however many lassos they might throw round my neck. But you're only a fledgling, delicate and tender, only just ready to try and fly the nest. You're not truly responsible for your actions yet. Then again…

TATYANA. Go on, what other obstacles are there?

BALUAN. You're a girl from that country where women order their husbands around. As your mother does… It turns out that your father, who has unlimited power over other people, crawls around meekly in front of his wife.

TATYANA. Yes, my mother always gets her own way.

BALUAN. That means the end of the world will soon be upon us!

TATYANA. The end of the world? How do you know?

BALUAN. Many moons ago or as we might say today – back in the 9th century – there lived a wise Kazakh poet by the name of Monke. It was he who said: "At the end of the world we'll be ruled by women". On seeing that nowadays there are more and more disrespectful, cantankerous women around, the end of the world can't be so far away...

TATYANA. You say that was in the ninth century? We're in the nineteenth now. That means he came out with that idea a thousand years ago...

BALUAN. That's how it adds up...

TATYANA. And we used to learn that there was no literature or culture to be found out in the Kazakh steppes.

BALUAN. Sadly, lying politics of that kind poisons the minds of young people.

TATYANA. Mergen, my mind hasn't been poisoned. I'm going to start studying everything differently from now on. I don't want to leave this place. Here I feel free. I think that there'll be endless problems for me back there.

BALUAN. If they give you a hard time, let me know. I would then carry off not just anyone, but your father.

TATYANA. So as to rescue your own friends and relatives you decided to kidnap me and now, so as to protect me from my own father, you're prepared to kidnap him?! (*Tatyana bursts into infectious laughter*) A first-rate adventure! Real Robin Hood!

A MAN ON A MISSION

BALUAN. I'm not going to ask you who he was…

TATYANA. It's fine that you're not asking! You don't know him and have no particular wish to. Mergen, that's just what I like about you! (*She laughs louder still and then Baluan joins in*).

At that moment Akylbai comes out from behind the rock. When he sees them laughing out loud, oblivious of everything else that's going on in the world, he stops in his tracks and gazes at them in astonishment.

Then Akylbai clears his throat to let them know he's appeared. He coughs as well. Yet Baluan and Tatyana, carried away like small children by their carefree laughter, remain oblivious. Unable to contain himself any longer, Akylbai then calls out.

AKYLBAI. Baluan. There's good news – *suyunshi!* Baluan, there's good news I tell you. Are you both out of your mind?

It is only now that the two of them break off laughing and look over towards Akylbai in astonishment.

BALUAN. Akylbai! At last! What news have you brought?

AKYLBAI. I tell you it's good – *suyunshi*. Hurrah!

BALUAN. Good fellow, well done! You're a real man! A true hero! Come on then, read it! What has the district chief written?

AKYLBAI. I can't read it. The letter is written in Russian.

BALUAN. Did the district chief write it himself?

AKYLBAI. It's in his very own hand!

TATYANA. In that case, I should probably read it. I can make out Papa's writing easily.

Tatyana takes the letter, recognizes her father's handwriting. Her voice by this time is rather nervous, slightly shaky even.

TATYANA. Papa!... Yes, it's his writing...

AKYLBAI. Young lady, calm down now. Soon you'll be seeing your father. Read it to us.

TATYANA. "This document has been issued to Baluan Sholak Baimyrzauli Nurmagambet. Settlers will not be moving into the territory of his summer or winter pastures situated on the shores of Lake Kairakty, where he lives. His parents, relatives and friends and also people from his village will be released from prison. Baluan Sholak Baimyrzauli can reside there and be at liberty in the Atbasar and Kokshetau Districts and he will not be prosecuted unless he commits a serious crime.

Signed by the Head of the Atbasar District – Terentii Dyakovich Dolgonosov on July 21, 1886.

AKYLBAI. Baluan, congratulations on your victory! The people from your

village have probably not yet heard that thanks to you they are to be set free. Let's go and bring them the good news.

Mikhail, who had walked up to the others without them noticing and stood silently to one side, while Tatyana was reading the letter, now joins in the conversation.

MIKHAIL. Those people have been informed. They are all rejoicing at the happy news and waiting impatiently to welcome their hero.

His words make the other three turn round suddenly and they eye him suspiciously.

BALUAN. Akylbai! Was it you who brought him here?

Baluan immediately runs over to pick up his rifle. Mikhail at the same time takes his revolver out of its holster

MIKHAIL. No I came here on my own!

TATYANA. Mikhail Trofimovich! Why have you turned up here? Have you been following us.

MIKHAIL. What if I had? Why would I not look for the man, who had beaten my coachman, hurled me out of my carriage like some useless chattel and then carried off a young girl. Ever since then I've been looking for him. I noticed that you had set off in the direction of the mountains and so I followed in your tracks.

TATYANA. What for?

MIKHAIL. I had not wanted to end up a living corpse at the bottom of the mountain and to have died in vain. I wanted to meet my end in a noble duel at the top of the mountain.

TATYANA. If you had decided to die defending your honour, that's up to you. There would have been no point in dying so as to protect me though…

MIKHAIL. There's no need to talk like that. You too are someone who loves taking risks, aren't you?

TATYANA. No! First of all, to take such a risk you should at least have won my affections. Yet, unfortunately, I don't have any such feelings for you. Secondly, both I and my name are stained forever. So it would be pointless to fight a duel at the top of a mountain for a girl like me. Both my father and his colleague, Troitskii, are convinced that a splendid career awaits you. So there is no need for you to besmirch your name among your colleagues. You would do better to concentrate on your dazzling prospects.

MIKHAIL. I have been thinking about all of that. When all is said and done, I came here because of you. For the last three days and nights I have been listening to all your conversations, lying over there behind the boulder.

BALUAN. What? What's he talking about?

TATYANA. What dastardly behaviour! It would seem that Shakespeare's Iago is an amateur compared to you, when it comes to treachery!

MIKHAIL. It's not treachery but jealousy! I'm ready to sacrifice everything for you.

TATYANA. I don't imagine the Governor-General will pat you on the back for that feat…

MIKHAIL. He'll understand. When I return I shall tell him all the details about everything that has been happening here. If he doesn't understand, then I shall turn my back on all that and come back to you.

TATYANA. What an honour you do me! For that I need to be well-disposed towards you, I assume…

MIKHAIL. What reason do you have for not being well-disposed towards me? What makes me inferior to that fugitive over there? What is it you don't like about me?

Baluan makes ready to aim his rifle.

TATYANA. Your ability to come out with such offensive words. And also I… I'm not the Tatyana I used to be. I am dishonoured.

MIKHAIL. That's all lies! You are a pure angel. You're deliberately saying all that so as to turn me away. I love you Tatyana!

Mikhail falls to his knees in front of Tatyana and tries to take hold of her hands, but she steps backwards, away from him.

AKYLBAI. Baluan, you have been in love with many beauties, but have you said "I love you" like this young man?

BALUAN. The people from their land are used to expressing their feelings openly, in words. They are not capable of real tenderness and caresses as we are: they confine themselves to occasional "Hmms".

MIKHAIL. It was not easy to listen to your conversations for three whole days. At one time an insane thought even crossed my mind: what if I were to kill you both, while you lay there sleeping in a tender embrace. Yet I held back. I was prepared to shoot Baluan if he had used force against you, but that did not happen. He behaved like a real man. My hopes were justified.

TATYANA. What hopes were those?

MIKHAIL. I had always thought that members of the people, which produced the great man, Chokan Valikhanov, could not be ignorant or wicked and so I was glad that my hopes bore fruit. Each hillock and mountain in this part of the world is extolled with a sense of awe in the works of Chokan. Tatyana, we are standing in the land where that great man was born!

TATYANA. Chokan? Valikhanov? I am ashamed to say that I have not heard of him.

BALUAN. You felt ashamed for me, when you commented that every time you mentioned a great man, I would ask "Who is he?" It turns out though that you had not heard of our great scholar and traveller, who graduated from the Omsk Military School, where you yourself are now studying.

MIKHAIL. (*to Tatyana*) When I get back to Omsk, I shall show you the classroom where he studied, the desk he sat at, even his books.

BALUAN. Are you really sure?

MIKHAIL. No man should lie when he is at the top of a mountain.

TATYANA. So that must be it. I had been thinking that the magpie had flown away before it had heard all I had to say. It turns out that you must have frightened it away.

MIKHAIL. Yes, I did frighten away the magpie. I did not want to listen any more to your tender words addressed to someone else.

BALUAN. In that case I'm grateful to you. We always welcome a true friend with a sincere embrace.

MIKHAIL. Lower down the mountain a crowd of people is waiting for us. They too must have worn themselves out looking for me. Nobody knew where I was heading. Tatyana and I – both given up for lost – shall go down and surprise everyone with our unexpected appearance.

BALUAN. Tanyazhan, this is where our intimate conversation at the top of the mountain comes to an end. These three days have brought about a unique change in my life.

TATYANA. And for me too these three days will be an endless source of sustenance for the rest of my life. Mergen, I shall never forget you! You mean so much to me… I can't find the strength in me to bid you farewell! (*Baluan wipes away Tatyana's tears with the scarf he had used before*). How fascinating life can be! You brought me here, using that scarf as a gag. We were bitter enemies and now we are parting as close friends. Farewell – lone plane tree at the summit of the mountain compelling me to begin my life again!

Tatyana ties the scarf to a branch of the plane tree.

BALUAN. Farewell Tatyana! Wherever you may be, may your heart always be pure. Do not let anyone dim your radiant feelings!

They make ready to leave.

MIKHAIL. I put my revolver away in its holster a long time ago, but why have you not brought your rifle down from your shoulder yet?

BALUAN. Life has taught me always to be on my guard! I have more enemies than friends and so I have grown used to wearing my rifle on my shoulder. I bid you farewell too. Do your best to make Tatyana happy! Akylbai will go down the mountain with you. Make sure, Akylbai, that you hand Tatyana back to her parents in person.

AKYLBAI. And you Baluan?

BALUAN. I shall stay here for a while alone. Don't linger any more. Set off on your way!

After bidding each other farewell, they all move on. Tatyana comes back once more to say good-bye. She embraces Baluan.

Baluan now stands alone. The magpie perches on the top of the pine tree.

BALUAN. The magpie with its striking wings has come back! Yet only a few days ago you offended a beautiful girl. She has gone now as well. You offended her and now she will not return...

Baluan picks up Tatyana's scarf, which had been left hanging on the branch of a pine-tree, and he buries his face in it, breathing in her scent.

Yesterday you were a gag and today you have become something infinitely dear to me! Farewell, radiant heart – an angel of a girl!

Once more Baluan buries his face in the scarf. His face shows that he is clearly moved and there are perhaps even tears in his eyes...

Written between June 8th and August 2nd in the year 2009. Almaty

A play in two acts by Dulat Issabekov,
Holder of the State Prize of the Republic of Kazakhstan

The Transit Passenger

Dramatis Personae:

Zeynep, a widow of pensionable age
Ertay, her son
Aytore, a lone traveller, aged about 60
A silhouette of **Aytore's late mother**

ACT ONE

A two-room apartment on the first floor of an old block built in red brick, situated on the fringes of Almaty. The airport is close by, and from time to time the roar of aircraft taking off and landing can be heard.

It is autumn, and outside it is raining hard. Zeynep is at home by herself. Just two months ago she started drawing her pension. In the corner of the room is a small table on which stands an old-fashioned telephone. Zeynep is restless and unable to settle, and evidently is impatiently waiting for somebody.

She goes over to the telephone to check that it is working, lifts the receiver and listens. At first she hears nothing and thinks the telephone is broken. But no – there is a buzzing in the earpiece. She puts down the receiver and paces up and down the room. She goes to the window and looks out. It is still pouring with rain.

ZEYNEP: They'll both be soaked to the skin! It's three hours since they phoned and said they were on their way. Where on earth can they have been all this time?

The cuckoo clock on the wall strikes four.

It's already four o'clock. So maybe the daughter-in-law's taken offence about something and changed her mind about coming? Should I phone them?

She goes to the telephone again, lifts the receiver and turns the dial a couple of times with her hand; then abruptly puts the receiver back down.

No, I won't do it. I'll only get that cantankerous mother of hers, and before we know it we'll be arguing. Better for me to make a nice pot of strong tea, so the pair can warm themselves up when they arrive.

She goes to the kitchen and puts the kettle on the stove. At that moment there is a ring at the door.

Aha! The troublemakers have arrived – my Ertay-zhan and his bride-to-be! *(The doorbell rings again.)* All right, I'm coming! They make me wait all day and then can't be patient for half a minute? Was it so hard for them to pick up the phone? *(Continuing to grumble, she opens the door.)* Well, damn the pair of you. Go on then, come in –…

Zeynep breaks off mid-sentence. On the doorstep before her is not her son Ertay and his bride but a stranger, a man of about 65, soaked and dripping from the rain. A stream of water is pouring down from the brim of his hat. Zeynep is taken aback.

ZEYNEP: You… who are you looking for?

AYTORE: Erm… how should I say? … It's a long story.

Startled, Zeynep slams the door shut.

ZEYNEP *(to herself)*: How odd he looks! They say that thieves go for people with that kind of miserable look. And what about the kids – they're really taking their time, just to make things worse.

The doorbell rings again. And then again. On the third time it rings constantly. Zeynep steps towards the door with only socks on her feet and presses her ear to the door.

ZEYNEP: Who do you want? Who are you?

AYTORE: I… I was looking for this building.

ZEYNEP: What building?

AYTORE: The one you are living in.

ZEYNEP: And what for?

AYTORE: I wanted to see the place.

ZEYNEP: You wanted to see it? *(Frightened)* But – why?

AYTORE: I haven't been here in a long time. I was feeling homesick.

ZEYNEP: Homesick? Are you in your right mind, talking to me like this? I'll call the police!

AYTORE: The police? *(Laughs softly)* I haven't been in this town for a whole fifteen years.

ZEYNEP: And what's that got to do with me? So what if it's twenty years, but why on earth should you be homesick for my flat in particular? There are plenty of houses in Almaty. And why didn't you call on my neighbours instead? Down on the ground floor is somebody just like you, an old man. He's languishing away because he's got nothing to do.

AYTORE: O my Creator! Whatever happened to the Kazakhs? There was a time when they'd invite any passing traveller in and offer hospitality, but these days they don't even let you in the house.

ZEYNEP: Times are different now. The Kazakhs have changed precisely because there are so many people like you – saying they're 'homesick'.

AYTORE: Maybe that's how it is. But I don't think you have changed. Your voice sounds sincere.

ZEYNEP: Ah, you sweet little… white-bearded old man! So you want to stir my pity, do you? Well I'm still not opening the door.

AYTORE: Look, understand me! I'm – I'm a traveller. I'm here for just two hours. I've come to look at your block. You see, twenty years ago I lived here myself. And so I decided that if the opportunity should arise, I'd go back and have a look. But clearly it's not to be.

Zeynep stops and ponders. The man's sedate and sincere manner is unfamiliar to her and seems to calm her down.

ZEYNEP: Are you... telling the truth?

No answer comes from behind the door.

Well, probably he really was homesick, if he hadn't been here for a whole twenty years. (*She opens the door a crack, trying to get a look at the stranger. He is no longer visible. She goes out onto the landing and sees the man going down the stairs, leaning against the railing, to the ground floor.*) Hey, you! ... Hello-oo! Old man! Wanderer!

The stranger silently turns round, then climbs back up to Zeynep's floor.

If... if you really are speaking the truth – then come in, come and look round my flat.

AYTORE: Thank you! I hadn't wanted to believe that everybody had suddenly turned so hard-hearted.

The pair walk up to the door. Zeynep still looks the stranger over with apprehension. He takes the door handle with one hand, and with the other he runs his fingers over the oilcloth that covers the outer side of the door.

I see nothing's changed! Sometime or other I bought that oilcloth and fitted it on the door myself. Hmm. Hello!

ZEYNEP: Hello...

The stranger takes off his wet hat and shakes it; drops of water fall onto Zeynep's face. She flinches in surprise.

AYTORE: My name is Aytore.

ZEYNEP: Well, and so what if it is? (*Wipes her face with her sleeve*) Does being called Aytore give you the right to go splashing water on a woman's face?

THE TRANSIT PASSENGER

AYTORE (*laughing awkwardly*): Ha, so sorry, forgive me! Looks like I've blown it already... I've been looking for this place for a long time, I got soaked through. Everything's changed round here.

ZEYNEP: From your appearance and the way you speak, you don't come over as evil. But you splashed me – it's a bad omen.

AYTORE: Again, please forgive me for my *faux pas*. I've just... come from the airport. I've got another flight soon. But how fast time flies... Life carries on and we all get older. As the years go by we look back over our past, and this fills us with yearning and sadness. The future is unfixed, but the past is precious. That's the way it is... and now I've turned up at an inconvenient time and started an awkward conversation. Please be generous and forgive me.

ZEYNEP: And then something really absurd will happen... I've never seen you before, I don't know you. And it's not as if there's a good reason to let you into the house, but I haven't got the heart to refuse you. And just look at you, it's as if you've just crawled out of a well. Well, there's nothing for it – come in. If you lived here once, then you'd better have a look round.

AYTORE: Thank you very much.

They enter the apartment. Aytore looks around, nods, and a smile breaks out on his face.

The place is still as I remember it. (*He laughs as he sees a metal post protruding from the wall near the entrance.*) I hammered that in myself when I was planning to put up some bookshelves here. But my wife didn't want books in the lobby, so I never put in the other post. I was going to pull that one out, but then events got in the way. And there it still is...

ZEYNEP: And where do you think it could have gone? I can see for myself, you banged it in rather well. A little while ago I wanted to pull it out but couldn't. I spent a whole day struggling with it for nothing. It's jammed in tight.

AYTORE: The walls are solid here.

ZEYNEP: Ah, well, never mind that post, it'll stay there another hundred years. You take off your wet clothes, you must be soaked to the skin.

AYTORE: Thanks. (*Takes off his raincoat and hangs it on a peg*) If you'll allow me, I would like to look around the other rooms.

ZEYNEP: Go on then, you've already come in after all…

Aytore takes off his shoes and is about to step further into the apartment, but Zeynep smartly thrusts a pair of indoor slippers in front of him.

AYTORE: Thanks very much. (*He pauses a moment before stepping into the living room*) Well, well, it's twenty years, whatever anyone says. It's disturbing…

Aytore wanders through the rooms. Zeynep, not sure what to do with herself, remains standing in the lobby. Aytore appears from the furthest room. He walks towards Zeynep, wiping his eyes and face with a handkerchief. He may be wiping away tears, or they may be drips of rain from his still-wet hair.

My name's Aytore. Hmm. Oh, yes, I've introduced myself already. My surname is Askarov. I'm just passing through – to use modern language I'm a transit passenger. I've still got (*looks at his watch*) three hours before my flight. I'd usually already be at Novosibirsk by now, but because of thick cloud at the airport there, as you can see, I've ended up in your house.

ZEYNEP (*laughing*): So I see.

AYTORE: But I'm on my way to Yakutsk. I'm going back from a holiday in Crimea. There are still two or three days of holiday left, so I decided to fly via Almaty. I fancied, just for a moment, breathing again the air of home. When otherwise would I have the chance to be here? After all, we don't live so near that I can just pop over in my free time.

ZEYNEP: Yakutsk ... but isn't that dreadfully cold, where the snow doesn't melt all year round?

AYTORE (*laughing*): Yes, that's it. Land of permafrost. It's where the Sakha people live.

ZEYNEP: But that's an awful long way away, isn't it?

AYTORE: Oh, don't. It's the edge of the world.

ZEYNEP: O Lord, how on earth did you end up out there?

AYTORE: Well, as somebody once said: 'Don't ask and I won't tell. If I tell, you will weep.' It's a long story, my dear.

ZEYNEP: So presumably you upset somebody and decided to move away.

AYTORE: That isn't far wrong.

ZEYNEP: But is it necessary to go and live at the end of the world just for offending someone?

AYTORE (*smiling sadly*): That's how it turned out. Must have been what was meant for me. Well, it's time I was off. (*Looks about him again as though leaving his own home.*) We moved into this flat... straight after the war ended. We were so happy at that time – not even the most talented writer, I'm sure, could describe our joy. Just imagine four years of being on your feet, under fire along the burning roads of the war, never knowing whether you would live or die, while your mother was ill at home along with your bride-to-be. There were just two days left before our wedding when my life turned upside down.

ZEYNEP: But did you get married anyway?

AYTORE: Yes we did. Right after the war.

ZEYNEP: That's very good. And so the mayhem that is usual in this world could begin.

AYTORE (*laughs cheerfully*): You've got a subtle sense of humour. Say, thank you so much. This has been like going back to when I was young, plunging into my past, and it's kind of like being born again. It feels as if all the years of my past are looking at me from every corner of this flat. I suppose you find the place a bit cramped these days, but I remember what it was like after being in the trenches – it felt as light and spacious as a palace. My mother – could I ever forget – cried for joy when we unrolled the carpet on the floor in that end room. She shed enough tears to fill three rivers. 'O Lord, thank you for everything!' she exclaimed. Then she said, 'I won't even murmur complaint if he takes me now.' '*Apa!*' I said, 'whatever are you talking about? We've just managed to survive to the good times, and already you're talking about dying. You'd be better to ask the Lord to be generous and give you a long life.' But she said, 'I prayed to my Maker that he would let me live to see you come home safe and unharmed. And he deigned to grant my request. And now I've been able to move into this light and palatial apartment. What else could I wish for? You know, the Lord doesn't like people who go on asking for things.' When I heard that I blurted out: 'Oh really, so you'd be ready to leave without even waiting for your daughter-in-law, who will be arriving in this house any day?' I remember now how my mother was taken aback at this. 'No, of course not, how could I possibly leave without having embraced the daughter-in-law I've waited for so long?' She said, all agitated. 'The Lord has granted me to have my wishes, and surely he won't consider the third to be excessive?' Can a person ever quench his thirst for life? We were just lads, we hadn't even grown moustaches yet, but the war had given us the kind of wisdom you see in old people. So I took my old mother in hand, so to speak, and we walked along life's road together.

ZEYNEP: I see you didn't give her any peace.

AYTORE (*bursts out laughing again*): You guessed… And when I said to her, '*Apa*, look, you've embraced your long-awaited daughter-in-law, and now you must live for the sake of kissing your first grandchild', she heaved a weary sigh and said: 'And I suppose that's already in the pipeline?'

ZEYNEP (*checks herself*): O my Lord, what a thing it is to let people talk! It can be awkward: here we are for such a long time, like the hunter and his prey, tied together by an invisible thread. And we have forgotten so much. People who don't know each other are usually wary when they meet, but a word brings them closer. When you called I was just sitting down for some tea. There's still time before your flight – why don't you join me for a bowl or two of tea to warm you up to your travels?

AYTORE: How strange… You can guess a person's hidden thoughts. Or you can see right through me, or for you nothing is secret. To tell the truth, I wouldn't mind some tea, even if it makes me late for my flight.

ZEYNEP: Let's go through, then… No, actually, it's not right to make a traveller who's come such a long way squeeze into my tiny kitchen. I'll bring the tea out here. Why don't you sit down and relax.

Zeynep shows Aytore to the couch, then spreads a cloth on the table in the middle of the room.

Well, wherever it is you live now, you were the first person to live in this flat. It's an order from God that you eat some food in your own home.

They both chuckle cheerfully. Aytore is left alone in the room. The clatter of crockery can be heard from the kitchen. Outside the rain is falling still harder; big drops thump the windows and then run down the panes.

AYTORE: (*to himself*): It's all as if it was yesterday... And it's just as though my poor ailing mother is about to come quietly out of that end room. And she has been confined to her bed for so long.

An image appears in the room in the form of Aytore's mother.

AYTORE'S MOTHER: Ah, you've arrived, my young colt? But why are you hunched up right on the corner of the couch? And why are you all wet?

AYTORE: I've been travelling a long time.

AYTORE'S MOTHER: You've been travelling? So that's why I haven't seen you for so long.

AYTORE: But you have probably sensed that I was thinking about you all the time?

AYTORE'S MOTHER: Sometimes I sensed it and sometimes I didn't. That's how it should be; the *ruh*, the human spirit, fades with time. I'm happy that my children and grandchildren are walking on the earth. They may forget about us, but the *ruh* will stay with them through their lives and protect them from trouble. You've come home from far away, you must be dying of thirst. Shall I bring you something to drink?

AYTORE: Don't worry, *apa*, I'm fine. You look after yourself. How are you feeling?

AYTORE'S MOTHER (*laughs softly*): How could I feel, son? After all, the spirit is protecting my children's house. It's all the same to the *ruh* how much time passes, a hundred years or a thousand. But I would like to breathe the scent of children, your children. Here you are at last, I've been waiting for you. I see you're going grey, son.

AYTORE: I'm older now than a prophet, *apa*. It's high time I got some grey hair. If you measure out this life from the cradle to the grave, you find that age comes extremely quickly. My great-grandson, whom you were unable to see when you were alive, is already a year old. (*Sighs heavily*) He has another sixty whole years to live before his head turns grey. This is how the life has turned out that you once prepared me for. And one day, at the appointed time, without fail, death will also find me. Then after that, we will be forgotten on this sinful earth, *apa*. All of us, like our distant ancestors, will return to the spirits and will soar in the heavens.

AYTORE'S MOTHER: Don't be sad, son. I see life has not been kind to you. But what can we do? I got to taste life in all its fullness. The only life a person has is the one determined for him by fate. He may be happy or unhappy with it, but it's the only one he's got. Just don't despair, my dear, think about how to preserve your offspring. That's the one thing that the spirits beg for from the people.

The image of Aytore's mother gradually moves away and disappears. Aytore's gaze is fixed on the apparition and stays there. Zeynep enters carrying a tray with tea things.

ZEYNEP: Weren't you bored, left here by yourself?

AYTORE: (*not sure what to say*): Erm… no, not at all!

ZEYNEP: It seems that coming here has thrown up a lot of memories for you?

AYTORE: How can I put it? They say that someone who loses his head laughs out of place, or a startled dog barks at random. I think I'm just a bit confused.

ZEYNEP: Why be confused, sitting in your own house? Have some tea.

They sit down at the table and drink tea.

AYTORE: How odd. Back in the Crimea I was drinking exactly the same Indian tea, from exactly the same kind of teapot. But tea made by a woman's hand has a completely different taste.

ZEYNEP: That may be so. The other day… (*The telephone rings*) That's probably Ertay my son. He should have got here by now, with his wife, so what's he doing still telephoning? Helloo, who's there? It's me. What's happened, why are you so late? You said you be here in the morning, but it's already getting dark outside. Is it your job? What sort of incessant work is this? Is my daughter-in-law there? … Who? You're waiting for your elder brother? Why should he come? My dears, you see him often enough, you could meet up with him tomorrow! OK, hurry up. Good. (*Puts down the telephone*) He's so vague, I'm sure it's making me grey. One minute he says he's going to live with his wife, and the next he's talking about coming to live here in the family home. Wherever his wife sends him, that's where he rolls up. Like tumbleweed, goes wherever the wind blows. The *jigits* of today are not like they used to be – our brave young men dare not say anything in defiance of their wives. They've become all soft and weak. It can be really annoying.

AYTORE: Is he your youngest?

ZEYNEP: How did you guess?

AYTORE: I just assumed. Anyway, my firstborn grew up a real tearaway. My goodness, when I think of the trouble he gave me. He nearly landed me in prison.

ZEYNEP: My God, what are you saying? And whatever were you guilty of?

AYTORE: I was accused of not giving him a proper upbringing.

ZEYNEP: And what offence did he commit?

AYTORE: Oh, don't ask, my dear. Just an ordinary, terrible act. He went swimming in the lake with a group of friends, boys and girls. They boosted their spirits quite a bit with vodka, and then in a rather tipsy state began to push each other into the water. My son and a friend of his ganged up on another young man, who seemed reluctant to leave the girls and go in the water. They asked him something like, hey, why won't you come swimming? Then they picked him up by his hands and feet, swung him a few times and threw him from the bank into the water. Then they waited for him to come up to the surface, but he didn't appear. They decided that he must be playing tricks on them, staying underwater deliberately. But he seemed to have disappeared completely. The others started to get worried and two or three of the boys dived into the water to look for him. Five minutes later they pulled him out. It turned out that he'd had a cramp and choked. He died in the ambulance on the way to the hospital. And what happened after that was simple enough: the ones guilty of the boy's death went to prison – I mean my son and his friend. Meanwhile there were tricksters after me as well: they had been waiting for an opportunity and used this occasion to get at me. The result was I was demoted at work. So you see, human life is full of struggle, but as you know, it also contains places for compassion.

ZEYNEP: But your son... Presumably he's grown up by now?

AYTORE: Yes he is. But ever since that time he's had no luck. It's like watching a camel trying to walk on ice: it falls down, then gets up, tries again, and falls again.

ZEYNEP: (*after a pause*): My eldest son... Also found it hard to get on his feet. He was a bundle of trouble since he was small, and later really started raising hell. He's spent his time inside as well.

AYTORE: Time inside? What for?

ZEYNEP: For getting into a fight, damn it all. And it's the same thing – it's because of drink. If they don't hurry up and pass a law that prohibits alcohol use, all our young men are going to drink their brains away. They can't hold their drink, and they can't enjoy themselves in a normal way. The minute strong drink touches their lips they start waving their fists. Our son had got into just such a disorderly state and didn't realise how worked up he was getting. He was working on the steppe near Kustanay on the wheat harvest and he got into a row with some soldiers. Allegedly one of the soldiers lost an eye and had his ear torn off. The police rushed from the town and arrested everyone who'd been in the fight. The investigation lasted several days. Apparently the father of one of the guys in the fight was a government minister – someone important. And they told me that this kid asked my son to assume all the guilt himself – that he should say that he was the ringleader, that he had pulled out the soldier's eye and torn off his ear. 'I can get you released', he apparently told his friends, 'if you let me stay free. But if they lock me up with you, there'll be no-one to get you out.' And without really thinking it through, our son agreed to it. "I was the ringleader of the fight and I maimed the soldier," he admitted during the enquiry and then signed the investigation report.

In the end they put my son in prison and released everybody else. And needless to say, nobody lifted a finger to try to get him released. I was left to pursue his case by myself. But what could I do on my own? Cry my eyes out? How many doorways did I beat down in tears, trying to get myself heard? What officials didn't I try to convince that my boy had been convicted in vain, that he couldn't have been the ringleader and anyway hadn't been involved in the fight, because he'd arrived on the scene after it was over. I heard from the police about somebody's eye being pulled out and their ear torn off. But all my efforts were to no avail. Everybody agreed that it was my son's fault for being so naïve as to accept the false charges and to sign the report, and there was nothing they could do to help. The law is the law, and a mere mortal can't interfere with it. What is written, what is pronounced, cannot be chopped down even with an axe. All in all my son was sentenced to six years ...

Zeynep wipes the tears from her eyes with the corner of her shawl.

AYTORE: So where did that... son of the minister vanish to?

ZEYNEP: Well, what could possibly happen to him? He's in clover. I went to see him and his father, the minister. They wouldn't listen to me. 'Your son got into a fight? He did. He admitted guilt? He did. So what you want us to do?' And after a while they wouldn't even let me near them.

AYTORE: (*with regret*) What corrupt swine. You know, types like that ride roughshod over the truth and scorn decency. Those people would betray their homeland tomorrow, or even their own mother. And the worst thing is that you can never uncover them or get them exposed. How many unscrupulous types there are in the world. You know, I've just about resigned myself to the fact that we'll never be rid of them... Now, don't take this as indelicate, but how old are you, little sister?

ZEYNEP (*smiles through her tears*): This is like on stage, where one old man calls another old man 'Uncle'. What sort of a little sister am I to you? Yes it does seem a bit indelicate to me to call a woman your little sister when she's already going grey.

AYTORE: Hang on a minute! Really, look how much we've already talked about – and I don't even know your name.

ZEYNEP: My name's Zeynep. But close people call me Azhe, which means Granny. Our great grandmother was called Zeynep, and according to our custom it wasn't allowed for me to be called that name as well. So they nicknamed me Azhe because it sounded close to my real name. Think of it, I was just a year old when they started calling me that - Granny! And now you want to call me your little sister.

AYTORE: (*laughs*) : That's funny...

ZEYNEP: Well, that's how it is, so there! And how much time have you got before your plane?

AYTORE: Oh-oh, Azhe, it seems like I've forgotten about my plane! (*Looks at the clock on the wall*) Good grief, how quickly the time passes. That's forty minutes already! And just a short time ago, when I was at the airport, every minute felt like a whole year. But I'd better start making a move. Anyway, it'll be awkward if one of your children turns up.

ZEYNEP: And that's been bothering me too. The young have quick tongues, they can hurt your feelings without meaning to. Otherwise you would be welcome to stay longer. Especially as the airport's close to our – or rather your – apartment, and there are plenty of taxis you can flag down outside. Well, maybe you would like to stay a little longer? I've got some meat I can put on for a meal.

AYTORE: Thanks for being so kind. (*Nods in the direction of the window*) The rain isn't abating. In that rain it'd be much better, of course, to sit here with you and drink this lovely tea. But tomorrow's Monday and you've probably got to get ready for work?

ZEYNEP: You really do keep wanting to make me look young! What work for me now? I left work long ago, and by the way I just started drawing my pension a month ago. That's the sort of little sister you've landed yourself.

They both laugh cheerfully.

AYTORE: Well, you hardly look like a pensioner!

ZEYNEP: What, am I a girl of marriageable age or something?

AYTORE: I can see that when you were a girl you gave the *jigits* a tough time. It's as though my uncle had a hard time with you...

ZEYNEP: (*weightily*): Well, what's true is true… I suppose that's why he was in a hurry to close his eyes for the last time, and left me alone with four children.

PAUSE

AYTORE: I'm sorry, forgive me. I didn't mean for my joke to turn out like that. Did he pass away a long time ago?

ZEYNEP: My elder son was eleven, and Ertay, the younger, was just four. He was – perhaps – the same age as you. And how old are you yourself? I suppose it's permitted to ask a man how old he is?

AYTORE (*chuckling*): Of course it is. I'm sixty. I realised just the other day that I was now old enough to be a prophet. It's odd to think, but if the Prophet were alive today, he would also be a pensioner.

Both laugh again in high spirits. Suddenly Zeynep drops a tea bowl onto the floor, and it shatters into small pieces.

AYTORE: That means good luck!

ZEYNEP: Please God! Look, it's still pouring out there. How will you keep yourself dry while you're waiting for a taxi? Sometimes in the evenings they just fade away.

AYTORE: Never mind. I'll just stop the first car that comes along.

ZEYNEP: All the same, make sure you don't catch cold. (*She gets up from the table, fetches an umbrella and hands it to him*) Here, take this with you.

AYTORE: But what about you?

ZEYNEP: Well as you can see, I'm staying in.

AYTORE: And tomorrow, and the day after? What will you do then?

ZEYNEP: It's unlikely these days, I think, that all the shops in Almaty will be closed at the same time.

AYTORE (*hesitates*): But umbrellas are hard to find these days, and they're expensive.

ZEYNEP: It's just as though you've wandered into a strange land and got out of your usual habits. Go on, take it, don't be embarrassed. It's no fun going home with an illness.

AYTORE (*takes the umbrella*): Thanks so much!

ZEYNEP: So you've seen your old flat and remembered your former life. I hope you feel better for it. And now you'll go home and tell your darling *baybisha*: 'I've just been to our old flat, where you once came as my bride. Now there's an elderly woman living there, just starting to draw her pension. She gave me tea and she sends you her best wishes.'

AYTORE: Not sure I know how to express my appreciation. Thank you once again!

ZEYNEP: Next time, bring your wife with you. Oh, and I don't think the collar of your suit has dried. (*She touches and strokes the collar of his suit with her finger*) No, it's still damp. I should have thought to take a hot iron to it. What do you think, take it off and I'll iron it quickly?

AYTORE: No, really, thanks! I've been enough trouble for you today already. Goodbye.

Aytore extends his hand in farewell, Zeynep does so too.

Well, we've told each other a bit about our sorrows, but we didn't manage to really get to know each other. I'm leaving, and you're staying here. Though our meeting was a coincidence, and you didn't know me before, but still, you treated me with hospitality. What else... can I say? I hope that next time we meet we can get to know each other better. (*He lets go her hand*) Or maybe you'll find yourself in our part of the world at some point?

ZEYNEP (*taken aback by his words*): Aha. Yes, I'll come. I'll definitely come and see you. (*Comes to her senses*) Everything covered in ice – well, nothing unusual, I can come and see you every single day.

Zeynep laughs at her joke. Aytore echoes her.

AYTORE: Well, keep well. I will pray to the Almighty that everything turns out well for you.

Aytore exits, and the door bangs noisily behind him. Inside the apartment is a deathly silence. Zeynep stands there as if in a daze. Then she goes into the kitchen. Seeing the broken pieces of the tea bowl on the floor, she takes a broom and a dustpan and sweeps the floor. For a moment she seems to hear Aytore's voice, saying to her, 'Don't you worry, there'll be celebrations in our street as well.' She flinches with surprise, and then, as though forgetting herself, goes up to the table where they had just now been conversing. She stops by the chair on which Aytore had sat. She runs her finger over the back of the chair, and then almost without realising it, sits on the chair. And at that moment it seems to her as though Aytore is still sitting opposite and grinning.

ZEYNEP: What's the matter with me? Am I going out of my mind?

She gets up quickly from the chair. She goes into the kitchen, but then she seems to hear somebody entering the apartment. She turns round abruptly. There is nobody there. She tries to pull herself together, and begins more or less to calm down. But at that moment she hears Aytore's voice again, close up, just behind her: 'Well, we've told each other a bit about our sorrows, but we didn't manage to really get to know each other.' Zeynep is overcome by fear.

Oh my God, that was his voice, you know. His words! What sort of delusion am I in? He's a total stranger, and yet I can't stop thinking about him… It's shameful! No, I need to find something to take my mind off it. I know – I'll phone her mother.

Zeynep turns the dial of the telephone. After a number of beeps, the other end of the line responds with a broad and unhurried 'Helloo!'

ZEYNEP: Aha, hello, is that Ertay's mother-in-law? This is his mother. How are you? How are you keeping, eh? I'm feeling not at all bad, thank you. I just wanted to find out what's going on with our young ones. They told me they were coming here this afternoon, but it's already evening. I'm fed up of waiting, my eyes are worn out with looking. Have they left or not? … What? He's sleeping? But why would he sleep in the evening? He just phoned me an hour ago and said they were setting off. What? … What's that? Under the influence? What on earth occurred to him to get drunk? Oh heavens… I mean, when he phoned he was sober! No, of course not, I don't think that you 'threw him to the ground and pumped him full of vodka'. What I mean is, he had given up drinking. Where is Ertay? Asleep? And is my daughter-in-law there? What? She's not at home? I don't get it – she lays her husband out on the bed, then goes off heaven only knows where. … So how can this be? Why? Why on earth would she go to visit her brother, but without her husband? And why couldn't Ertay come and sleep here? Go and wake him up, then pour cold water on him!

There is a pause. It seems that the mother-in-law has gone to wake Ertay.

ZEYNEP (*to herself*): Oh Lord, I hope she doesn't really pour cold water on him! (*Into the telephone*) Hi, er, better forget about the water. Let him sleep! (*No response from the other end*)

I hope he doesn't get a fright when he wakes up… Yes, hello, how is he? Is he not getting up? … Did he say he'd phone as soon as he gets up? You mean he's not sleeping? He says he wants to sleep?

THE TRANSIT PASSENGER

Good grief, why does he torment me so much? Just let him come here and show his face! OK, that's fine, don't get upset, mother-in-law. Let him call me when he gets up. I won't trouble you any more. Take care of yourself, goodbye. (*Puts down the telephone and starts pacing up and down the living room. She talks to herself.*) He's got no self-respect! His wife goes out visiting, but he, half-wit that he is, lolls about on his bed at home. Whenever will he come to his senses, when will he find himself?

The telephone rings loudly.

Aha, that's my boy, he's woken up and got out of bed! (*Runs to pick up telephone*) Ertay, my dear! ... Who? Is that you? I didn't recognise your voice on the telephone. I'd only heard your name once before, and already started to forget it... Yes, I was on the phone, that's why it was engaged. Business with my son ... No, he still hasn't arrived. He's asleep. No, it's various things. He's collecting some things together, he'll never manage it... Is your plane on time? What? Delayed another three hours? It seems you're not having an easy time today... After you left here – you know, I wasn't quite myself. Oh my goodness, what shame... I feel uncomfortable somehow. And this rain, it just won't stop! I'm starting to worry that there may be floods. What? I said I'm afraid. Afraid of what? I don't know. For three years now it's felt as though my house is surrounded by something and there is danger lurking... This is what the times are like now – nothing but troubles. And I've started being afraid of everything. We used to get thunderstorms in April, but now we have thunder in summer and autumn as well, even in winter. It seems even nature has got confused. Can you hear the thunder? It's really booming round here, it's as though the sky has been torn in half... You can't hear it? OK, listen. (*Zeynep holds out the receiver towards the window, then brings it back to her ear*) No, I didn't go outside, I just held the receiver up to the window, so you could hear the rolls of thunder. Could you hear it? No? Well, never mind, they probably have thunder in Yakutsk as well, and you'll hear it there.

So what are you going to do now? Ah, you're going to a hotel? Good idea, go and get comfortable… No, what makes you think I should take offence? God save us! … I don't know. Ertay promised to ring. What? I don't understand. You wish you could speak without feeling agitated? I still don't understand. I see … And why ever not? What's shameful about that? You're acting like a girl who's having to enter a stranger's house for the first time… I said, you're just like a girl who's never crossed a stranger's threshold. That's what they say about somebody who fills everything with shame. You've obviously forgotten a lot by living so far away. My door is always open to people who wish to enter with good intentions. And to tell the truth, this is your house as well, isn't that right? Good, then come back.

Zeynep puts down the receiver. Her face is pensive.

Well Zeynep, you've invited someone to dinner, and there isn't a scrap of meat in the house. (*She looks inside the fridge and straight away slams the door shut*) The cupboard is bare. I need to get to the shops before they close. How much money have I got left? (*She opens her purse and counts the money inside*) Three hundred *tenge*. Well, two kilos of meat cost two hundred *tenge*, half a kilo of sugar another fifty and two hundred grams of butter the same. That will leave me fifty *tenge*. What can I buy with that? A glass of milk, a handful of sweets, two apples – and that's it! And then, when I lay everything I've bought out on the table, it won't look much of a spread. But he's a stranger, from far away, how on earth will he know what I can afford? He'll probably think the Kazakhs have changed their customs. But hang on, if I spend all my savings today, what am I going to eat tomorrow? It's another eleven days to pension day. Am I going to live on air and water? And what if, come eleven days, they don't pay the pension and start saying forever 'come back tomorrow', and that nonsense goes on for a couple of weeks? It's already become awkward borrowing from the neighbours. Anyway, they're having to tighten their own belts. My head is spinning… But now I think

I'm beginning to understand people who go hungry for a month after receiving a guest. Just one visitor! (*Looks at the clock on the wall*) O heavens, look, it's already late! I'll go mad from always thinking about tomorrow. It would be better to go and see the neighbours again.

She puts on her coat, hurriedly fetches a shopping bag and exits the apartment.

* * *

The same scene. The stage is empty. Enter Zeynep, soaking from head to foot.

ZEYNEP: I gave him my umbrella, as though I was never going to go outside again. Now I'm soaked.

She takes off her outdoor clothes and places some packages on the table. Evidently she has not managed to buy very much.

Well, that's all the shopping. I borrowed a whole five hundred *tenge* from the neighbours, but there still isn't enough here even for one person. And that five hundred *tenge* is my whole monthly pension! (*Laughs*) Oh well, there's no point grumbling, better to get on with the dinner. (*She moves away from the packages.*) But just a minute, I was out quite some time, what if he came here and rang the bell while I was out, and then left again? Why didn't I think to leave a note? They are right when they say that a lame sheep bleats after supper… Oh my Lord, I forgot to buy any bread or milk! How are we going to manage? (*Opens the packages*) I'll just have to ask the neighbours again… Why is he taking so long?

The doorbell rings. Zeynep jumps.

ZEYNEP: O Lord! (*In agitated excitement she checks her appearance, then feverishly starts setting crockery on the table.*) The door's open, come in!

Aytore enters the apartment.

AYTORE: A certain stranger is going to be bugging you all day, I suspect. (*He shakes the umbrella.*)

ZEYNEP: Well, you're not someone who'll be here very often. Come in, be my guest.

AYTORE: Thank you. You know, I think the sky above Almaty must be worn out.

ZEYNEP: That's entirely possible. It's three days since I saw a blue sky. Have a seat.

Aytore sits down on the same corner of the couch where he sat before and begins unhurriedly to comb his wet hair.

AYTORE: It's funny, but this time I came in here in a completely different mood.

ZEYNEP: Maybe because it's familiar – walking into your own house.

AYTORE: No, it's nothing to do with that. It's more about the way you relate to people. I think that people like you are becoming museum pieces.

ZEYNEP: So do I need to be pickled in a jar of alcohol?

AYTORE (*bursts out laughing*): You what? Hey, what I mean is that these days you are a rare kind of person.

ZEYNEP: Oh, come on. What do you really mean?

AYTORE: Do you want me to be honest? To tell you the truth, I really wasn't sorry that the flight was delayed.

ZEYNEP: Are you fed up of flying?

AYTORE: No, I don't mean that.

ZEYNEP: So what do you mean?

AYTORE: I wanted to see you.

ZEYNEP: Uh?

AYTORE: I really wanted to see you again.

ZEYNEP: God preserve us! Why this again? What did you want to see me again for?

AYTORE: (*laughs*): I'm not sure I even know.

ZEYNEP: Good grief, but I need to go out to the shops.

AYTORE: You don't need to trouble yourself so much just for some traveller.

ZEYNEP: Well, I was getting ready to go to the shops before you arrived. I've been stuck at home all day, waiting for my son. But he's asleep… What am I saying? He's not asleep, but he's been held up by various things. Okay, I'll only be a few minutes… Shall I put the television on for you?

AYTORE: No need, thanks.

ZEYNEP: Well, have a look at my photo album. You may see somebody there that you know.

Zeynep hurries into the hallway. From there she hears Aytore's voice:

AYTORE: Do you think you'd be able to buy me a bottle of light dry wine?

Zeynep stops dead, thinking of her precarious financial situation.

ZEYNEP: Wine? But that's expensive, you know.

AYTORE (*with a guilty smile*): Here, take this money for the wine.

ZEYNEP: Shall I spend it all?

AYTORE: No! I'm not a merman. Just one bottle's enough.

ZEYNEP: You haven't understood me right. I don't need your money. I was already thinking of buying some wine. You really have forgotten a lot about our customs. Did you ever see a Kazakh guest offering money for drinks? Though you might have bought some wine on your way.

She checks herself, realising that she has said too much.

AYTORE: I wanted to buy some wine myself, but to tell you the truth, I felt shy. Look, won't you accept this money as a *korimdik* – a gift in honour of your home?

ZEYNEP: I can't take it, that's not how I was brought up.

AYTORE: Well, then, let's go to the shops together.

ZEYNEP: And do you still not understand? What will I say to the neighbours, who live only in order to know about everyone and everything? No, you stay here, I'll go to the shop by myself.

Zeynep picks up her shopping bag and goes out. Aytore is left on his own. He leafs through the photo album. The telephone rings loudly in the corner. It goes on ringing for a long time. Aytore does not know what to do. He goes back to looking at the album, then the telephone rings again. Now it goes on ringing and does not stop.

AYTORE: Maybe I should say that the householder is not at home? (*Lifts receiver and listens. An unknown male voice is gabbling loud and fast at the other end.*)

VOICE: Hello, Mama! Why didn't you answer? Were you asleep or had you gone out? What's wrong, are you having an argument with Rosa's mother? Do you think I can't look after myself? Hello? Hello? Why don't you say something, Mama? Mama? Mama!

THE TRANSIT PASSENGER

Aytore replaces the handset without speaking. The telephone begins to ring again straight away. This time Aytore ignores it. A minute later Zeynep returns, talking to herself.

ZEYNEP: So how does it feel to be in your old house?

AYTORE: When you're by yourself you think about many things.

ZEYNEP: Well, there isn't much to choose from in our shops. I got what I could find. Now I'm going to start making the dinner, but you sit here and relax.

AYTORE: No, I got plenty of rest by the Black Sea. I'll give you a hand.

They go into the kitchen..

By the way, your son phoned. I didn't pick it up the first time, but he rang again.

ZEYNEP: And what did he say?

AYTORE: He wasn't interested in who he was talking to, he just let off a stream of talk about his problems.

ZEYNEP: Was everything all right with him? Oh my goodness, what did you and he talk about?

AYTORE: Don't worry, I didn't utter a single word. I don't think he even realised who had answered. I daresay he'll ring again before long.

ZEYNEP: As I was going to the shop I was wondering how you'd got hold of my phone number? I don't recall giving it to you.

AYTORE (*starts to laugh*): Aha, I resorted to a clever dodge. When I went back to the airport I saw somebody from Flat 5. I think he'd come out for a smoke. To my good fortune, he happened to know your phone number.

ZEYNEP: I see you aren't just a regular type. Here, chop these onions... If I'm not mistaken, you're heading home without calling on any old friends and acquaintances in Almaty. Haven't you got any left?

AYTORE: Of course. But I don't think any of them misses me. People today have lost their sense of attachment. They meet somebody after thirty years and can't even find a few warm words of greeting in themselves. The other thing is I've lost track of their telephone numbers. I don't know who lives where. And the city has changed beyond recognition. It wasn't easy even finding this building.

Do you know, by the way, that we used to heat this flat with coal? Come and look over here. There used to be a stove pipe that ran out from here. In the mornings we cleared out the ash, and then we hauled coal upstairs to the first floor in buckets. In those days not every district had its own telephone – never mind every flat! – so if you needed to make an urgent call, you'd run to the airport or to somewhere nearer the centre of town. We ran, full tilt, hardly better than barefoot and on black ice and in sleet and snow. Looking back now, that distant time seems incredibly precious. Or maybe it's always like that: everything we have experienced becomes dear to us?

ZEYNEP: But sometimes it's more like we don't want to remember.

AYTORE: Yet all the same not having to erase what's happened in our lives. I had a difficult childhood, but I think of it now with a warm sadness. I don't think about the times when I cried or when I was bad or mischievous in particular, but I see my childhood times overall as something pure and undisturbed. We wanted to get on with living and to grow up as quickly as possible, sometimes we thought that would happen tomorrow and we couldn't wait for the next morning. I remember once taking a pen and ink – that's what we used in those days – and drawing round the shape of my hand

and fingers on a piece of paper. And it was amazing – next morning I placed my hand over the outline, then ran to my mother. 'Mama, look, my hand no longer fits this outline! So am I grown up now, a man, a real *jigit*? My mother kissed me and said, 'Yes, of course, my little sunshine! You've got bigger since yesterday and are now a real *jigit*. And will I now be a victim of these little fingers?' Where's my unforgettable mother now, I wonder, and what did I ever do for her? There's a small mound in the cemetery, but it is a long time since I visited her grave. And I probably wouldn't be able to find it any more, it was an inconspicuous spot. But my life – well, here it is, wandering about in foreign lands…

Overcome with emotion, Aytore breaks off.

ZEYNEP: Come on, now, don't get upset. (*Her voice now also starts to tremble tellingly.*) And what happened next? (*Forces herself to laugh.*) I said, what happened after that? Did you go on tracing your hands on paper?

AYTORE: Of course I did… Back then I thought that the world was held up by the hands of grownups, and that they upheld all the truth in the world. It seemed to me that grownups alone were the bearers of good and order, and could stand up to evil and violence. They all lived for the people, I thought then, and were called to bring beauty to the land they called home. They all had the powers of the legendary Tolagay, who could move mountains. And so we couldn't wait to grow up ourselves… When we were young we didn't realise that good and evil, love and violence, often went hand in hand and that in life the top people in society often used evil and force. And now I think about it, and it seems good to have lived in ignorance… This is how it is in life: as children we hurry to grow up, but life as an adult turns out to be dull and lacking colour. (*Nods and gives a brief laugh.*) A bit like this colourless Romanian wine. (*Some water boils over from the kettle onto the hot surface of the stove with a hiss.*) What's this? The kettle's boiled already? Have I been talking that much? I've probably been leading you up the garden path.

ZEYNEP: You're an interesting person. You probably won't believe this, but it turns out that I've never before talked with somebody like this in private, one to one. With a man, I mean. You must have some kind of magical gift.

They sit down, still talking, at the table where they had recently been sitting.

ZEYNEP: It's strange that my son hasn't phoned. Maybe we didn't hear it ring because we were talking?

AYTORE: No, the telephone hasn't rung.

At this moment the doorbell abruptly rings.[1]

ZEYNEP: (*gives a start*): O God! In this house the doorbell and the phone are enough to give anybody the jitters. What can we do? What if it's one of the children?

AYTORE: I don't know. I'm powerless in this matter.

ZEYNEP: Well of all things, how can you be so unconcerned? His mother-in-law said he was drunk and asleep... Suppose he says something in the heat of the moment that offends you... We'll be disgraced if it's him and his wife. They won't understand a thing!

The doorbell rings again.

ZEYNEP: Coming! I'll be right there! (*On tiptoes she brings Aytore his raincoat and hat.*) Put these on and stand there like someone who's just walked in.

AYTORE: And as whom should I stand here?

---

1 Ru version gives as telephone, but seems clear it is the door

THE TRANSIT PASSENGER

ZEYNEP: Good question, who indeed? Maybe you're the plumber? No, you don't look like a plumber. Well, with that tie – maybe you're from the housing management office? But they don't go round to people's flats at night. ... Aha, got it – you're an agitator!

AYTORE: Well, what should I be agitating for? Or who?

ZEYNEP: I don't know, you think of something.

AYTORE: There aren't any elections on at the moment…

ZEYNEP: Really? I hadn't thought. All right, you've called here by mistake.

The doorbell rings without stopping..

Well that's it, there's no time to think of anything else. Just stand there looking thunderstruck and look around like someone who doesn't know me.

Zeynep goes to the door. Aytore puts on the hat and raincoat and stands stock still in the middle of the living room. He can hear Zeynep talking to somebody in the hallway. She comes back into the room.

AYTORE: Who was it?

ZEYNEP: Your friend… Good grief!

AYTORE: What friend?

ZEYNEP: You know – the one from Flat 5. He said he came to apologise to me for giving my phone number to a stranger.

AYTORE: Oh my goodness! And there I was in a panic thinking it was Ertay.

ZEYNEP: These are the kind of neighbours I've got. A frog couldn't cross the path without them knowing about it. Well, why are you standing there like that?

AYTORE: I'm standing as if thunderstruck, like you told me to.

ZEYNEP: You call that thunderstruck? What, with your hands clasped together behind you?

AYTORE: Well, how am I supposed to stand?

ZEYNEP: Like this? (*Tries to demonstrate and almost loses her balance.*) As if thunderstruck? … So what should that be like? … I remember us going into the woods for firewood once and my mother scolding me: 'Well, why are you just standing there looking all thunderstruck?' What did I look like? Like this, I think…

She loses her balance again and almost falls. Without thinking she leans against Aytore. They laugh at themselves together.

END OF ACT 1

ACT TWO

The same scene as before. Zeynep is busy with household tasks. Aytore enters. He goes up to her discreetly and gives her some flowers. Zeynep is delighted.

ZEYNEP: I can just imagine what would happen if one of the children saw us enjoying ourselves so much. God save us! Let's go back to the table, the tea's probably cold by now.

AYTORE: And what would be the problem if they did see us? We'd make our acquaintances. I'm not some sort of burglar, you know! We'll tell them like it is – I used to live in this apartment.

ZEYNEP (*chuckling, sits down at her place and pours tea for Aytore*): What's the good of that, pray? My boy's a bully, he could just blurt out, 'Look at you, having fun with some old man, but you're always grumpy with me'. Better if you tell them how you ended up living so far away.

AYTORE (*as though he has not heard her*): I've a feeling that some visitors have come to my house in Yakutsk.

ZEYNEP: Well, what if they have? Your spouse will be there to receive them.

AYTORE (*after a pause*): We always used to be glad to have visitors. How is that here these days?

ZEYNEP: We're still pleased to have them. Is it not the case that I'm entertaining somebody right now that I've never met before?

A long, unfamiliar silence descends.

AYTORE (*Gets up from his seat*): So why did I move so far away? And what did I find that made me stay there so long? To tell the truth, I've been wanting to pour my heart out to somebody for some time, to get the weight off my chest. Of course I can always tell people about my ordeals but where can I find someone who really understands? That's something I don't know… In the last two or three years my life's afflictions have been tormenting me almost to death. But maybe the problem is just age? It could be that the body, rather than the mind, just senses that much of life is past and there isn't much left? While I was in the Crimea I had a long and heartfelt conversation with an old man. He knew a lot and was a thoughtful person to talk to. A Kazakh, in fact – originally from Arys near Chimkent. Have you heard of a town with that name in those parts?

ZEYNEP: Of course I have. How could I not have – I'm from there myself! Arys is a large town, it stands on a crossroads of old caravan routes.

AYTORE: My goodness, it's a small world! Who would have thought it? You know, it seems to me that a person becomes sensitive when he lives a long way from where he comes from. (*He pours wine into his glass and drinks a little.*) For sure, some people are happy to settle down wherever they make it good, but I can never stop thinking about my homeland. (*Laughs*) I doubt whether anyone's as attached to their homeland as we are, the Kazakhs. I remember when I was a child, two of our relatives decided to move away. What a fuss, when they loaded their modest belongings onto the carts! Practically the whole village turned out, the men had tears in their eyes and the women were keening and lamenting. Those relatives said their goodbyes as though they were going to their deaths. But they were only going to live some seventy versts from us. That's the Kazakhs for you! But I live on the edge of the world, as you pointed out so accurately. I ought to have come back, but there is a reason that prevents me doing so. Still my heart aches. Round here I've got plenty of relations and friends. Well, I used to have. That was twenty years ago. I don't know how many of them are still left. They say that you can tell a person's entire life from their eyes, but I seem to have grown old: I don't feel drawn even to call in and see my close friends and relatives.

ZEYNEP: Maybe the reason preventing you is something in yourself? Maybe you're just hard-hearted by nature?

AYTORE: You're right. I was born that way.

ZEYNEP (*noticeably embarrassed*): Forgive me, I wasn't thinking about what I was saying.

AYTORE (*growing calmer*): What is there to apologise for? You're not far from the truth.

ZEYNEP: I don't know. But look, here you are praising the Kazakhs, but do they deserve it? As far as I can see they don't take life very seriously. If a Kazakh man marries a Chinese girl, everything in the house becomes Chinese. If the man's Chinese and the girl's Kazakh, the same thing still happens. It's like that proverb – if you hit a bird with a stone, you kill the bird; hit the stone with the bird, and the bird still dies.

AYTORE: Well, I think I was that bird! (*Suddenly angry*) But how many times today have I said I miss my homeland? Do you really think I couldn't have got a flight direct from Simferopol to Yakutsk?

ZEYNEP (*also angry*): Why have you got so worked up, and why are you raising your voice? Even my husband never spoke to me like that.

AYTORE (*taking control of himself*): You're a true woman, Zeynep.

ZEYNEP: That doesn't interest me any more.

AYTORE: Please be generous and forgive me. All the same, you're not a stranger to me, mistress of my former apartment.

ZEYNEP: Just look at him! He said his piece and now he's gone back on his word. What will happen now?

AYTORE: What's going to happen now?

ZEYNEP: Well you started this conversation!

AYTORE: Ah, yes… (*Pours wine and drinks*) Man's a visitor on this earth, a guest of God. And knowing this, he waits for good news every morning, and every day he expects miracles. He expects all this as he would a long-awaited guest. It makes no difference whether he is an all-powerful khan or an indigent beggar. I told you just now that I'm not short of friends and family in Almaty. But I haven't got the strength to go wandering the streets. It makes me feel as though I'm walking on my son's bones.

ZEYNEP: Oh heavens, what on earth are you talking about? What bones?

AYTORE: Remember, I told you about my son, who ended up in prison? Life was not kind to him. After that he seemed to sort himself out, and soon enough he got work as a bricklayer. He earned reasonable money, enough for himself at any rate. This made me feel better too, and I began to forget about the reprimand they'd given me at work for 'not giving my son a proper upbringing'. I was made deputy director of a geological enterprise, and people said that I was actually running it myself. Today a whole ministry has been set up on the basis of that organisation. And then, just when my career was taking off, everything turned upside down.

ZEYNEP: Well, what happened?

AYTORE: Certain jealous elements started bombarding 'the authorities' with a mass of anonymous letters. The ones that claimed to be my friends swore their eternal friendship… But I was accused of giving jobs to my relatives, of getting drunk and inciting sedition in public, issuing bonuses and awarding them wherever I wanted, and they said I was morally degenerate, lived with two wives and so on and so forth. They started taunting me, demanding explanations and intimidating me. They came down so hard that I was eventually unable to justify my innocence...

Late one night the telephone started ringing at home. My wife answered it, listened and then broke down wailing loudly. They asked us to go to the police station straight away. There they showed us a jacket belonging to our son, stained all over with blood. It turns out that they found us thanks to a notebook in the jacket pocket.

ZEYNEP: But was he still alive?

AYTORE: They knew nothing about him whatsoever. My wife collapsed unconscious. And how hard it was for me to see my wife and daughter grieving so much! It broke my heart seeing them clutching the bloodied jacket and crying their eyes out, I almost lost my mind. Our lives were ruined... In the evenings our house – this apartment in which you and I are sitting now – felt cold and like a prison, and not like a human dwelling at all.

ZEYNEP: Oh my Lord! But did they find your son?

AYTORE: They did. A year later.

ZEYNEP: Where?

AYTORE: They raked his bones out from under the asphalt while they were building a road. There was proof of his identity in the back pocket of his trousers. It was still clean, as if it has been issued only the day before. They found half of the body – below the chest...

ZEYNEP (*horrified*): Good grief, what are you saying? Stop! Don't say anything else. How savage all this is!

AYTORE: That's what the times are like, I'm afraid. People have become savage.

A deathly silence hangs over the room. Zeynep weeps.

ZEYNEP (*through her tears*): Why do you not say something?

AYTORE: There's nothing else for me to tell you.

ZEYNEP: I've had enough concerns of my own, and now here are all yours as well… How hard is life for the stepchildren of fate, how many tears, how much suffering? Here you come, as though from a different world, telling me about yourself… and then you say, 'There's nothing else to tell you'. So now it's up to me to bear the burden… My own as well as someone else's grief. But it seems nobody's ever been concerned for me.

AYTORE: Forgive me, maybe you can tell me how I should comfort you? Up until now we were not closely acquainted…

ZEYNEP (*in a cutting tone*): We weren't close, you say? We're strangers to each other. My, how strange people sometimes are. But then, I can't remember anyone even in my close family ever offering me comfort. Although… I didn't exactly take care of myself either. I thought it was a sin to be concerned only with my own worries. But it seems that conscience, compassion, gratitude, guilt and remorse were forgotten long ago. Ever since I was small I looked after my mother, who was unwell. I also tried to help endless brothers, sisters and cousins to get a start in life… I did everything I could so that they wouldn't resent me, I worked night and day. But none of these people could find it in themselves to say to me, 'You've been through water and fire to look after us. Why don't you take a little more care of yourself?' Later they all forgot about my efforts completely. My mother died in my arms. 'We've all been such a burden to you', she wept in her last minutes. 'We've been like *sungyla*, those weeds that grow around melons and suck away all the goodness from the earth around them until they wilt. You didn't get what you deserved in life. But my daughter, you lived up to all my expectations. Piety is selective, it may be present in just one child out of a whole large family. And this single child ends up carrying all the hardships and burdens of those around her. That was your fate, my sweetest. But remember that good deeds don't always turn out for the best. May God reward you...' And the way it turned out – it was just as though mother had looked into the water and seen what would happen with me, and that's what did happen. I don't remember whether anybody has ever repaid me in kindness.

AYTORE: She was a prophet.

ZEYNEP: Who do you mean?

AYTORE: Your mother.

ZEYNEP: Yes, she was a prophet. Although it's well known that good is not always repaid with goodness... So who was responsible for the death of your son?

AYTORE: That's a long story. I wouldn't want to burden you with it, but since you're interested... That act of meanness was carried out by the people who were after me. Apparently my son discovered the person who'd organised all those anonymous letters, and confronted him in a dark hallway and shook him by the collar. The guy was frightened and confessed. But that wasn't the end of it – he went on harbouring malice and eventually got his revenge on my son. And I couldn't prove that a crime had been committed.

ZEYNEP: And what about the workmen surfacing the road? Did you meet them?

AYTORE: A lot of water had passed under the bridge since he was killed, we'd lost a lot of time. The workmen in that gang had changed and it was difficult to find many of them. And on top of that, I didn't feel able to stay here any longer. Like I said, just walking down the street, I had the sense of hearing my son's bones crunching underfoot. So one day we simply gathered our things and moved to Yakutsk. I had an old friend living there, and we went to be near him.

ZEYNEP: And what about your wife?

AYTORE: She passed away… a year ago. After they found my son's remains under the asphalt, she wasn't herself for some time. I think she lost her mind, she was oblivious to everything. She started wandering the streets of Yakutsk looking for his remains. I had to give up work to keep an eye on her, so that I wouldn't lose her as well. But in the end she succumbed… One day she went out looking for our son. It was a polar night, dark even in the daytime, and there was a blizzard like you've never seen… We never found her, never had the chance to give her the six feet of earth that is appointed for every person…

ZEYNEP: Well, that's just life, isn't it! (*Wipes her tears with the corner of her shawl.*) She's here today, and tomorrow she's gone. You're born, you grow up, you try to achieve something in life, and like I said, you'll go through fire and water to achieve it. And sometimes, in the middle of all that endless effort, you don't realise how the time has flown. Yet in this short gap between birth and death, how much trouble people still manage to inflict on each other! Tell me, what for?

Zeynep weeps. Aytore puts his hand on her shoulder, trying to comfort her. Neither of them notice that they have moved closer together.

AYTORE (*thoughtfully*): I know how tender and delicate women are, and yet at the same time so strong and courageous. But nobody can see into their soul. You might gather all the geniuses of the world together and solve the mysteries of the universe, but they could never really understand a woman.

ZEYNEP: What are you talking about?

AYTORE: I'm talking to myself, out of sympathy for you. I care about you – I share your feelings.

ZEYNEP: You share my feelings?

AYTORE (*laughs softly*): I do. Does it not happen that a person sometimes feels drawn to somebody? That's happening to me now. Once there was a time…

ZEYNEP: Never mind your 'once there was a time', but do you really sympathise with me?

AYTORE: Yes. Is there anything reprehensible in that?

ZEYNEP: O my Lord, such disgrace! Have you really gone so wild, have you lost all sense of shame? Really, at your age, meeting a woman for the first time, especially a woman of a certain age… You've definitely lost the plot.

AYTORE (*selflessly, with a cheerful laugh*): I see, now you're saying it too! Lost the plot, a dead duck! You know, it's true, something really has happened with me. And now all that remains for you to do is to throw me out of my old home, and then there really will be nothing left in these parts to detain me. My last hope will be lost.

ZEYNEP: Don't ever say such things! You must never live without hope. I don't believe that any troubles should keep you from your native land. Come back.

AYTORE: What for? And who for?

ZEYNEP (*astonished*): Do you need to have a reason to return to your homeland? What grievance do you have?

AYTORE: But how can I come back? I've got no house here, no job, no means of supporting myself.

ZEYNEP: Do you suppose all that should be handed to you on a plate? Look, your homeland is your tribe, your people. Why, out there on the edge of the world, do they offer you the meat of a fat sheep and say to you, 'Greetings, dear brother Kazakh, come and sit here in the place of honour!'?

AYTORE: No, of course not.

ZEYNEP: So what are we really talking about? This is your homeland, this is where your people live. If they have only water to live on, then you live on water with them. If they drink poison, you drink poison with them. Living with them, as one of them, you don't suffer. But wanting everything to be arranged for you isn't the point, and besides, it doesn't seem right for a man. Anyway, it's hardly a life of luxury here these days.

AYTORE: You're probably right. You're very clever, Zeynep. Some of what you've said has really hit the spot.

ZEYNEP (*checks herself*): Oh goodness, with all this talking we've let the tea go cold again. I'll heat it up. (*Switches on an electric samovar*) And as for my prodigal son – still neither hide nor hair. Where's he been all this time?

AYTORE: Parents worry about their children, but the children don't care. He'll probably turn up when he remembers his mother.

ZEYNEP: That's how it always is. The parents spend their entire lives worrying about their children, but the children grow up and scatter to the four winds. Especially the boys. You'd think they'd managed to get themselves born without needing a mother at all. They never stop to think that their parents get anxious if they don't hear from them. A son might turn up occasionally for a funeral, to throw his handful of soil onto the coffin, but sometimes they haven't even got time for that. The poor daughters, though, they nurture their feelings towards their parents all their lives. My late mother used to say, 'To be frank, the only one who really cares about their mother is the daughter'.

AYTORE: Do you think so?

ZEYNEP: They say that after you die, everything that you did in this life is weighed on a scale. On one side go all your good deeds, while the evil you committed is placed on the other. If your good deeds weigh more than your bad, you are sent to heaven, but if it's the other way round, you go to hell. But this world is full of sin, so most people are laden with their faults when they die. One day, it is said, there were two parents whose sins were greater than their good deeds. They were to be sentenced to hell, but just then their daughter came running up to them, groaning, and said, 'Let me carry all your sin. I'll go and burn in hell instead of you.' And saying these words as though uttering an incantation, the girl took off her shawl and tossed it into the scale pan containing the parents' good deeds, which tipped the balance. So she spared them terrible suffering. So there you have it: that's the nature of a daughter. She goes to hell to save her parents.

AYTORE: Thank you for telling me that. (*Agitated, he wipes his face with his handkerchief. He then goes up and sits opposite Zeynep and takes her hand.*) I knew that ever since Adam and Eve, since the male and female principles first appeared, that the suffering of woman has been a thousand times greater than what men have to endure. But you said it so expressively and so profoundly that something lit me up inside.

ZEYNEP: My daughter was the only support I had in life, and I expect it'll be her who keeps me company in the next world as well. I'm talking about my daughter Nazip... (*Also becoming agitated*) Ever since she was small, my own flesh and blood, she grew up knowing hardship and poverty... She died when she was just twelve. Tell me, is there anything harder for a mother than the death of her own child? She didn't use to say much, but felt life keenly. Her illness didn't seem to last long – she was in bed for only two days. Just two days! … And even in her last minutes she didn't lose her composure. '*Apa*', she said calmly, looking me in the eye, 'I was thinking of giving you three shawls for the next world. Here they are.' She pulled three new shawls out from under her pillow, each one neatly folded four times, then smiled quietly. 'But there isn't even a speck of sin on you. And so I suppose I'll give them to somebody who's destined for hell, it'll save one miserable soul from torment.'

I didn't realise she was going to die – the thought never crossed my mind… But then, what could I have done even if I had guessed that this was my daughter's last hour? I finally understood she was dying when she said to me, '*Apa*, when you take me to be buried, I want you to hold my hand in yours. Please don't leave me alone…' And then she died, she who was my very soul.

AYTORE: Hmm. What caused her to die?

ZEYNEP: It was my fault.

AYTORE: How?

ZEYNEP: It happened like this. Just before that I fell ill and couldn't leave the house. But the children were at various schools. I wasn't well enough to go and collect my daughter from school. And it seems she got on the wrong bus and got lost in town.

AYTORE: So what happened?

ZEYNEP: Some people brought her home next day.

AYTORE: Where had she been?

ZEYNEP (*through tears*): She sat up the whole night in some dilapidated building or other. If only I hadn't been unwell…

AYTORE: She must have caught a terrible cold.

ZEYNEP (*raises her head abruptly*): What, do you even need to know that?

AYTORE: Forgive me, it seems I've said something tactless.

ZEYNEP (*after a pause*): People have degenerated completely. They say that when the Almighty is displeased with man, He cuts all their humanity off from them. And this is obviously what has happened. Just look at how intolerant people have become of one another. They haven't got hearts in their chests at all, but stones. How on earth could anyone treat a young girl so cruelly? My poor lamb! ...

AYTORE (*softly*): I can't ask any more questions.

ZEYNEP: Why, go ahead and ask. We've no longer got anything to hide from each other. Some savage creature or other took advantage of her.

AYTORE (*covers his face with his hands*): What monsters... Whatever has happened to people today? But please, please, don't lose heart! I beg you!

ZEYNEP: Well, what is there left for me in this life except to endure the blows that fate deals me?

AYTORE: Did they find the perpetrators?

ZEYNEP: No. And there was no one to look for them. The lot of ordinary people is not a happy one. We are probably the most patient and submissive of people.

AYTORE: So why does this cheapen human life with every passing day? Does the earth not have patience for us?

ZEYNEP: I don't know. What can you say to an old woman who's lived miserably all her life? Now my grandmother, she was a singular woman. She wouldn't allow women to give birth far from home. She tried to prevent her daughters-in-law going out of the door when they were pregnant. If any of them attempted to go and visit her own family, she would get everybody up on their feet looking for her and did not calm down until she herself had brought her home. She said that a child born away from its family home would inevitably grow up cruel and heartless. We, stupidly, laughed at her. She must have known some kind of secret and abided by it, otherwise why would she have got into arguments with people? (*From the kitchen comes a hissing sound as the contents of a saucepan boils over.*) Oh grief, now look, I've forgotten the pan. The meat will have been done long ago.

AYTORE (*pensively*): 'A child born away from its family home will inevitably grow up cruel and heartless'. Where did she get that idea? Why haven't I heard it before? Or do we take these simple statements to be superstitions and avoid them like the plague? How exactly right it is though! It seems to me that we Kazakhs are copying foreign ideas more and more instead of using our own, and that's becoming our trademark – imitation! Everything we have… like native gold, we're losing everything we have with every step.

ZEYNEP'S VOICE (*from the kitchen*): Why are you sitting there like the ambassador of an enemy country? Come in here, you could at least chop some onion. You haven't forgotten that you've still got a flight to catch? Hurry up.

AYTORE (*going into the kitchen*): I can chop both the onions and the meat. Give me a knife.

ZEYNEP (*starts with surprise*): Oh Lord, you were so quiet coming in!

She drops the knife in surprise. Aytore picks it up from the floor and runs his finger along the blade.

AYTORE: Well here's a fine state of affairs. This isn't a knife, it's a blunt axe!

ZEYNEP: In a household without men, knives turn into axes and an axe ends up as a hammer.

AYTORE: Spot on yet again! No, you're not just a woman, but the most genuine treasure. You know so much! But if you're so clever, then tell me: where is a Kazakh's stomach?

ZEYNEP: On the top of his head.

AYTORE (*cheerful*): Ha, you missed the mark this time! A Kazakh's stomach is on these fingers. It is never full unless they are being burnt by hot meat.

They both laugh, grinning at each other. Their glances are warm. Aytore finds a sharpening implement and proceeds to sharpen the knife.

What a lot of meat you've boiled for just two of us! We'll never eat all that in one go.

ZEYNEP: If the meat all fits into one cauldron, the Kazakhs don't regard it as a lot. And we've just got a little saucepan's worth. In any case it's not right to make judgements about food like that. Saying that somebody's prepared too much food is like revealing that your ancestors had humble origins.

AYTORE: You're not someone to argue with. All the same, let me just say that in parts of Europe, say, our dinner for two would be more than enough for a delegation of thirty.

ZEYNEP: Is that so? Well, what can you do – if they saddle two Kazakhs with the work of thirty Europeans, then you and I will simply have to resign ourselves to the task.

They laugh at their words. They carve the meat, place it in a dish and take it into the living room. Aytore uncorks the bottle and pours wine into two tall glasses.

AYTORE (*raises his glass*): To our second meeting in our old house!

ZEYNEP: Thanks.

They clink their glasses. At that moment the doorbell rings.

Well, fancy. I was just thinking, how is it that we haven't been disturbed yet!

She gets up from the table with mixed feelings of grief and discontent.

AYTORE (*startled*): What should I do?

ZEYNEP: Stay there. (*Goes to the door*) Who's there?

ERTAY'S VOICE. Mmm. It's me!

ZEYNEP: Ertay, is that you?

ERTAY: Yes it's me!

ZEYNEP: Oh Lord, his speech is slurred.

She opens the door. Ertay enters, soaked from head to foot, his raincoat sagging from him.

ZEYNEP: Just look at you! And where did you manage to get so drunk? I heard you were asleep!

ERTAY: Where's – Where's Rosa? Is she… here?

ZEYNEP: How should I know where she is? I thought she was with you. You told me yourself you were waiting for her brother.

ERTAY: No! She's here. She ran away from me and you're hiding her.

ZEYNEP: O heavens! Why on earth would I hide my daughter-in-law in here? What's wrong, have you fallen out again?

ERTAY: You said it…

THE TRANSIT PASSENGER

ZEYNEP: So what's the problem? What's lacking in your relationship?

ERTAY: I'll show her! She called me a beggar. I'll have her beg for mercy. She... I wanted to kill her, but she ran off. I went looking for her outside but couldn't find her. They told me in the other house that she'd come here.

ZEYNEP: Oh well, let them say whatever God puts into their heads, you can't gag them. And give that up about killing her. You'd only go to prison. Come on, take your things off.

Ertay enters the living room without removing his shoes. Seeing the stranger at the table, he stops.

ERTAY: And what type have you got here? Some old geyser... But... I thought... it was Rosa in here. (*Draws his finger across his throat to suggest decapitation*) I wanted to cut her head off. Do you understand?

AYTORE: Thank you for noticing I'm the wrong person.

ERTAY: What the...? He's saying thank you! Is he cultured or what?

Ertay seizes the wineglass in front of Aytore and knocks the contents back in one gulp.

Aahh!... Your health!

AYTORE: Thanks.

ERTAY (*to his mother, who stands and looks on, bewildered and saying nothing*): So Rosa really hasn't been here?

ZEYNEP: No, she hasn't been here.

ERTAY: So where is she?

ZEYNEP (*almost in tears*): Why do you keep asking me? How on earth should I know?

ERTAY: OK, I'm off then. (*Picks up his mother's glass and downs the contents in one. Nods to Aytore*) Well, ciao, Michael Jackson!

He walks unsteadily towards the door.

ZEYNEP: Ertay… Ertay-zhan! Where are you going? It's cold out there, it's raining…

Ertay quickens his pace and exits almost at a run. Zeynep is distraught. She sits down at the table with a remote expression.

AYTORE: Looks like I've caused you complications.

ZEYNEP (*starts*): What? Did you say something?

AYTORE: I feel awkward, as though I've caused you an inconvenience.

ZEYNEP: None of this is your fault. (*Serves the meat onto plates.*) Here, have some dinner. Don't worry, there's no reason to.

AYTORE: It's time I set off for the airport.

ZEYNEP: Yes, it probably is. But at least drink some of the hot broth from the stew. I put some *kurt* in it – the little balls of dry cheese they love out on the steppes. And I suppose it's a long time since you tasted our national soup.

She hands Aytore a bowl of sorpa *(mutton broth). He drinks it up in one gulp, but in a somewhat different manner from that shown recently by Ertay.*

AYTORE (*trying to remain upbeat*): Delicious! And after *sorpa* with cheese I can't manage anything else. You know, I used to have a friend the same age as me. Every time he'd been abroad he would say 'In such and such a country they worry no end about what they eat. But they haven't come up with anything like our *kurt*, which will keep its flavour for a hundred years. They just build pyramids and domes that are no use to anyone.' We laughed at his words. I said to him, 'Do you think they'll ask you in the next world what you ate in this one?' He just said, 'Well, they definitely won't ask me what I built!'

Zeynep goes on sitting aloof, not paying attention to him.

ZEYNEP (*as though talking to herself*): What face should I be presenting to the children now? What will I say to them? And will they listen to me?

AYTORE (*in a guilty tone*): It's always like this with me. As soon as I am drawn strongly to somebody, something immediately gets in the way. It's been like that all my life.

ZEYNEP: It seems you didn't have your feet tied together when you were a boy?

AYTORE: How do you mean?

ZEYNEP: Don't you know that tradition?

AYTORE: No... never heard of it.

ZEYNEP: Anyone would think you'd grown up in a vacuum, like corn in the shade – you never saw anything worthwhile, never learnt kindness and don't know anything about anything. How have you managed to preserve your original purity so intact?

AYTORE (*not angered, but giving a confused laugh*): Well, if you are so omniscient, perhaps you will care to enlighten me.

ZEYNEP: When a child is just starting to walk, they tie his feet together so he can't walk, like hobbling a horse. Then they ceremonially cut the tie. It's a whole big celebration, a feast. The point is so that the child will get on in life, doesn't stumble and doesn't fall as he goes on his way.

AYTORE: And is it not possible to do this now?

ZEYNEP: You're exactly sixty-four years late.

AYTORE: Then there's nothing to be done. Hey, thank you for your hospitality! I'm very grateful to you. Indeed I am grateful to fate that it is you who lives in the house where I used to live and that it's awoken in me a sense of wanting to see the old place, which gave me the possibility of meeting and talking with you. Yesterday I was reading a magazine and came across these lines of a poem:

> In unending clouds of stinking smoke
> A new puff of smoke was born in suffering.
> Lived its life in the dark, then died in sorrow.
> There it is – the likeness of life…

That's it, pretty much exactly. And in the middle of this unending succession of years of darkness, meeting you has seemed to me to be the one beacon of light to have illuminated my whole life.

ZEYNEP: Come off it! What are you talking about actually?

AYTORE: Sorry. I don't like that kind of language either. When you meet somebody who does nothing but brag, it's quite uncomfortable. They have no shame. But I tend more to blame the people who listen to talk that is full of flattery and deception. If it were not for such simple-minded people, empty words like that would just evaporate by themselves. I hadn't realised just now how highfalutin I'd become. … Anyway, let me say it again – thank you a thousand times for being yourself and for being the occupant of my old home.

Zeynep is about to object but Aytore halts her with a gesture.

AYTORE: I know, I know! You want to say I've gone too far. But surely I'm permitted in my life to pour out my soul to one person at least. That person turned out to be you. I wouldn't normally have told you all this, but you and I will never see each other again. Never! As far as I see it, your lot in life has been like mine, with no shortage of sorrow. That's evidently been our destiny.

ZEYNEP: There was an old man in our village, called Barakat. He was as poor as could be, all skin and bone, with tendons tough enough to make rope. He used to look after the livestock of a wealthy employer. I remember him one day, leaning heavily on his stick and saying: 'The world contains eighteen thousand living creatures. And to create just one of those, the Almighty had to love it. I thank the Almighty that he loved me and created me as a man who carries a stick and looks after animals. He could have made me into a dog, a pig, an ant or a worm, a mosquito or even a midge.'

I used to listen to him when I was a child. And now I think: these revelations of his contain a lot of meaning. As we strive for what is far away we lose what's right in front of us. And by trying to go deep we don't pay attention to what is on the surface.

AYTORE: True. And we haven't gone far or dug deep. Pity.

ZEYNEP: We are given our due by our deeds.

AYTORE: But something else is a pity as well which is that there are fewer and fewer women left in the world like you. In another forty or fifty years, of course, we will see entirely different women – the ones that know the world from watching television. Have you noticed that it's already getting hard to find a grandmother who knows how to tell her grandchildren stories?

ZEYNEP: There's a Kazakh proverb: 'The hearth renews itself in forty years, and the country renews itself in fifty'.

AYTORE: Absolutely right. (*In a rush of emotion Aytore clasps Zeynep's shoulders, embraces her and then straightens his arms.*) Very soon our place will be taken by the young, and in fifty years they too will be replaced. And we... as you've just said, we will become like a hearth that has gone cold. Our dust will wander somewhere between earth and heaven – provided that is, that there remains any dust from us. But look, enough of all this melancholy. Even without it, life doesn't exactly spoil us. I would like to propose a toast to you.

ZEYNEP: As you like. I'll put out an appetiser.

She starts busying herself with the plates, but Aytore takes her hand.

AYTORE: I repeat – I've said all this to you because we will never meet again. Come on, have a sip of wine with me.

ZEYNEP: I have never drunk wine in my life.

AYTORE: Never?

ZEYNEP: Never.

AYTORE: Didn't you even drink it when you were young?

ZEYNEP: Not even then.

AYTORE: Human beings are dubious creatures.

ZEYNEP: What's so surprising about that? It's simple – I've never drunk wine, I don't even know what it tastes like.

AYTORE: Well, why don't we find out? Why don't you try a little wine for the first time in your life?

ZEYNEP: Just give a man an excuse to drive women off the path of righteousness. Very well, then, I'll try it.

Zeynep clinks glasses with Aytore, then screws her eyes up tight and drinks up the contents of the glass.

AYTORE: And you call that the first time?

ZEYNEP (*surprised*): But it's just like water! How do people get drunk on this?

AYTORE: They certainly manage it!

ZEYNEP: Well, shall we drink some more?

AYTORE: Certainly. Here's to you!

ZEYNEP: To me?

AYTORE: Yes, to you.

ZEYNEP: Do you know, today is the first time anybody has ever raised a glass to me.

AYTORE: Surely someone has drunk a toast to you at some point or other?

ZEYNEP: No. And what's it for?

AYTORE: Oh God, how have you survived this long? Look, let's drink to your health again.

Zeynep again drinks the glass to the bottom.

AYTORE: Hmm, that's not bad for a beginner.

ZEYNEP: Well, we're about to say goodbye after all…

AYTORE: It's funny, but I get a feeling that I've known you a long time. It's like I'm sitting in my own home.

ZEYNEP: Well you are sitting in your own home!

AYTORE: Indeed. Well, I must go. It would be awkward if Ertay comes back.

ZEYNEP: How long we've spent over our dinner and now it's all down the drain.

AYTORE: And what if we do meet again by some chance?

ZEYNEP (*ponders*): This is how it is: people meet, they talk, they get familiar with each other, and then they go their separate ways.

AYTORE: And often their paths don't meet.

ZEYNEP: That's true.

AYTORE: I used to have a friend who was a poet. He died young. I still remember something he admitted to me. 'Every woman is an undiscovered planet', he used to say. Not an ordinary planet, but a planet of sorrow. A woman's soul can be wounded. Women are vulnerable because they are made of innocence and chastity. Humanity has not yet evolved into a society that values women, and no man has ever yet been born who is capable of caring for them. There is no such thing as a bad woman, but there are bad men.

'They say that when the sea recedes and becomes shallow, and the water in it has almost turned to brine, certain silvery fishes preserve their lives by burrowing into the silt. And their habits and appearance gradually change. What we have done has made the seas recede and the coasts are coated with a crust of salt, and ultimately the women we see are maimed and crippled. We are eternally indebted to women for the fact that in them we have killed purity and tenderness. There are no bad women – there is simply no such thing. The worst that do exist are known by people as hags or witches, but even they do not arise from a decent life. The reason for them – yet again – is our stupidity and ignorance, the dog's life that we men have made for ourselves.'

ZEYNEP (*agitated*): Why are you telling me this?

AYTORE: Because I share your feelings. You are one of those rare women who has preserved her purity and innocence.

ZEYNEP: Here we go again, the old song.

AYTORE: My friend also used to say: 'The Creator decided to 'delight' man with yet another heavy burden – the capacity to understand others who were like himself. By understanding another, he comes close to that person's woes and troubles, but is unable to help him. He begins to suffer from his sense of his own impotence, and his chest becomes empty. So you should never look into a person's soul; the more you open the hiding places of another soul, the deeper you fall into the abyss. You can never reach the bottom of the abyss, but even if you did, you would find only one bitter truth – that no person on this earth is happy. Human life is filled with misfortune and suffering. What a heartbreak it is to realise that even the days of a child who has only just appeared on God's earth are numbered. And so we shouldn't indulge ourselves in sorrowful reflections.' What do you think of his argument?

Zeynep stands, close to tears.

ZEYNEP: You needn't have told me all that. Sometimes I just want to get on and live and to turn away from everything. Then you can feel free of care.

AYTORE: I wouldn't have said it if I wasn't leaving. Well, come on, let's say goodbye. (*Gets up from the table and starts putting on his coat.*) So, shall we shake hands? I think that our two meetings today deserve it.

ZEYNEP (*sadly*): It would have been better if you'd never come into this house…

AYTORE: Let me shake your hand. It has fed me today.

ZEYNEP (*putting out her hand*): God bless you. Have a safe journey. And may you know happiness wherever you live.

AYTORE (*looking aside*): Well, our dear old home, may God preserve you. ... Ahh, I don't think I told you the story about that post. One day I only just managed to pull my wife out of the noose she had tied. She was about to hang herself from that post.

ZEYNEP (*horrified*): Oh Lord, what are you saying now? Are you also one of those men who...?

AYTORE: We are all sinful.

ZEYNEP: How can that be? I thought you were respectable. That's why I was ready to bare my soul to you... I mean, to treat you with respect.

AYTORE: Life is full of possibilities. For example, we have just had a long intimate talk, we've had dinner together and I even proposed a toast to you. But what if my wife had been alive and found us together? She would have got upset and tried to end her life. Would you think she was right?

ZEYNEP: God forbid! Can somebody really take their own life for that?

AYTORE: Well, do you see? That is exactly what once happened. I was walking home from work and I saw a woman sitting on a bench, holding a child. She was crying inconsolably. She was about thirty-five and seemed nice enough. I went up to her and asked her what the matter was. Apparently she had three children and her husband was working. Then suddenly her husband, to whom she had been loyally faithful, abandoned her and the children. And the day before that happened she'd received a telegram from Aktyubinsk informing her that her mother had died. She had no way of getting there and nobody to leave her children with for a few days, and so here she was, crying in the street out of humiliation and resentment. I offered her some money but she refused it point blank. So I offered to lend her the money and wrote out a receipt. Then I bought her a plane ticket so she could go to her mother's funeral. I even ended up looking after her children in her house until she got back to Almaty.

ZEYNEP: What happened after that?

AYTORE: When she got back she came and thanked me with tears in her eyes.

ZEYNEP: And then?

AYTORE: What happened next was the inevitable. Evidently someone told my wife about all this and she went into a fit of hysterics. That's when she tried to hang herself from this post.

ZEYNEP But what happened after that?

AYTORE: Nothing very interesting.

ZEYNEP: But that woman... what was your relationship to her after all this? How did it end up? Why are you standing there with that expression as though none of this is to do with you?

AYTORE: Well, we moved away... after my son was killed.

ZEYNEP: But you didn't move away that same day!

AYTORE: We were friendly, of course, before we went, and one day she even came to see us and brought the children.

ZEYNEP: And you haven't tried to find her while you're passing through now?

AYTORE: I tried. Apparently she died a year ago.

ZEYNEP: May she rest in peace...

AYTORE (*looks at his watch*): Oh-oh, I'm already late. Goodbye!

Aytore kisses her hand and goes out. Zeynep stands in the doorway and listens to his footsteps for a long time. She is alone again. It is pouring rain outside. Suddenly the outer door is flung open noisily and Ertay enters. He hurries into the living room almost at a run. His hangover has evidently worn off a little.

ERTAY: Where?

ZEYNEP: Who do you mean?

ERTAY: Where's that old guy?

ZEYNEP: What do you want him for?

ERTAY: I wanted to make his acquaintance.

ZEYNEP: He's gone. By the way, he was the previous tenant in this flat. He came to have a look at it.

ERTAY (*chuckles ironically*): You're wrong, Mama! He's not so crazy as to come here to admire his old flat.

ZEYNEP: Well it seems that such eccentrics do exist.

ERTAY: And you treat these eccentrics to dinner and wine?

ZEYNEP: Forgive me, son, that's how it finished up.

ERTAY: Don't worry, Mama. (*Suddenly embraces his mother with great warmth.*) It's been on my mind recently… You probably think we don't feel anything and can't apply our minds to anything, right? Well actually we do understand something. We understand completely. You… you lived only for our sake. You never thought about anything else.

ZEYNEP: Ertay, my boy, what are you talking about?

ERTAY: Don't you understand? In the last two days I've realised what I had never thought about before in all my twenty-five years.

Forgive me, Mama. Now I… Now we won't allow you to be hurt any more.

ZEYNEP: Where's your wife?

ERTAY: I don't know… I'm not… going back to her. She insulted me. She insulted all of us! From now on I'm going to take care of myself, Mama, and listen to you. You are so precious to me! There's nobody else on earth like you, Mama!

He hugs his mother and weeps. Zeynep strokes his wet hair and kisses his forehead.

ZEYNEP: And so does this mean you'll be marrying for the third time in your twenty-five years?

ERTAY: I don't know yet, Mama. Maybe I won't marry again. Whatever you say, that's what I'll do.

ZEYNEP: You what? What's this you're on about?

ERTAY: She said she didn't want to have the son of a beggar. She wants to marry someone else… They hit me – Rosa's brother and her husband to be…

ZEYNEP: What do you mean, they hit you? When I phoned, her mother said you were asleep.

ERTAY: No… I was unconscious.

ZEYNEP: A curse on the lot of them! (*Weeps*) And your big brother Bektur can't help – he's so far away.

ERTAY: I spoke to him yesterday. He's in Kholmsk on Sakhalin island. Bektur's coming back soon, Mama. He says he needs to come back to his homeland while he's still *compos mentis*. And after all, he's the captain of our ship! He'll sort out my offenders at a stroke. I will meet him myself and tell him everything.

The telephone rings. Zeynep answers.

AYTORE'S VOICE: My flight's about to take off. Have you heard from Ertay?

ZEYNEP: Yes I have.

AYTORE'S VOICE: Did he phone or has he come?

ZEYNEP: He's come.

AYTORE'S VOICE: I just wanted… We're boarding now, but I just wanted to hear your voice one more time.

ZEYNEP: I'm touched.

AYTORE'S VOICE: What's the matter? Your voice sounds strange somehow.

ZEYNEP: It's just… When did we ever know peace?

AYTORE'S VOICE: Well, goodbye! Be happy!

ZEYNEP: Safe journey.

Zeynep replaces the receiver on the hook. She does not move. She seems not to notice that she's crying.

ERTAY: Mama! Mother, my dear, what's the matter? Why are you crying?

He drops down before her on his knees. Zeynep pulls him back up onto his feet.

ZEYNEP (*angrily*): Get up! Don't you dare get down on your knees. Don't you ever go down on your knees for anyone!

ERTAY: But this is you, Mama! I was on my knees in front of you.

ZEYNEP: It makes no difference. You can respect someone without getting down on your knees.

ERTAY: I promised you, Mama, that I would act according to what is right. Just please don't cry. You've had a hard time with us and you must be tired. Well, from this moment on we are going to take care of you. We'll still find happiness, Mama! Sometime in the future we'll buy a plot of land outside town and build a big house with two floors. We'll live together. By then Bektur will be back from Sakhalin. He said in his last letter that he was sorry for having insulted you before he left. Let me read a few lines from his letter.

'Ertay, you're the youngest of the three of us, can you please try to explain the situation to Mama. I have offended her badly and will be guilty of this for the rest of my life. But if she will forgive me, I will come back. Out here I've got a big house of my own, by the sea. I could swap it for an apartment in Almaty. My wife has agreed to move, she realises that she was in the wrong before. We're changing our eldest son's name from Charles to Sharip and our daughter's name from Eleonora to Eligai. We speak our own Kazakh language at home. The children have just written their grandmother a letter. I'm enclosing it with this letter. Read it to Mama for me.'

(*Reads in a little girl's voice.*) 'Dear Grandma, we miss you so much! Why don't you come and visit us? All of us, papa, mama and us, are coming to see you in the summer. Love from Sharip and Eligai.'

Zeynep breaks into loud sobs and sinks onto the couch.

ERTAY: Mama, I wrote them a letter recently. It said: 'Mama forgave you long ago. She's very pleased that you've decided to move back to Almaty.' That's what I wrote. You don't mind that I did this by myself, do you, Mama? You won't get angry with me, will you? Promise?

ZEYNEP: Well why should I, son? You did exactly right. Clever boy! My clever little bundle of mischief!

The roar of an aircraft is heard passing directly over the house. It is as though Aytore's voice can be heard somewhere: 'Goodbye! Be happy…!'

ZEYNEP: Goodbye! Travel safely!

ERTAY: What? Who are you saying goodbye to, Mama?

ZEYNEP: Oh, nothing. I must have been deep in thought. Life is full of mysteries, my boy, and we're not able to turn away from them.

Ertay tenderly embraces his mother and lays his head on her shoulder.

THE END

DULAT ISSABEKOV
Holder of the State Prize of the Republic of Kazakhstan

The Monument

(A COMEDY IN TWO ACTS)

Alma-Ata, 1989.

Dramatis Personae

ASHTEN – a plumber
ZHANAIDAROV – First Secretary of the District Party Committee
ESIRPEKOV – Secretary of the District Party Committee
SATANOV – First Secretary of the Regional Party Committee
SALAKHOV – Sculptor
MASHANOV – Sculptor
KULYASH – Wife of Ashten

TWO INSTRUCTORS

KURMASH – Interpreter

Mr. CHARLTON & Mrs. CHARLTON – Members of an English Delegation
MR. CONRAD

JOURNALIST

GIRL IN WHITE DRESS
HER DANCING PARTNER
SERGEANT

PART ONE

Scene 1: *On the stage is a platform. On the platform an orator. We do not need to know who he is, but he is an inspired speaker. Every now and again recorded applause can be heard.*

The orator: Comrades! Nowadays we celebrate all manner of public holidays and events. We also need to celebrate anniversaries and key jubilees through our labour, modestly and without pomp. Today we are celebrating the 99th anniversary of our very own leather factory. The previous speakers recalled with pride the achievements of the last 99 years. Why have we assembled today in this hall? The reason, Comrades, is that we need to agree on how best to celebrate the centenary of our factory, which we shall be celebrating next year. (Pre-recorded cheering: "Here, here!", That's the way!") How ought we to conduct these celebrations? Surely not as noisily and grandly and with such loud cheers as in the past? You would surely agree? I have a proposal, Comrades. Our part of the world has been rich in livestock for as long as we can remember. Even before the Revolution it was famous for its herds. That is why the meat factory was built in our district. But where you have meat, you will have hides. We can't gobble up animals complete with hides and fleeces. We had to build a tanning factory. Of course, that took a long time and to start with a tanning workshop was built. That formed the basis for setting up a factory for treating leather and that was how the largest enterprise of its kind in our country was born. When celebrating the centenary of our factory we should not forget the trail-blazers, the very first tanners.

(*Enthusiastic applause*)

A journalist comes on to the platform.

JOURNALIST: I am from the district newspaper. I have been studying the history of this factory for a long time. I plan later to write a novel about the development of leather production in Kazakhstan. That's for the future. Now though, I want to turn your attention to the fact that in the last few years we have started forgetting the working man, started appreciating and respecting him less than in the past. Yet we ought to go down on bended knee before him. Who laid the foundations for this factory? Who ran the first workshop? Who was the first tanner? We need to find him and erect a monument to him in front of the factory!

Voice from the crowd: Comrade correspondent! The factory's a hundred years old. When the workshop opened, the first tanner would have been, let's say, twenty. Where are we going to go and find him now?

JOURNALIST: He who seeks shall always find. If we can't find the man himself, then we must at least honour his descendants. The working man must always be at the centre of attention, Comrades!

ZHANAIDAROV: Those in favour of erecting a monument to the first tanner, raise your hands. (*A forest of hands*)

Supported by an absolute majority. Now that's decided, the next thing is to get in touch with Alma-Ata, with the Union of Artists. We need to invite two sculptors out here, preferably the best available.

Voice from the crowd: It depends what kind of monument you want. If it's only a bust, then one should do.

ZHANAIDAROV: You have I'm sure seen the kind of monuments erected to actors or writers: they're depicted sitting or standing and sometimes even reclining on their side. But I don't think it would be proper to cut off a working man's lower half.

Voice from the crowd: For sure! No scrimping on our simple working man!

ZHANAIDAROV: The vote was unanimous. I now declare the meeting closed. All we need do now is wait for the sculptors from Alma-Ata.

Scene 2: *Zhanaidarov's office. Enter the head of his Ideology Department, Esirkepov.*

ESIRKEPOV: I have good news for you, Comrade Zhanaidarov!

ZHANAIDAROV: You have? Out with it then!

ESIRKEPOV: The long-awaited sculptors from Alma-Ata have arrived. They're waiting in reception.

ZHANAIDAROV: Well done, Esirkepov! Since you've been with us, ideology here in the district has been on the up and up. Call them in!

Two men enter. They have deep-set eyes like burnt holes in a blanket. Both have beards. One has hair pulled back in a plait. The other has a shaven head. Zhanadairov winces at the sight of them.

The new arrivals shake hands and then place their hands on their heart in greeting. They introduce themselves.

SALAKHOV: Boris Salakkhov.

MASHANOV: Timur Mashanov.

ZHANAIDAROV: Prior to now... have you been... in sculpture?

SALAKHOV: Of course. Our work graces many a collective- or state-farm office.

ZHANAIDAROV: Well done! Who have you depicted already... or should I say sculpted?

MASHANOV: Chickens, camels, cows, pigs, sheep... you name it.

ZHANAIDAROV: M-m... and what were your rates?

SALAKHOV: On average 20-25 roubles for a chicken.

ZHANAIDAROV: Twenty-five roubles for just one chicken?

SALAKHOV: On average.

ZHANAIDAROV: But my friends, for 25 roubles you can buy 5 live chickens!

SALAKHOV: Here we're talking works of art, which can't be measured in terms of money!

ZHANAIDAROV: It's expensive!

ESIRKEPOV: And how much is a man worth?

MASHANOV: Nothing. When it comes to sculpture though, that's expensive of course.

ESIRKEPOV: On average, how much?

SALAKHOV: If the individual is of only local as opposed to international importance, then we could agree to create such a sculpture for 50,000.

ZHANAIDAROV: Fifty thousand?! Esirkepov, have you got a heart pill with you? (*He places it beneath his tongue*). That's the monthly income of a whole collective farm!

ESIRKEPOV: Can't you do it any cheaper?

MASHANOV: As it is, we're charging you our cheapest rate.

ZHANAIDAROV: This monument is just what we need!... Fifty thousand for a wretched tanner! They're not taking us for a ride are they, Esirkepov?

ESIRKEPOV: What can we do? The people has decided. Everyone knows about it.

ZHANAIDAROV: The people, the people!... What have they got to do with it? They'll make a noise for a bit, but then they'll calm down! They know about it in the Regional Committee?! (*Turning to the sculptors*). All right, that's settled. When will it be ready? (*To Esirkepov*) When do we need it by?

ESIRKEPOV: For the autumn, for October 24th – the centenary of the factory. Will it be ready by then?

MASHANOV: Definitely.

SALAKHOV: No problem.

ZHANAIDAROV: Off you go then. (*Pointing to Esirkepov*) He's got the contract.

MASHANOV: We have to settle some aesthetic questions. How d'you want the sculpture to look? Just a worker cast in bronze, standing still or engaged in the creative process of tanning leather? Do you need a portrait likeness? Of someone still alive among his descendants? If there are any of course? Incidentally, what was his name? What did he look like? When was he born and when did he die? And so on...

ZHANAIDAROV: Put all those questions to him, to Comrade Esirkepov? You can all go now.

They leave.

Scene 3: *The House of Culture in the local town. One of its spacious rooms has been turned into a workshop for the sculptors. Near a large window a thin ordinary-looking man is standing on a raised platform– motionless and holding above his head the skin of a sheep of the Edilbaev breed. The sculptors are hurrying to complete their first rough model.*

SALAKHOV: You wretch, we wore ourselves out looking for you. It turns out that you live right here, under the very nose of the District Party Committee. It was lucky at least that Home

Maintenance Team No. 2 remembered that you work for them as a plumber.

MASHANOV: Who'd have thought it The grandson of the first tanner – the founder of leather production in Kazakhstan – is a plumber! So is it true that your grandfather was called Melden Zheldybaev and that you're the spitting image of him? Are you sure you didn't make all that up?

ASHTEN: Not a word of it. I remember everything just as my father told it me.

MASHANOV: So we're using you as a model for your grandfather's portrait. D'you at least realize that you're going to go down in history now?

SALAKHOV: Yes, you're a lucky fellow Ashten! If it wasn't for us, nobody would have known about the sozzled plumber, who crawls about in cellars, drinking himself silly?... Don't put your arms down! That's right, hold them up like that! You mustn't just stand there, but look at the skin as if you can't take your eyes off it. That's more like it! And don't sway from side to side!

(He pours some wine into a glass and hands it to Ashten, who downs it in one and then 'freezes' in his majestic pose).

MASHANOV: You, Ashten Zheldybaev, are now the most famous man in the District, d'you realize that? They're talking about you everywhere and about nothing else. "Prototype! Life model! They're making a statue of him!"

SALAKHOV: "A real character!" is what they're saying. And yesterday I was the first to entrust a mission to the two Party instructors: "Make sure that Ashten does not have to queue for booze and for as long as the work lasts is issued with vodka from the District Committee canteen on the basis of a bottle every second day. So that no-one should suspect what's going on, the vodka must be poured into a bottle labelled "Sary-Agach Mineral Water". You see what a privileged person you are now, thanks to us! I wouldn't be surprised if tomorrow you weren't made President of the USA, dear Mr. Plumber! But tell me, if the Americans were to summon you one day, bring you to the White House and say: "Rule America, Ashten, you can be our President" - would you agree?

ASHTEN: Why not? Ruling a country's a piece of cake. Of course, I'd agree.

SALAKHOV: You're a cheeky fellow, there's no denying it, but that's why I warm to you. That's the spirit, Ashten! Only your right arm's come down. Lift it up again! Or would you like another glass of "Talas" wine, Comrade President?

ASHTEN: I'm only standing here doing nothing. Pour away.

MASHANOV: I appreciate people with no inhibitions, no complexes. Come on then, life model, old chap. It makes me happy to drink with you.

SALAKHOV: Come on then, Monument, grow and reach for the sky! (*They drink*).

MASHANOV: And what a welcome they gave you yesterday in the wine shop. The queue let you go to the front and the women started making eyes at you. The one who reeked of onions couldn't take her eyes off you. That look of hers was saying: "My love, my sunshine, Ashten! I've been looking for you my whole life long, where have you been hiding? What happiness to see you come out of your cellar and do us the honour of standing in one and the same queue for red wine! At last I've found you and I'm never going to let you go. Oh my real live monument! Did you notice her deep brown eyes?

ASHTEN: You mean the one with an Elastoplast on her forehead?

MASHANOV: That's the one, so you noticed her?

SALAKHOV: By the way, didn't she whisper something into your ear? When you failed to melt from her fiery breath? Probably a declaration of love? Come now, out with it!

ASHTEN: She asked if I'd share the price of a bottle of vodka

with her and another person...

MASHTANOV: Very right and proper. A woman's never the first to declare herself. "Let's share a bottle" – that's how it all begins.

(*Ashten throws the skin to one side*).

SALAKHOV: Oi, Ashten, what's the matter with you? Why did you drop the skin?

ASHTEN: And why are you taking the mickey? I'm going to ring the District Committee. I've had enough of your monument.

(*Both the sculptors rush over to dissuade him*).

MASHANOV: Come now Ashten, think again! Nobody's taking the mickey. You just thought they were. There's no need to ring the District Committee or to give up on the monument. If you're not careful, the spirits of your ancestor will be angry with you. Calm down, you're just tired. We're tired too. Let's down another drink and the three of us can take it easy.

(*He thrusts a glass at Ashten*)

ASHTEN: All right then – for the sake of the ancestors.

SALAKHOV: Now you're behaving like someone who respects the spirits of his ancestors!

MASHANOV: After all, we've got quite a lot to show for today's work. (*He unfolds the canvas, on which Ashten can be seen lifting up the skin*). If your grandad were to come back to life now, he'd have fallen down dead again, struck by the likeness.

ASHTEN: People who've seen him say that he was just like me, an exact copy.

SALAKHOV: Excuse me, of course, but perhaps it should be the other way round, with him as the original and you as the copy. After all he was a hundred years older than you.

ASHTEN: Perhaps you're right. (*Outside the workshop, music can be heard*) What's that music?

MASHANOV: All round here people are practising for the centenary. Girls and young fellows from the factory are learning ballroom dances.

ASHTEN: (*smiling*) Ballroom dances. I just love ballroom dancing. (*He grabs the sheep-skin, spins round in a dance and disappears outside the door with it*)

SALAKHOV: Listen, that's our model vanishing!

MASHANOV: He mustn't cause any trouble (*They rush into the adjoining hall, but Ashten has already made 'trouble': after wrapping the sheep-skin round the shoulders of a girl in a white dress, he grabs her waist and starts spinning her round. She starts squealing and soon the scene in the hall is one of shouting and confusion*)

ASHTEN: My lovely, I've been looking for you all my life... D'you know who is standing before you? None other than Ashten Zheldybaev who provides the real-life model for the monument in honour of his grandfather.

THE GIRL: Lout! Drunken swine. Help! (*Her dancing partner comes to the rescue*)

DANCING PARTNER: Where have you sprung from, you wretch?

ASHTEN: I'm no wretch, I'm a monument... or rather its model.

THE MONUMENT

DANCING PARTNER: A right model you are! How long ago did you escape from the madhouse? (*The girls run off squealing. Soon the siren of a militia vehicle can be heard*)

ASHTEN: Who's escaped from the madhouse? You don't mean me? You won't get away with that!... (*He grabs the young man by his lapels and the sculptors rush over to try and separate them*)

MASHANOV: Lads, go easy on him, we're to blame. We'll take him off to the workshop now. Ashten, come on. We can dance back in there. Come on!

ASHTEN: But I want to dance here!... (*Enter two militia-men*)

SALAKHOV: You've ruined everything, Ashten. You'll be our undoing.

MASHANOV: A fortnight in the cooler. How can we get the work done without him. What can we say to the District Committee?

* * *

At the militia station. After making Ashten sit down, a sergeant draws up a report prior to taking Ashten into custody for a fortnight for drunk and disorderly behaviour.

SERGEANT: Your name and surname?

ASHTEN: Ashten... Zheldybaev...

SERGEANT: Year of your birth?

ASHTEN: 1965.

SERGEANT: Where d'you work and what as?

ASHTEN: As a plumber for Home Maintenance Team No. 2.

SERGEANT: Ethnic category?

ASHTEN: Kazakh.

SERGEANT: (*under his breath*) You'd be better off dead than a Kazakh like that! People like you should be swept off the face of the earth.

ASHTEN: Don't you dare insult me like that... D'you know... Do you know who you're talking to?

SERGEANT: We're used to people like you... Genghis Khan.

ASHTEN: No, I'm not... Genghis Khan... I'm...

SERGEANT: All right, all right. Just sign here.

ASHTEN: For what?

SERGEANT: For disturbing the peace and confirming that everything's been reported properly.

ASHTEN: I wasn't disturbing the peace...! (*He puts his hand out to pick up the telephone and almost falls over*) I want to phone the District Committee... Can I?

SERGEANT: You're sure you don't need the UN? Pérez de Cuéllar is probably at home, waiting for your call.

ASHTEN: Yes... I mean it... I need to ring the District Committee (*He stretches out his hand towards the receiver and almost falls over*).

SERGEANT: We'll hear what they have to say. That'll be a laugh!

(*Ashten totters over to the telephone and dials the number*)

ASHTEN: Hallo... Hallo... Is that the District Committee? The duty officer? It's me... Ashten... Zheldybaev, yes... The very one... the monument... or rather its model. Me... they want to lock me

THE MONUMENT

up. Yes... for a fortnight... (*He turns to the Sergeant*). The address? What's the address of the station?

SERGEANT: The district station. Every idiot knows where it is.

ASHTEN: The district militia station. Every idiot knows. All right. (*After putting down the receiver, he walks over to an armchair and settles down into it*). Genghis Khan...this'll learn you.

SERGEANT: Did you really ring the District Committee?

ASHTEN: You've made a habit of not believing people... Now you'll see if I was joking or not... Tomorrow you'll be kicked out of here...

head over heels. You'd better be careful who you mess with.

(*A car draws up outside. The duty-officer from the District Committee comes in and shows his badge. Then he heaves Ashten up by the armpits and leads him out*).

SERGEANT: (*Almost in tears*) Why, O why did I get tied up with him... my poor head (*He looks out of the window*). He's getting into a black Volga and the number's a District Committee one. We're done for!

* * *

Office of the First Secretary of the District Party Committee, Zhanaidarov. A meeting is in progress.

ZHANAIDAROV: Comrades! The monument was not ready by October 24th. We wrote to the Regional Committee and assured them that it would be ready by the November holiday. That deadline was not met either. We swore we would erect the monument by the New Year, but once again failed to keep our word. The Regional Committee was beside itself with rage. On one occasion our office was even inspected and I personally was carpeted. So, Comrade Esirkepov, please report on the true state of affairs regarding the monument as of now!

ESIRKEPOV: It's finished, First Secretary, quite finished.

ZHANAIDAROV: If it's finished, why isn't it standing in front of the factory?

ESIRKEPOV: Everything's finished. It's just that the monument's eyes and one of its ears aren't finished. We'll need to wait another little week.

ZHANAIDAROV: (*Red in the face by now*) My dear fellow, surely they don't need a whole week just to make two holes for eyes and stick on an ear?...

ESIRKEPOV: It's creative labour... not something you can hurry over.

ZHANAIDAROV: Just you listen to me... What's difficult about that? If it was only a question of eyes, I'd make the holes myself. Or even you can go and do it!

ESIRKEPOV: But there has to be a complete match with the original, otherwise it's no good.

ZHANAIDAROV: Make them match then! Where is he... whatshisname?

ESIRKEPOV: Ashten Zheldybaev.

ZHANAIDAROV: That's right, Zheldybaev. Surely it's not a problem transferring those goggle-eyes of his to the monument? Or is there something special about them? Perhaps his ears stick out at a strange angle?

ESIRKEPOV: No there's nothing special or difficult about it, but...

ZHANAIDAROV: But what?

ESIRKEPOV: But he's stopped opening his eyes. He's drinking himself silly on "Sary-Agach Mineral Water" and sleeping. Round the clock.

ZHANAIDAROV: Drunk on nothing but mineral water?! Oh yes…

ESIRKEPOV: He hasn't opened his eyes for a whole week now.

ZHANAIDAROV: Give him a shake, then wake him up! At least get working on the ear in the meantime. I doubt if he's hiding his ear under his pillow? What kind of artists are they, if they can't even fashion his eyes from memory? They must have seen those eyes a thousand times!

ESIRKEPOV: They peered into them endlessly…

ZHANAIDAROV: That's it then! There's no time to lose. I want them to finish them off today. (*The telephone rings*)

Yes, it's First Secretary Zhanaidarov on the line (*Suddenly all his self-importance vanishes: he is completely taken aback, starts to cringe and looks as if he's about to crawl into the receiver. The call is from the First Secretary of the Regional Party Committee*)

Good day to you, Tursun Satanovich! How is your health, how are you feeling? I heard you'd caught a cold – a cold they told me – how are you feeling now? Have you shaken it off? It's very unreliable weather, not really spring, but not summer either. Make sure you take precautions. Against what? Against draughts, of course, what else. People need you, local people, who themselves selected you as a candidate for a People's Deputy. Congratulations, by the way. Of course, you'll get through, beyond any doubt. As for that other alternative candidate, the tractor-driver – what's she getting involved for? She ought to know better than to challenge you! What are you saying? She refused to stand down as a candidate? Such an obstinate woman. Things have gone too far with this democracy lark, we're all going to the dogs! Surely she knows who she's up against! What would she be able to do, even if she was elected as a deputy? If she'd realized that, she would have driven off on her tractor into the steppe to do what she's good at. Of course, we're worried too... What did you say? The monument? How could I possibly forget the monument?! It's well worth it. Yes, by now. It's really majestic, on a pedestal. Right in front of the leather factory, yes. Fine. It looks fine. Everyone's praising it. We hadn't got round to telephoning you, that's all. We're very sorry about that of course. Wha-at? What's that you're saying? Visitors coming here to the District? And you're coming too? But of course, that's wonderful. We'll be very happy to see you. Foreign visitors? Where from? From England? What a great honour for us, we're looking forward to it... God help us and preserve us!...

(*He goes on holding the now silent receiver for a long time and has obvious difficulty recovering from the shock*)

That's definitely what people would call divine revenge!

Who would have thought it! Why couldn't those wretched Englishmen sit quietly at home?! They have to go poking their noses left, right and centre, even deciding to have a look at our god-forsaken backwater. We sit around here for hundreds of years and can't even get as far as Alma-Ata, let alone England!...

(*He gets us from his chair and starts pacing agitatedly up and down his office*)

ESIRKEPOV: What's up? Is everything quiet?

ZHANAIDAROV: What d'you mean "quiet"!? Your bureaucracy and relaxed way of doing things may cost me my life! You heard with your own ears that I had to lie and say the monument was ready. I couldn't ask for a further delay because of one ear and two

THE MONUMENT

eyes missing from that statue. What shall we do? Representatives of a leather factory from England are coming out here and the First Secretary of the Regional Committee himself is accompanying them. They'll be here this evening. In the morning they intend to visit the factory and have a look at the monument. What do you have in mind?

FIRST INSTRUCTOR: What if we were to say that at night some riffraff destroyed or damaged the monument?

ZHANAIDAROV: That's a load of rubbish. They'd say we had to catch the criminal and who could you go out and catch?

SECOND INSTRUCTOR: Why not let it stand there with one ear? After all Venus de Milo has survived for centuries with both arms missing.

ZHANAIDAROV: But the eyes, the eyes, what are we going to do about those? Your Venus can stand about for as long as it takes without arms. But if a tanner has lost both eyes, how is he going to tan leather? That ruse is not going to work. Has anyone else got any suggestions?

FIRST INSTRUCTOR: This god-forsaken rain goes on and on just making things worse. It's been pouring for days and won't stop...

ZHANAIDAROV: What's rain got to do with it?

SECOND INSTRUCTOR: I support the idea. How long are the English going to linger by the monument? I reckon ten minutes or at the most twenty. And we, for our part, will hurry them along. We'll invite them up into the mountains, to admire exotic scenery. Europeans are mad about anything exotic: they're ready to forget about food and drink as they rush after it. So, let Ashten stand there on the pedestal for twenty minutes, just as he is – the real-life model. It's not for nothing we've been letting him wallow in vodka the last six months. Nothing's going to happen to him in that short time. Then we'll lead the delegation away and he'll jump down from the pedestal and walk quietly back home.

FIRST INSTRUCTOR: (*laughing*) He might not jump down, but stay up there. He's not in any hurry to do anything. If push comes to shove, we can hire another plumber to take his place (*Laughter is heard in the background*)

ZHANAIDAROV: Comrades, stop laughing. This is no laughing matter. Who has got any ideas?

FIRST INSTRUCTOR: There's no need to wrack our brains. We need to adopt the idea already proposed. We have no other choice.

ZHANAIDAROV: All right. Let's say that we've accepted the proposal and put Ashten himself on the pedestal. But he's not a statue, he's a real live person. What's going to happen if he suddenly starts coughing or sneezing when the English delegation is there… then what?

FIRST INSTRUCTOR: He won't cough!

SECOND INSTRUCTOR: He won't sneeze!

FIRST INSTRUCTOR: We shan't let it happen!

ZHANAIDAROV: What d'you mean – shan't let it happen! What are you going to do – block his mouth and nose? And everything else?!

SECOND INSTRUCTOR: Leave all that to us. We shall take steps to ensure that he won't let anyone down or put our country to shame in front of the outside world.

ZHANAIDAROV: Well… I'll put it to the vote. Who is in favour of placing Citizen Ashten on the pedestal in front of the leather factory on a temporary basis before the foreign delegation leaves, in

THE MONUMENT

other words of using a live model instead of the sculpture currently being worked on? Would they please raise their hands. (*Everyone raises their hands all together*) Count the votes, Esirkepov.

ESIRKEPOV: (*After counting*). The results of the vote are as follows: one against, two abstentions and seven in favour.

ZHANAIDAROV: So, the proposal has been accepted by a majority of the voters. So Comrades, it has been duly decided by the District Party Committee that the plumber from Home Maintenance Team_No. 2, Ashten Zheldybaev, who has been providing the model for the statue of the first tanner, Melden Zheldybaev, must stand in person for half an hour on the pedestal in front of the leather factory. This question has now been resolved and we can all go our separate ways. (*All those present rise from their seats*).

ESIRKEPOV: Ashten is sleeping at the moment. According to his wife he opens his eyes at the end of the television news programme "Time", has a drink from his "Sary-agach" bottle and then goes back to sleep again. We need to make sure that at that particular moment two or three of our people are near him, so as to explain to him the task he has been set by the District Committee. It has to be done very carefully though, as if you were pulling a hair out of rising dough.

ZHANAIDAROV: Who's going to go and see him?

SECOND INSTRUCTOR: We'll go. We're ready for anything to promote the prestige of our Party and People. The people and Party are united as one!

ZHANAIDAROV: Well done! A party which has soldiers like you, can face up to any problem! Let's get started! (*They all set off in different directions*)

* * *

Ashten's flat. He's lying on his bed dead drunk. A bottle of "Sary-agach Mineral Water" is standing on the bedside table. His wife Kulyash is giving him a piece of her mind.

KULYASH: To Hell with that monument of yours. It wasn't enough that you used to come home drunk out of your mind, now you're in on the act with those – what d'you call them – sculptors and with the backing of the District Committee, what's more! At first they at least only gave you a bottle every other day, but now there's one delivered every god-given day! It's a wretched business the way they're deliberately turning you into a drunk!

ASHTEN: A white dance, a ballroom dance!... The girl in a white dress... You... you will be mine! Oh what a ball!

KULYASH: Ballroom dancing is the last thing you need! The girl in the white dress can't do without you! She wouldn't look twice at a drunk like you!

ASHTEN: Ballroom dancing, how I love it!... White shoulders, little white hands on my shoulders! Soon they'll be twined round my neck! Don't joke with me: I kicked a militia-man out into the world without his uniform... Oh, how I love ballroom dancing...!

KULYASH: Stop ranting. You'll wake the children. They've got nothing to wear and winter's only just round the corner. They're running round barefoot and you couldn't care less. We're reduced to bread and water and you just lie there in a drunken heap... (*Sniffing*). What kind of God let me run into you?

ASHTEN: Let's go dancing!...

KULYASH: Oh Ashten! Zheldybaev! Open your eyes and ears, listen to what I'm going to say. "Run from a husband who's useless, just like a tree that's shadeless", as the saying goes. I'm taking the children and leaving – d'you understand? I'm leaving this house for good. You can stay here, drinking yourself silly, till you really do turn into a statue! (*A knock at the door*)

Come in, the door's not locked!

(*The two Instructors from the District Committee walk in*)

FIRST INSTRUCTOR: Greetings, dearie!

SECOND INSTRUCTOR: Good evening! So Ashten's home... We're in luck! (*in a cautious voice*) Greetings... In we come...

ASHTEN: Let's go dancing!

KULYASH: Don't pay any attention. For sometime now he's been talking nonsense. Excuse me though, who might **you** be?

FIRST INSTRUCTOR: We are from the official staff of the District Party Committee. Here's our ID (*He shows her their documents*)

KULYASH: There's no need for all that. I believe you. Forgive me, it's not very tidy round here... I'll lay the table right away...

SECOND INSTRUCTOR: Don't you worry, dearie. We haven't got time to linger. We have to discuss some urgent business with Ashten in private.

KULYASH: Go ahead and try if you can. He's drunk out of his mind. (*She walks out*)

FIRST INSTRUCTOR: Oh Ashten, what a state you're in!

ASHTEN: Let's go dancing!... The girl in the white dress...

SECOND INSTRUCTOR: Ashten Zheldybaev! Lift up your head! We've come to you from the District Committee!...

ASHTEN: Go to **He-e-ll**!

FIRST INSTRUCTOR: Come now, Ashten, calm down! The First Secretary of the District Committee sends you his greetings…

ASHTEN: He can go to Hell too!

SECOND INSTRUCTOR: (*in a scared voice*). Come now, come now, Ashten! How could you send our District leader that far? You might end up with the militia on your heels!

ASHTEN: The militia? D'you think I care? Don't you start joking with me!

FIRST INSTRUCTOR: No-one has the slightest intention of joking with you, Ashten. We've come to see you about a decision taken by the Bureau of the District Committee (*Ashten raises his head in surprise*).

ASHTEN: The Bureau? But I'm not a party member. Why have they sent you to see me?

SECOND INSTRUCTOR: You must understand, Ashten… A very serious situation has come about. An unexpected foreign delegation is coming here.

ASHTEN: What's that to me? Let them come.

FIRST INSTRUCTOR: They're coming to look at the monument.

ASHTEN: Let them look, if they must.

SECOND INSTRUCTOR: How can they look at a monument, if there isn't one?

ASHTEN: How should I know?

FIRST INSTRUCTOR: Ashten, may you be blessed for seven generations to come, but just respect this one request of ours and comply with it.

THE MONUMENT

ASHTEN: What request?

SECOND INSTRUCTOR: We should say the Bureau's decision perhaps and this is what it involves: while the visitors from England are being shown round the compound of the leather factory complete with statue and because it – that is the statue – is not finished, it is required that Ashten **Zheldybaev** should stand on the pedestal for half an hour…

ASHTEN: Wha-a-at?

FIRST INSTRUCTOR: Calm down now, Ashten! You must understand: there's no other way out. You're our only hope, you're the only one who can save the honour of socialism from the jaws of capitalism!

SECOND INSTRUCTOR: In the name of our whole system you are entrusted with this task. The authority of the socialist camp is at stake.

ASHTEN: Camp? You want to send me away to a Camp for Re-education through Labour? You know what you can do with that idea…! My head's splitting!

FIRST INSTRUCTOR: Your head you say?! That's a trifling matter for us… Just a moment (*He takes a bottle of "Sary-Agach" out of his brief-case, uncorks it and pours some into a glass*).

Here you are, down it in one! (*Ashten throws back the contents, sniffs at his clenched fist and collapses straight back on to the bed*)

ASHTEN: Let's go dancing!… Oh, the girl in the white…

SECOND INSTRUCTOR: So you liked the girl in the white dress, Ashten? The one who was dancing the other day…? Take it as read that she's yours, that she'll soon be twined round your neck?

ASHTEN: When?

217

SECOND INSTRUCTOR: Any time. You just say the word. If the District Committee takes a decision, all she can do is go along with it. She'll come along and she'll twine…

ASHTEN: Re-e-ally?

SECOND INSTRUCTOR: The District Committee never disappoints.

ASHTEN: Done! I'm ready to stand there not just for half an hour but for a whole hour… just as long as she… But remember, not a minute longer! As soon as the hour's over, I'm not going to take any notice of your District Committee or the girl in white. I'll just jump down and make off home. D'you get me?

FIRST INSTRUCTOR: (*preventing Ashten from saying any more*). Of course, Ashten, rest assured! You stand there for your half-hour and then off you go, wherever you like… that is, back home of course. May we rot in hell, if we ever reproach you for anything after this!

SECOND INSTRUCTOR: At this rate you'll soon be the First Secretary of the Regional Committee yourself!

ASHTEN: What of it? He's a Secretary in his own eyes and for you, but not me. If he's so clever and forbidding, why did he fail to sort out just one monument and then make a mockery of a live human being? Who needs a leader like that, eh?

FIRST INSTRUCTOR: Come now Ashten, you shouldn't even say things like that! He doesn't even know about all this!

ASHTEN: Oh, let's go dancing! My lovely, the girl in white!… For your sake, my beauty, only for you did I say Yes…

SECOND INSTRUCTOR: Thank you, Ashten… We declare our gratitude to you for not letting the Party down.

THE MONUMENT

FIRST INSTRUCTOR: Perhaps a monument will be erected to your very own self one day.

ASHTEN: Oh, let's go dancing!...

* * *

A large hall in a hotel. It may once have been Zhanaidarov's office. A reception is being held for the English delegation. Satanov, the First Secretary of the Regional Committee, is addressing the assembled company, Leaders of the District Party Committee are also present.

SATANOV: Dear Comrades! Dear guests from England! In the endless expanses of our country you will not find a single spot where culture does not flourish and where the people's prosperity does not go from strength to strength. We are extremely glad that from the whole garden of plenty that is our Homeland you have chosen this very spot for your visit. During the three days of your tour you will acquaint yourselves with the life and customs of our people, with the conditions in which they work. In a short time our people has achieved great feats, hitherto unknown. In the past there was nothing here, empty clay-pans and bare steppes. But now, as you can see, a splendid modern city has grown up.

Here in our region as well as the Kazakhs there are representatives of 130 other peoples and ethnic communities living and working side by side with each other in peace and friendship, like children of one happy family. As a symbol of the great solidarity of the people, one of our factories last year started producing a special sausage containing meat from sheep, goats, cows, horses, pigs, chickens and camels. It was named "Friendship Sausage" and this evening you will be able to try some for yourselves.

MRS. CHATLTON: Ooh! Fantastic!

SATANOV: You've said it. Our very life out here borders on the fantastic. By way of conclusion, I should like to add…

ESIRKEPOV: Excuse me, I have a small announcement to make. Some changes have been made in our programme. Dear guests, we shall be showing you the statue of our first tanner this evening after supper and not tomorrow afternoon as had originally been planned. That is because tomorrow we have to set off to the mountains early in the morning to a gathering of shepherds. Knowing how the English love horses, it has been decided to organize a special *baiga* or race in honour of our guests.

DELEGATION MEMBERS: Amazing! First rate! OK!

ESIRKEPOV: As for the monument, this is how we shall proceed: before we set off, each of you will be given an album of photographs taken from various angles. The photographs are unique because this is the world's first monument erected to the Unknown Tanner. Indeed such a thing is only possible in socialist society and could never have occurred in the capitalist world. This makes us proud.

We shall now call on the leader of the English delegation, Mr. Charlton, to speak next. He heads the foreign relations department of the English leather company "Seven Hides", Mr. Charlton.

MR. CHARLTON: We have been given a very warm welcome in the land of Kazakhstan and enjoyed an unprecedented level of hospitality. We have been delighted to experience the modest diligence of Soviet men and women, the sincere friendship extended to us, to all members of the English delegation. My wife and I, your guests from England, wish to express our profound gratitude for the honours and respect shown to us (*Applause*). We are particularly impressed by the care shown by the Soviet leaders to modest working people, by their love of history and the advancement of the arts. Long live humanism! Long live progress! (*Applause*)

SATANOV: So my friends, in half an hour we shall have dinner in the banquet hall of this hotel and then after dinner we shall show

THE MONUMENT

you a local attraction – the monument to the first tanner in the region. (*Members of the delegation leave the hall*)

Esirkepov! Why has there been a change in the programme?

ESIRKEPOV: But I explained why, Comrade Satanov, otherwise we won't get to the shepherds' feast in time. And in addition - as you yourself know - there's nothing to regale foreign visitors with here in our town.

SATANOV: What about your celebrated "Friendship Sausage"?

ESIRKEPOV: We've got it ready, but it would be embarrassing to give our visitors just sausage.

SATANOV: At responsible moments like these, everything ought to be discussed and organized in advance, down to the very last detail.

ESIRKEPOV: That was duly done, Comrade Satanov. It's just that we didn't have time to inform you of everything.

SATANOV: Just you look out, Esirkepov. On your head be it!

ESIRKEPOV: All will be in order! (*He takes the Instructors over to one side*). Go straight to Ashten and warn him about the change in the programme. The English visitors are going to have to view the monument at night. In daylight they might have noticed that it was a real live person. Look, we're in luck, a sleet shower's just begun. Perhaps we'll pull it off! Hurry round to Ashten now!

SECOND INSTRUCTOR: All will be in order (*The Instructors exit quickly*)

ESIRKEPOV: Allah, you must save us! The last thing I want is an official reprimand over this monument!

SATANOV: Comrade Secretary, you don't mean to say you're praying? What kind of communist can you be after that?

ESIRKEPOV: Comrade First Secretary, sometimes even a communist can be in need of God. As they say – someone, somewhere, some time. I've never had to welcome such important guests before and that's making me pray to the Almighty to ensure that everything goes smoothly.

SATANOV: All right… We must prove to the world, at every step of the way, that our socialist order is superior. Let's join the guests.

ESIRKEPOV: Yes, it's time (*They leave*)

* * *

Ashten's flat. He and his wife are having supper. Enter the First and Second Instructor from the District Committee.

FIRST INSTRUCTOR: Ashten, you're having supper, I see. Enjoy your meal.

ASHTEN: Thank you. Do sit down. Why have you come round at such an inconvenient time? Has something happened? Or is everything quiet and calm?

SECOND INSTRUCTOR: If everything was quiet and calm, we wouldn't be running round here with our tongues hanging out. Urgent instructions from the District Committee.

KULYASH: Perhaps you've failed to fix up Ashten with a second wife, the girl in the white dress?

FIRST INSTRUCTOR: Don't be offended at us, my love. In politics you have strategy and you have tactics. That was a tactical move on our part.

ASHTEN: What, so tactics in Kazakh means – con trick?

SECOND INSTRUCTOR: Come now, Ashten… Tactics is when there is a change in the means of achieving a goal.

ASHTEN: Don't you pull the wool over my eyes. Where are those rogues – the sculptors?

SECOND INSTRUCTOR: They should be here any moment. They've already done the eyes. That only leaves the ear.

ASHTEN: So what d'you want from me?

SECOND INSTRUCTOR: You see, Ashten. There have been unexpected changes in the programme. The English delegation has decided to set off early tomorrow morning to a shepherds' gathering. That's why they want to see the monument today, literally in half an hour's time.

ASHTEN: But it's snowing. I'll freeze to death.

FIRST INSTRUCTOR: Just dress up warmly.

ASHTEN: No, I'm not going.

SECOND INSTRUCTOR: Ashten, what does this mean? Surely you don't want to put socialism to shame in front of the capitalists? That would be a political error on your part.

ASHTEN: Are you going to arrest me? Send me to the camps?

FIRST INSTRUCTOR: These last few days you've started using dangerous language. I think these sculptors have been having a bad influence on you…

ASHTEN: Why d'you keep nagging me? Surely with the whole district to choose from you could have found somebody else. And if you want to demonstrate the advantages of socialism, you could have got up on the pedestal yourselves?!

SECOND INSTRUCTOR: But you're the model… the prototype!

ASHTEN: Surely it's all the same to the Englishmen, who they stare at?

FIRST INSTRUCTOR: You shouldn't talk like that, Ashten. You are the descendant of your famous ancestor, Melden Zheldybaev – a worthy descendant, who is the model for the monument. We could stand there, of course, but the Secretary of the Regional Committee might recognize us.

SECOND INSTRUCTOR: Then again, it's better to stand there at night, than to have to stick around in the daytime. You haven't considered the moral and psychological advantages of the nocturnal setting. So I would advise you…

ASHTEN: All right, you've brought me round. But the rate for a call-out at night is higher.

FIRST INSTRUCTOR: (*hands Ashten an envelope*) Three ……..

ASHTEN: Three thousand.

SECOND INSTRUCTOR: Three hundred.

ASHTEN: Isn't that on the mean side? (*He pulls on his trousers*).

FIRST INSTRUCTOR: Have you no shame, Ashten? When you come down from that pedestal, you'll get another three hundred. Six hundred roubles for a mere half-hour. That's six months' wages for you, Comrade plumber! (*Ashten who had already put one leg into the trousers, starts taking them off…*)

SECOND INSTRUCTOR: (*grabbing Ashten's trouser leg*) Come now, Ashten (*He prods him in the side to make him laugh…*) You were just joking weren't you? Tell me you were!

THE MONUMENT

FIRST INSTRUCTOR: Of course he was joking. I don't even know how those words could have possibly tripped off his tongue. I humbly beg you, please forgive me (*He bows down low, but without concealing his disdain*)

ASHTEN: That's more like it! (*He puts on a padded jacket and pulls on his boots. The Instructors take hold of his arms and lead him forth like a bride*)

KULYASH: (*calling after him*) Look out or else you might really turn into a statue!

ASHTEN: (*calling back to her*) Off I go ! Don't get involved in Party affairs! Women shouldn't meddle in politics!... (*They leave the stage*)

KULYASH: Oh, Allah, what's got into him? He wasn't like that in the old days... (*She is almost in tears*)

End of PART ONE

PART TWO

A square in front of the factory. A light wind is blowing and snow is falling. Ashten is lit up by projectors and holding a skin in his proudly raised arms. The English delegation and Party officials from the District and Regional Committees are all in attendance. They are walking round the pedestal, looking up at the monument in admiration.

MEMBERS OF THE DELEGATION: Most striking! A rare monument! Astonishing! Thrilling! Amazing work!

ZHANAIDAROV: (*to the Instructors*): Don't let the delegation linger here for long, try and lead them away quickly! (*To Mr. Charlton*) Mr. Charlton, please remember, we only have half an hour! We need to get going, I think.

MR. CHARLTON: No, no. You can't hurry when trying to appreciate works of art.

MR. CONRAD: It's a pity, a great pity (*After bringing out his camera, he prepares to take photographs*).

SATANOV: What does he regret?

ZHANAIDAROV: He regrets that he won't be able to have a good look at the monument in daylight. Comrade interpreter, explain to him please that we have another village feast ahead of us. It will be impolite if we turn up late. (*The interpreter translates*)

MR. CONRAD: O...ho! Another *dastarkhan*! ....!

ZHANAIDAROV: (*Radiant in expectation*) Yes, we Kazakhs love eating meat!

MR. CONRAD: O-ho! Scotland... I... Scotland. We like eating at night too!

THE MONUMENT

INTERPRETER: (*To Zhanaidarov and Satanov*) Mr. Conrad says that he is from Scotland and that the Scots also like eating meat at night – when they have any of course (*Everyone laughs*).

SATANOV (*To Zhanaidarov*) I have to leave, I'm afraid. I have to leave for Moscow on the 8 o'clock plane. Show the guests round properly with every consideration. The monument isn't bad, not bad at all. The man on the pedestal looks so real, drawn straight from life. Tell the sculptors responsible to come and see me, when they're in the regional capital. Perhaps we'll nominate the work for a State Prize.

ZHANAIDAROV: Fine, fine… May Allah preserve us! Fine, fine…

SATANOV: Comrade Secretary of the District Committee, what's come over you all of a sudden?

ZHANAIDAROV: Me… I'm just feeling anxious… Please don't be angry, if our welcome has not been up to standard…

SATANOV: (*patting him on the shoulder*) When the English have gone, come and see me. I want to register an official vote of thanks for your successful ideological work.

ZHANAIDAROV: May Allah protect us and have mercy on us. Of course I'll look in. May the Lord spare us a reprimand… They've deserved a vote of thanks, of course.

SATANOV: You don't look very well, are you sure you're not ill?

ZHANAIDAROV: Yes, yes – I have been feeling a little under the weather since yesterday (*A forced cough*).

SATANOV: Look after yourself, Comrade Zhanaidarov. Take care of your health. You're a person who's important to the Party.

ZHANAIDAROV: Thank you, Comrade Satanov. For the sake of the Party, we're prepared to give up the ghost…

SATANOV: But, as I said, make sure you get better. I wish you a speedy recovery! (*He shakes Zhanaidarov's hand and then turns to the English*) Dear guests, may I have your attention for a moment. I have to go back to my headquarters on urgent business. I wish you a pleasant time during the rest of your tour of the district. It will be an honour for me to receive you in my town two days from now. All the best!

(*He leaves and the English shout their loud farewells after him. Mr. Conrad continues to photograph the monument from various angles. Suddenly he calls out and freezes with his camera still raised*)

MR. CONRAD: O-oh! (*He says something rapidly and excitedly in English. Zhanaidarov, who has come over faint, grabs at his heart. The English, shouting and pointing upwards, crowd around him*).

THE ENGLISH: What's that?

ZHANAIDAROV: What d'you mean "What's that"? It's a monument.

THE ENGLISH: (*to the interpreter*) The skin the statue's holding is swaying… We can't believe our eyes!… (*Zhanaidarov, stuck for an answer, looks over at Esirkepov*)

ESIRKEPOV: Well…er…how shall I put it? This was how our sculptors envisaged it. It's no easy undertaking when a figure is depicted holding a plaster skin or one made of iron instead of a real one. So we decided they should use a real sheep-skin. It would bring art at least one step nearer to life.

MR. CONRAD: Ah! So it was planned? How resourceful (*He takes another photograph*) The latest innovation in monumental art!

THE MONUMENT

MR. CHARLTON: And they call this the provinces! You won't find such high-class art in England! Nor in Moscow, nor in Paris!

MRS. CHARLTON: How lucky that we came here! (*The sheep-skin, blown down by gusts of wind, floats through the air and lands right in front of Mr. Conrad*).

ZHANAIDAROV: (*moving over to the pedestal, he says to Ashten in a barely audible whisper*) You wretch, you could have waited till the guests left!

MR. CONRAD: What was that? (*To the interpreter*) What did our host say?

INTERPRETER: He's put out because the sheep-skin, which usually stays firmly in place, came adrift precisely when guests were here. The workmen must have fixed it badly (*The Scotsman says something excitedly to the Interpreter*).

ZHANAIDAROV: What's he saying?

INTERPRETER: He wants to acquire the skin as a souvenir. He's prepared to pay £500 sterling for it. He wants to know what you think.

ZHANAIDAROV: Oof!... Is that all it was? Let him have it for nothing. Whatever else we might be short of round here, sheep-skins are a-plenty. (*The Interpreter translates*).

MR. CONRAD: What a kind Russian!

INTERPRETER: He's not Russian, he's a Kazakh!

MR. CONRAD: Oh yes, a Kazakh. For free, that's good. Scotland loves what's for free…

(*Good-natured laughter follows. Ashten's muffled voice can be heard*)

ASHTEN: Take them away quickly or I'll be stiff with cold!

(*The English look round in surprise, not understanding where the voice is coming from*)

ZHANAIDAROV: Ashten, I'm going to make it look as if I'm talking to Esirkepov, but you listen. They don't understand Kazakh anyway. Even if you turn into a block of ice, stand there just a little longer and be quiet. We'll soon all be leaving.

MR. CONRAD: Thank you, thank you. It's a wonderful souvenir (*He packs the sheep-skin into his bag on which the word "Adidas" can clearly be seen*)

MR. CHARLTON: I must tell you all how deeply moved I am today. I am so fortunate to have seen with my own eyes such a rare statue. When I say I am happy beyond words, I mean it with all my heart. I do not think I am alone in this. This day will have left us with the most vivid and impressive cultural experience of our trip. Thank you so… so much!

MR. CONRAD: I too should like to say a few words. When we arrive home, we shall of course remember this remarkable encounter for a long time and tell people about it. This simple sheep-skin, which fell down from the monument by chance, will from now on be kept in the British Museum, a treasured possession of the whole British people. There is no doubt that the Museum will offer me ten thousand pounds sterling for it. In response to your generosity I feel obliged to leave you five hundred pounds as promised. (*He brings out his wallet and starts counting out the money*) This money I now hand over to Mr. Zhanaidarov! (*He holds out the money*)

ZHANAIDAROV: The sheep-skin is our present to you Mr. Conrad and Soviet people do not accept money for presents (*He puts the money back into Mr. Conrad's pocket*)

ASHTEN: You wretch! (*The English people look around again in surprise*)

THE MONUMENT

ZHANAIDAROV: (*Speaking as if he is addressing Esirkepov*) Come now, Ashten, our position is no better than yours. You can see for yourself – they're not going. Hold out for just another five minutes

(*The monument responds with what could be a groan or a sigh of regret*)

ZHANAIDAROV: Be quiet you! The last thing we need is for you to start joining in an argument from up there.

ESIRKEPOV: Mr. Charlton, I'm sorry but we're behind schedule already (*He taps his watch*)

MR. CHARLTON: Yes, yes. We need to go.

(*The English group leaves the stage talking loudly. Alone at last, Ashten jumps down from the pedestal*)

ASHTEN: What nonsense – letting the hard currency vanish!

Zhanaidarov accepts bribes quite happily every day...

(*He pulls a small bottle of vodka out of his pocket, takes several gulps, drops it and staggers off stage*)

* * *

A hotel room, where Mr. Conrad is installed. Having already settled down for the night, he suddenly jumps up with a squeal as if the blankets are on fire.

MR. CONRAD: Adidas, Adidas. Help someone, help! (*He searches feverishly for his bag*)

(*The Interpreter comes in*)

INTERPRETER: Excuse me, Mr. Conrad, is something wrong?

MR. CONRAD: I've left my bag somewhere. I'm so damned absent-minded. It's got my souvenir in it, my souvenir. I probably left it near the monument (*Runs out*)

(*Mrs. Charlton comes in*)

MRS. CHARLTON: Mr. Translator, you speak splendid English. Where did you learn to speak it so fluently.

INTERPRETER: I graduated in languages. Ever since I was a child, I have been studying English with great diligence and devotion.

MRS. CHARLTON: And how many languages do you speak? Unfortunately I don't speak any apart from English.

INTERPRETER: I have mastered many – English, Russian, Uzbek, Turkish, Kirghiz, Tartar, Azeri, Turkmen, Karakalpak, Nogai, Khakas, Bashkir and, of course, Kazakh.

MRS. CHARLTON: You're a polyglot. What a gift! But when did you find the time to study all those languages?

INTERPRETER: "Where there's a will, there's a way", as the saying goes.

MRS. CHARLTON: Oh, I forgot the most important thing. What's your name?

INTERPRETER: They call me Kurmash.

MRS. CHARLTON: How should I address you in full?

INTERPRETER: Kurmash is fine. That's enough. We Kazakhs don't use patronymics as well.

MRS. CHARLTON: Nor do we. It's the same all over Europe and America. But, you're a real youth of the East. A real Genghis Khan!

THE MONUMENT

INTERPRETER: Unfortunately, the only person you people know about from the whole of the East is Genghis Khan.

MRS. CHARLTON: Tell me, Kurmash… The sculptors, who made the monument which we saw – to which school of art do they belong?

INTERPRETER: To which school? (*Under his breath*) Most likely the local secondary. (*Out loud*) They belong to the school led by the famous Soviet sculptor, Konenkov.

MRS. CHARLTON: Would it be possible for me to talk to them?

INTERPRETER: They live in Alma-Ata. I think you would have a chance to meet them before your flight leaves for Moscow.

MRS. CHARLTON: Then I would feel that we had completed all the tasks we had set ourselves for this trip of ours.

INTERPRETER: We shall try and fulfil your wishes as far as we can, Mrs. Charlton.

MRS. CHARLTON: Elizabeth…

INTERPRETER: Elizabeth! What a pretty name!

MRS. CHARLTON: Tell me, can eastern men love women who aren't Muslims!?

INTERPRETER: And how!

MRS. CHARLTON: Can I ask you a practical question?

INTERPRETER: Of course, Mrs. Elizabeth.

MRS. CHARLTON: Tell me, would it be possible to get hold of another sheep-skin – a souvenir like the one Mr. Conrad has?

INTERPRETER: As many as you like. Ashten's shed is overflowing with them.

(*Realizing what he nearly let slip, the interpreter becomes highly agitated*)

MRS. CHARLTON: Ashten, who's that?

INTERPRETER: That's the warehouse supervisor at the fur and leather factory. He has a special reserve of fresh sheep-skins so that a new one can be used for the monument each week. If you wish we can get hold of one like that for you.

MRS. CHARLTON: You are so kind, Mr. Kurmash. In the name of our delegation and on behalf of my husband, Mr. Charlton, allow me to express our profound gratitude.

INTERPRETER: There's no need, Mrs. Elizabeth. We're happy to do you this service. (*He kisses her hand*).

(*Enter Mr. Conrad. He is soaked through and splashed with mud from top to toe. He comes in looking tired as he wipes his bald head*)

MR. CONRAD: No, I didn't find it.

INTERPRETER: No, you didn't find the monument. You must have lost your way.

MRS. CHARLTON: Good night, Mr. Kurmash. Good night, Mr. Conrad (*She bows her head slightly and leaves*)

INTERPRETER: Even if you were intent on doing so, it's impossible to lose your way. Only two streets from here the giant factory looms up like a mountain. Didn't you see it?

MR. CONRAD: Yes I saw it.

INTERPRETER: The monument stands in front of that very same factory. How could you possibly have missed it?

MR. CONRAD: (In a frightened voice) It's not there. There's no monument.

THE MONUMENT

INTERPRETER: What d'you mean – no monument?

MR. CONRAD: Just that – no monument. The factory's there, the square's there, the pedestal's there, but there's no statue of a worker.

INTERPRETER: You must have been on the wrong side then...

*   *   *

Hotel. Hullabaloo. The English visitors appear as if they have been dragged from their beds.

MR. CONRAD: Sensation! Sensation! The monument's been stolen!

The monument's disappeared from the square!

MRS. CHARLTON: It can't have! Robberies don't happen in the Land of the Soviets.

MR. CONRAD: I've just come from the square. I saw with my own eyes that there was no statue! (*The Interpreter hurries off to call someone on the telephone*)

MR. CHARLTON: Mr. Conrad, if your assertion is wrong, this could put Great Britain in an awkward situation!

MRS. CHARLTON: Worse still, it could lead to cooler relations between our two countries!

MR. CHARLTON: Or even undermine the creation of a single European Union.

MR. CONRAD: As God is my witness, I'm telling the truth!

MR. CHARLTON: When people are telling big lies, they start calling on a powerful God for a witness.

MRS. CHARLTON: Perhaps you simply failed to find it?

MR. CHARLTON: Or you're not feeling well?

MR. CONRAD: I'm completely all right and I was on that very same square, which we all left two hours ago. The square's where it should be, the factory's where it should be and so is the pedestal, but there's no statue.

(*Zhanaidarov comes in. The English visitors cluster round him enthusiastically and shower him with questions. There follows an improvised briefing*)

MR. CHARLTON: Tell me, Mr. Secretary of the District Committee, do robberies take place in your country?

ZHANAIDAROV: No, there have not been any in the past and there won't be any in the future.

MRS. CHARLTON: And do communists lie?

ZHANAIDAROV: Never. Not just communists but members of the Young Communist League wouldn't lie either.

MR. CONRAD: But isn't what you're asserting now a genuine lie?

ZHANAIDAROV: I do not answer such provocative questions.

MR. CONRAD: How d'you explain the fact that the monument in front of the factory has disappeared?

ZHANAIDAROV: The monument has not disappeared. There are only rumours to that effect. It is simply a machination on the part of those who have come to our country with hostile intentions.

MRS. CHARLTON: But the Adidas bag which Mr. Conrad left behind by chance in the square has not been found.

ZHANAIDAROV: Firstly, we do not know who left what there in the square and, secondly, so as not to consider other people thieves, we ourselves need to be vigilant.

THE MONUMENT

MRS. CHARLTON: Bravo, bravo. A very resourceful answer! (*She writes something down in a notebook*).

MR. CONRAD: And how d'you explain what I did find (*He shows them a small vodka bottle*). I found it there in the square by the pedestal in the bushes. Who was drinking vodka and then left the bottle behind?

ZHANAIDAROV: In the first place, nobody in our country drinks vodka. I hope you've heard about Gorbachev's decree in 1985, about the campaign against drunkenness and alcoholism?

MR. CHARLTON: We've heard and even read about it. We have nothing to amend or add to that.

MR. CONRAD: And we saw the result of this campaign in Moscow – long, very long vodka queues.

ZHANAIDAROV: (*with a sarcastic laugh*) That queue hasn't reached us yet. There's no getting away from the fact that Moscow's four thousand kilometres away from our District.

MRS. CHARLTON: Well said! Mr. Zhanaidarov, you're a very resourceful man. We people in England value resourcefulness particularly highly (*She takes notes again*).

ZHANAIDAROV: Thank you, thank you! (*He makes a sign to the Interpreter*) Now, as they say, best see for yourselves. The statue will be standing where it stood before. Let's go to the square. There's a car waiting for us downstairs. Let's set off (*They all move over to the door*)

MR. CHARLTON: (*To Mr. Conrad*) Mr. Conrad, if you are mistaken, it will be a disgrace not just for us, but for the whole of England!

MRS. CHARLTON: I too feel out of sorts, when I think about that. (*Out loud*) Mr. Kurmash, keep me a place next to you!

INTERPRETER: With pleasure, if Mr Charlton doesn't object.

MRS. CHARLTON: In England people don't get jealous about wives, do they Richard?

MR. CHARLTON: (*Slightly taken aback*) Absolutely correct, my dear (*To Mr. Conrad*) May God help us. Off we go, Mr. Conrad (*They leave*).

* * *

Semi-darkness on the stage. All that can be seen are the silhouettes of certain individuals. Agitated voices can be heard.

ZHANAIDAROV: How are things over there? Are you ready?

ESIRKEPOV: It would seem so. Thank God. Yes!

ZHANAIDAROV: On with the floodlights.

(*Six floodlights pick out Ashten in the darkness. He is standing proudly on the pedestal with his sheep-skin held up on his raised arms*) Ladies and gentlemen! You now have a rare opportunity – to admire the rare monument. You see, no-one had stolen it. While you were out looking for it, staff from the factory had time to replace the sheep-skin held aloft by the statue (*Pause*)

MR. CHARLTON: (*To Mr. Conrad*) What an embarrassment, Mr. Conrad. Don't you think so? (*Mr. Conrad clutches at his heart and collapses*).

MRS. CHARLTON: O-oh, he's fainted. Quick, take him back to the car (*The two Instructors pick up Mr. Conrad and take him off*).

(*To Kurmash*) Mr. Kurmash, couldn't you possible present me too with a sheep-skin held up by the statue? But so that my husband shouldn't notice… He doesn't like that, he regards it as international small-mindedness.

INTERPRETER: Proposal accepted... I'll see to it straightaway...

MRS. CHARLTON: No. no, not now whatever you do. Later... I'm just astonished at how kind and responsive you people are.

INTERPRETER: It's part of our nature, Mrs. Charlton – we can't refuse a guest anything... Especially when such a beautiful woman is doing the asking...

(*Elizabeth holds out her hand and Kurmash kisses it passionately. Noticing Mr. Charlton looking at them, he comes over all embarrassed*) You say Europeans don't get jealous about their wives – what a wonderful quality.

MRS. CHARLTON: Yes, that's how it is Sir... (*She laughs*). Yet, being unwilling to follow the example of jealous Asia, European men often lose out... It appears that your people has a tradition for carrying off brides?

INTERPRETER: Yes, yes, sometimes a youth will kidnap his beloved.

MR. CHARLTON: What degradation!

MRS. CHARLTON: Why degradation? It's wonderful! A moonlit night, the endless steppe and your lover carries you off on a fleet-footed horse into the distant unknown...

MR. CHARLTON: All women want to become heroines of Walter Scott's novel about Rob Roy. Romance, romance and yet again romance! And how do you make up for this lack of romance?

INTERPRETER: We fight.

MRS. CHARLTON: Why?

INTERPRETER: But why not? We always have to fight against something.

MRS. CHARLTON: Life without romance is tedious and uninteresting. (*Unexpectedly*) Richard, Richard!

MR. CHARLTON: What's happened, my dear?

MRS. CHARLTON: Look, look over there! There's something shining... something shining in his pocket (*They all stare at Ashten*)

Mr. Zhanaidarov, what's that shining... in the statue's pocket... What can that mean?

ESIRKEPOV: ...It's a piece of ice. We have an extreme continental climate, you know. Extreme heat or extreme cold. After the last snowfall, ice formed in some of the deep folds of our clothes...

MR. CHARLTON: It looks pretty in the light from the projectors.

ZHANAIDAROV: (*To the two Instructors*) Turn off the projectors, before we have a disaster on our hands.

FIRST INSTRUCTOR: We wanted to turn them off ourselves, but the controls jammed! Just our luck...

ZHANAIDAROV: Where are the electricians?

SECOND INSTRUCTOR: They say it'll take at least twenty minutes to repair. (*Zhanaidarov gives an angry shrug*)

ESIRKEPOV: What can be done?

FIRST INSTRUCTOR: The electrician says we'll have to link up two phases. There's no other way he says. Then the projectors will blow once and for all...

ESIRKEPOV: Let them blow for real, for all I care! Do something and fast. (*The Instructors run off*)

MRS. CHARLTON: Where have those gentlemen run off to?

THE MONUMENT

ZHANAIDAROV: To find out how Mr. Conrad's feeling... We can't just abandon a guest and not see to his needs.

MRS. CHARLTON: Of course, of course. That's a very proper decision. By the way has Mr. Conrad's bag turned up?

ESIRKEPOV: But of course... What did you think would have happened to it? We'll bring it to the hotel ourselves...

MR. CHARLTON: You know, I like this statue even more this time than the last. I'm going to take another photograph of the man...

ESIRKEPOV: (*In a frightened voice*) What man?

MRS. CHARLTON: The man on the monument, of course.

ESIRKEPOV: Oh yes, please go ahead.

(*Mrs. Charlton lifts up her camera to take another photograph. At that moment all six projectors explode one after the other with a terrible bang. The square is plunged in darkness. Bewildered voices can be heard, all hell is let loose. The two Instructors run in*)

ZHANAIDAROV: Well done, lads! So quick off the mark! If only you could always manage that!...

TWO INSTRUCTORS: (*Panting and out of breath*) A single word from you, Comrade First Secretary and we'll always be ready to lay on the end of the world!...

ZHANAIDAROV: Comrades, ladies and gentlemen! We have a slight technical hitch. It'll all be sorted out very soon. Lads, switch on the headlights and let the guests get into the cars... (*The car lights are switched on*). Dear ladies and gentlemen, please take your seats! (*The visitors move off stage talking loudly. Esirkepov remains by the monument*).

ESIRKEPOV: Ashten, come on now! Give the bag back to the foreign guest immediately!

ASHTEN: But you see… my little boy really needs an Adidas bag!

ESIRKEPOV: Tomorrow I'll issue you not just one but two bags like that from our warehouse. But give me the Adidas bag that's not yours!

ASHTEN: All right then, but make sure it's two. I'll take them. (*He comes down from the pedestal*)

ESIRKEPOV: Then again… Why did you climb up on to the pedestal with a bottle in your pocket?

ASHTEN: If it hadn't been for that woman, nobody would have noticed. What's really bad is that the five hundred dollars went up in smoke! That was a real let-down!

ESIRKEPOV: I see there's no limit to your cheek. We nearly found ourselves in a right mess, thanks to you.

ASHTEN: D'you think I had an easy time of it?

ESIRKEPOV: But now listen. On the way here the visitors expressed the wish – out of the blue – to visit the home of an ordinary worker. We had to opt for you. Tomorrow the visitors are going to have breakfast at your place.

ASHTEN: You don't really mean it? It'll cause chaos at home. My wife will have it in for me…

ESIRKEPOV: Don't worry about any of that. Everything's ready. A telephone has been installed in your flat and furniture has been delivered. The table is being laid.

ASHTEN: What d'you mean? All that for just one hour?!

ESIRKEPOV: That's no trouble for the District Committee! Get back home now. Don't go off anywhere without our permission… Have you got that? And you're not to have a drop to drink in the meantime, d'you hear?

ASHTEN: All right, I'll go along with it.

ESIRKEPOV: Make sure you do!… Till tomorrow!

ASHTEN: Bye for now! (*They go off in separate directions*)

* * *

Ashten's flat. It has changed beyond recognition, as if transformed in a fairy-tale. A large candelabra hangs from the ceiling. There are carpets on the floor and hanging on the walls and a touch-dial telephone. The table is laden with all manner of delicacies, champagne, various kinds of cognac and vodka.

ASHTEN: (*Comes in and almost faints in amazement. He recovers himself with difficulty*) Listen, Kulyash… aren't we lucky, eh?

KULYASH: (*Laughing nervously*) Yes… we're lucky. But all this frightens me, Ashten!

ASHTEN: Don't be scared, you silly! We've got first God on our side and then the District Committee!

KULYASH: But even so… Haven't they gone too far? I hope it won't end badly…

ASHTEN: You're not looking bad either… so prettily turned out (*He looks her up and down and spins her round*) You know… you remind me of a certain girl… Was it in a dream or for real?

KULYASH: You notice all sorts of things when you're sozzled (*Ashten walks shyly over to the table*)

ASHTEN: Look at that now! It's a miracle! Oranges! Tangerines! Bananas! And what on earth's that?

KULYASH: Coconut juice.

ASHTEN: And that?

KULYASH: Walnuts. And over there we have a pineapple.

ASHTEN: Someone's pulling our legs!... It's pure magic! O-ooh and there's "Friendship" sausage (*He sits down at the table*). The vodka's not the ordinary kind (*He reads the label*) "Ambassador", what will they think of next?! (*He takes a tumbler out of his pocket and fills it*). I've been poisoning myself with this wretched "Wheaten Vodka" (*He brings out a half-empty bottle of it from his other pocket and pushes it to one side*). Now I'm going to try "Ambassador" vodka for once in my life (*He downs the tumbler's contents*). Now that's the real thing.

KULYASH: I still can't believe my eyes. Pinch me, perhaps I'm just dreaming. (*They pinch each other*).

ASHTEN: No, it's not a dream. It's for real. You have a drink too. Be my guest.

KULYASH: No we mustn't. We've got to receive the visitors in the morning. You ought to be going to bed. You can hardly see straight

ASHTEN: (*Slightly tipsy*) Our first Secretary says… "At the next elections," he says, "We'll nominate you as a candidate for election as a People's Deputy". "If you die," he says, "We'll erect a monument, not to your grandfather but to you in person". What d'you think: should I die or become a deputy?

KULYASH: You shouldn't talk such nonsense. I don't need you as a deputy or any monument after your death. Even though your drunken stupors may last weeks, the children still need a father.

ASHTEN: You said I was drunk for weeks on end. You mean me? What have you been saying? (*He pours out more vodka and downs it again*). Listen, let's sing a song...

KULYASH: Are you in your right mind? It's past midnight. You'll wake the children. That's enough, don't drink any more. I've put clean sheets on the new bed...

ASHTEN: Have you now?

KULYASH: Yes, to be sure.

ASHTEN: That's a surprise! A real surprise! (*Kulyash leads him off into the bedroom*) Let's go dancing! Let's go dancing! The beauty in the white dress!...

"The Party leads the people,

The Party leads the people..."

(*On reaching the bedroom door, Ashten suddenly turns round*)

KULYASH: What more d'you need, you wretched fellow? You've been drinking all day, surely that's enough? Come to bed.

ASHTEN: Kulyash, you go to bed... I'm going to sleep with all this luxury here for me, like nothing I've ever seen before...

KULYASH: No, I'm not going to leave you on your own. We'll lie down to sleep together. Come on.

ASHTEN: I'm not going to lie down... with you. I have to say, if I'm honest, that I've fallen for another...

KULYASH: Who have you fallen for, you wretch?

ASHTEN: A girl... in a white dress...

KULYASH: A girl in white? And she? Does she love you?

ASHTEN: She will... there'll be no choice.

KULYASH: What d'you mean... there'll be no choice?

ASHTEN: It's a resolution by the Bureau... of the District Committee.

KULYASH: About what? What resolution?

ASHTEN: An ordinary one... It was decided: everything that Zheldybaev wants is to be carried out without question!...

KULYASH: But it probably doesn't apply to love, that resolution?

ASHTEN: It applies... we'll make sure it applies... I shall now (*He goes over to the telephone*). Hallo! (*After clearing his throat*) Who's that? The flat of the District Committee Instructor? It's Ashten Zheldybaev here. Listen, what about the agreement? What d'you mean, which agreement? The Bureau's resolution – have you forgotten? It's not a resolution about what, but about who. About the girl. Yes, the girl in the white dress. And it was on headed Party writing paper, wasn't it – complete with an official round stamp. It was all agreed! All right...and listen... where's the rest of the money. Tomorrow, together with the Bureau's resolution? .... All settled. Bye for now! (*He puts down the receiver*).

So you see, that's Zheldybaev for you! Now you've understood who Zheldybaev is. Who was I yesterday? An ordinary plumber... a fly, a mosquito. But today?! I might even become a Deputy! Then win one of those alternative elections and be a member of the Village Soviet, then the District Executive Committee, the District Party Committee or even the Regional one... If your lucky number comes up, the sky's the limit...

* * *

Night. The square in front of the factory. On one side of it Ashten appears and on the other the two Instructors from the District Committee.

THE MONUMENT

FIRST INSTRUCTOR: I hope you're happy about the spirits of your ancestors, Ashten Zheldybaev? Thanks to them you've become a person whose name is constantly being mentioned by the District leaders.

SECOND INSTRUCTOR: You're already taking liberties, speaking to us in an unacceptable tone.

ASHTEN: What's the point of beating about the bush? Give over the last three hundred roubles.

FIRST INSTRUCTOR: (*Looking at the Second Instructor*) Who'd have thought it? I've forgotten to bring them along with me yet again. I left them in the office, in the safe. Tomorrow morning I'll bring them round to you at home.

ASHTEN: Make sure you do… And where's the Resolution?

SECOND INSTRUCTOR: Resolution? Which resolution?

ASHTEN: The District Committee's. About the girl in the white dress.

FIRST INSTRUCTOR: (*Casting a knowing look at his colleague*) Ah, so that's it! I've got it (*Hunts in his pocket*). Here it is - there are two copies. The girl in the white dress has one and the other I shall now solemnly present to you! (*He hands Ashten a piece of paper*)

ASHTEN: For real? (*He takes the paper and reads*) "This Resolution acknowledges a citizen of the Communist District, resident at House 20, Socialism Street, as the real-life model for the monument erected in front of the leather factory. In view of the national significance of this monument currently being erected, the District Committee will attend to the everyday needs of the model, namely Ashten Zheldybaev. All his requirements regarding food items, clothes, furniture and other household goods, must be satisfied immediately". But there's not a word about the girl in the white dress here, is there?!

SECOND INSTRUCTOR: No that's correct. That was overlooked. Give me the paper (*He takes the paper out of Ashten's hand and adds something*). Now it will read as follows: "…requirements regarding food items, clothes, furniture and LOVE must be satisfied immediately"! Something else needs to be added as well: "All those who fail to comply with this Resolution will be regarded as persons who do not support the domestic policy of the Soviet government". So you see, Ashten, with a document like this you can go up to any girl who takes your fancy and none of your requests should be turned down (*He returns the paper to Ashten*).

FIRST INSTRUCTOR: I could do with a paper like that! …Today you are going to be filmed for the TV programme "Time". The whole world will see you. A TV camera is not like the eyes of ordinary people. You need to be prepared. Let's rehearse. Climb up on to the pedestal.

ASHTEN: What about the school-leaving certificate that was promised? Did you mean it for real?

SECOND INSTRUCTOR: We do not use words loosely. Everything will be in order: your school-leaving certificate, university degree and, with God's help, you'll end up a Deputy to the local Soviet. You already have the Resolution regarding the girl in the white dress. What else d'you need? Climb up into position quickly!

ASHTEN: And what about my wife, if the girl's willing?

FIRST INSTRUCTOR: As regards the wife?... We'll have to take advice on that.

SECOND INSTRUCTOR: By then the Supreme Soviet will perhaps have passed a Decree permitting polygamy. In the mean time you need to take up your elevated position on the pedestal! (*Ashten climbs up onto it with a dreamy smile on his face*)

THE INSTRUCTORS: (*Running up to Ashten first from one side and then from the other, as they try to be helpful*)

- Stand like this!
- A tiny bit straighter!
- Hold the sheep-skin tighter!
- Try not to blink!
- Breathe through your nose, not your mouth!...

Two men approach. They are Salakhov and Mashanov.

FIRST INSTRUCTOR: But we had already set up a police checkpoint so that no trespassers should be allowed through! Who let you in?

SALAKHOV: We're the sculptors. Didn't you recognize us? These men are here to unload it. We've brought the statue and we're going to set it up now.

(*Salakhov looks at the monument and both sculptors collapse in a faint. The two Instructors have difficulty bringing them round, splashing them with water*) Is this a dream?

SECOND INSTRUCTOR: It's no dream. We were told it would be a long time before you got here.

MASHANOV: (*Unable to talk his eyes off the monument*) And where's that sprung from?

ASHTEN: (*From up above*) Greetings, colleagues. It's **me**, Ashten!

(*Both sculptors faint again. The two Instructors revive them*)

SALAKHOV: At last I've grasped it. Instead of a statue they used a live model. We could do with as rich an imagination as our leaders'...

SECOND INSTRUCTOR: For God's sake, don't say a word about this to anyone. We beg you most earnestly. Out of the blue a delegation from England turned up. We reported to the Regional Committee that the monument was already in place and so we had to find a solution. Today people from the "Time" programme are coming here to do some filming.

MASHANOV: Forgive us, Ashten, it's all my fault and Salakhov's. It was only today that the casting works at last delivered our order. It's a miracle we got here...

ASHTEN: Never mind, lads. It could happen to anyone!...

SALAKHOV: (*to the Instructors*) Now help us find a pick-up crane and a few workmen. Then we'll be finished by this evening. On our way here we went to see the First Secretary of the Regional Committee. He also promised to come, straight after the workmen...

FIRST AND SECOND INSTRUCTOR: (*Both at once*) Who, Satanov?!

SALAKHOV: Yes.

FIRST INSTRUCTOR: That's all we need! We've had it! (*Both Instructors faint. The sculptors pour water over them*)

MASHANOV: (*To Ashten*) Come on Ashten! What are you doing up there, get down!

ASHTEN: What's for me to do down there? I like it better up here.

FIRST INSTRUCTOR: I said all along you'd be the death of us all. That's just how it's turned out. Ouch, my heart! The Region's

First Secretary on his way --- and the people from the "Time" programme!...

SECOND INSTRUCTOR: Who on earth was it who had the bright idea of putting up a monument to some old man whose ashes have long since rotted in the ground!... Why did we need all this fuss?!...

FIRST INSTRUCTOR: Come on, we need to go and see Zhanaidarov. But how are we going to relay this news. You tell him...

SECOND INSTRUCTOR: No, you. After all, you're his nephew.

FIRST INSTRUCTOR: But you're his brother-in-law. He's not going to tear a strip off you.

SECOND INSTRUCTOR: All right, we'll decide all that when we get there. We need to hurry. What will be, will be... (*They leave hastily*)

ASHTEN: (*calling after them*) What am I meant to do?

FIRST INSTRUCTOR: Don't be a nuisance. Do whatever you like! (*They all exit*)

* * *

Ashten still on the pedestal. He is singing. His wife appears and she is in tears.

ASHTEN: Kulyash, Kulyash, what's the matter with you?

(*She says nothing at first*)

KULYASH: Our home's empty again. They've stripped out everything!...

ASHTEN: Stop howling. What does it matter if it's all gone. All those things weren't ours anyway.

KULYASH: It's not about that at all.

ASHTEN: What is it then?

KULYASH: They were making us look like fools, Ashten. They put us to shame in every way they could!

ASHTEN: There was no shame. They put themselves to shame.

KULYASH: Don't you understand anything? Look read this! (*She hands him a sheet of paper*)

ASHTEN: The Bureau's Resolution? I've got a copy of my own.

KULYASH: So you're going to drop me and marry the other girl?

ASHTEN: No… er… I… did that in revenge for you slapping me in the face… She's so beautiful and proud… I wanted to teach you a lesson, to stop you turning your nose up at me…

KULYASH: What d'you mean? Through a resolution of the District Committee?

ASHTEN: How could I have done anything otherwise?

KULYASH: Beautiful is she? More beautiful than I am? P'raps she looked like a fairy through your sozzled haze?… Come now, just open your eyes and see what she really looks like? **I** shall bring her here now… (*She makes as if to leave*)

ASHTEN: (*Rushing after her*) Kulyash, Kulyash – where are you going? I don't need anyone, d'you hear? (*He tears the paper up into small pieces*) What a mess they've made of everything! You're losing your wits Ashten! That girl in the white dress was the last thing you needed!

THE MONUMENT

KULYASH: Come on Ashten dear, let's go.

ASHTEN: No! I like it here (*He starts singing again*)

KULYASH: Ashten, get down from the pedestal! Stop singing!

(*Ashten goes on singing. His voice grows louder and louder*)

Ashten! What's the matter with you, Ashten?

(*Ashten continues to sing louder and louder. Perhaps he is crying as well*)

THE END

DULAT ISSABEKOV

Baroness Alison Suttie, House of Lords, British Parliament, UK

I had the great opportunity to go to Kazakhstan for the first time last September.

We were there to participate in the Festival of languages in Astana, where I had the privilege to meet Dulat Issabekov

When I was told that we were to see his play, 'The Transit Passenger', three days in a row I thought this may be a test of endurance! The first evening we saw the play in English, the second evening in Russian and the third evening in Kazakh. However, instead of being a test of endurance it was actually a wonderful experience to understand the impact of different languages and different cultures on the same play. Each evening we had the opportunity to witness a uniquely individual interpretation of this wonderful play.

'The Transit Passenger' is a play about life, about growing older, and it is a play about the anxiety of being left alone with your memories. By the time when I saw the play in the original Kazakh language, beautifully acted - even though I didn't understand a word of Kazakh - I had tears in my eyes…

Lightning Source UK Ltd.
Milton Keynes UK
UKOW04f1522010917
308397UK00001B/259/P